nanotales

nanotales

ziv navoth

Ziji

Published by Ziji Publishing
www.nanotales.net

Distributed by Turnaround Distribution Services Ltd.
Telephone 020 8829 3000

ISBN 978-0-9554051-1-2

Printed by Creative Print and Design, Wales.

To my parents, for giving me a past

and to Maya, for giving me a future.

#1

There were 97 advertising executives in the hotel, all competing for external telephone lines. Their mission was simple: come up with an advertising campaign for a war that hadn't taken place.

They had 12 hours to prepare, and they used them to call friends, family, assistants and anyone who ever fought in a war, or simply served in the military.

The challenge was given by the firm's founder, who over the course of 30 years had built an empire employing thousands of people and serving some of the most prestigious companies in the world. Each year, the firm's top executives would gather in an hotel and discuss the firm's results and its plans for the year ahead. Each year, the chairman issued a new challenge, and each year 97 or so executives would pour their years of experience into 12 concentrated hours of creativity.

The competition wasn't one taken lightly. The previous year, the winner was made vice-chairman of the firm in less than a month, and the year before the winner was given a bonus of over $10 million. The firm's current CEO won his position three years ago by developing the best advertising campaign for an imaginary company that sold air ('Because you deserve to know whose air you're breathing').

The methods used by the advertising executives to develop their campaigns were as diverse as their numbers. One executive sent a helicopter to fly in a former chief of staff. Another drove for three hours to interview a known militia leader who had been imprisoned during a previous war. And yet another executive meditated with his spiritual advisor.

The winner of the competition was set to be announced by 9am. The timing was intentional. Executives were expected to spend the 12 hours before the ceremony working, not sleeping. Their commitment could be quickly ascertained by even a cursory visit to the hotel's kitchen. There, one floor beneath the ground, a staff of 15 kept refilling coffee pot after coffee pot, before whisking them off to 96 rooms.

And with all this activity it was not surprising no one noticed that one room was conspicuously missing from kitchen's food order log: room 1903.

If one were to peek into room 1903, one wouldn't see much that would be of interest. It was a spacious room, much like the others, boasting a TV set, a large bathroom and a king-sized bed. But unlike the other 96 rooms, room 1903 was dark, its sole occupant tucked in bed.

Like his colleagues, the executive in room 1903 was present hours earlier at the main dining room, where he too had heard the chairman issue his challenge. Like his colleagues, he too wanted badly to win this year's competition. But while his colleagues had left the dining room in a flurry of activity, each running his own race against time, the executive from 1903 went to his room, took his clothes off and slipped into bed.

Sleep did not come easily. He tossed and turned, got up to take a shower, then another one. But nothing could stop his mind from racing. To lose this year's competition would be unfortunate. But to abstain from it would be a disgrace.

When the phone rang the sun had already risen. For a brief moment the executive in 1903 broke into a cold sweat, worried that he had missed the ceremony altogether. But when the voice on the other end of the line turned out to belong to one of the hotel telephone operators, announcing his wake-up call, the executive calmed down, if only for a while.

The executive from room 1903 stepped out of bed and began dressing. He put on a fresh pair of socks, a new pair of underwear, a starched white shirt, polyester suit and blue tie to match. He looked at himself in the mirror one last time and left the room.

Downstairs, the main dining hall buzzed with activity. Placards, signs bearing slogans, and even a small group of soldiers in fatigues, were all assembled.

At precisely 9am, the chairman of the firm took to the stage and congratulated the executives on their effort to develop the best pro-war campaign. It was hard to keep the room quiet, but the chairman's closing remarks did just that. This morning, said the chairman, in addition to the winner of the competition, there will also be losers. Ten losers, in fact, that would pay for their sub-standard campaign with their jobs.

The executive from room 1903 lowered his head, as did most of the other executives. Though each had convinced himself of his own victory, all knew that their peers were highly capable individuals. Capable enough to do a job that was as good, if not better, than themselves.

By the time the executive from room 1903 was called up to the stand, twenty of his colleagues had given their brief presentations, with three of them discharged from their positions, there and then. So it wasn't without trepidation that the executive from room 1903 climbed the stairs to the main stage.

'If your client had hired you to launch a pro-war campaign,' asked the chairman for the twenty-first time, 'what would you do?'

The room was silent. Each executive in their own mind was asking whether they were about to see another one of their colleagues lose his job, and whether they themselves wouldn't be next in line.

The executive from room 1903 remained silent. The chairman, who was eager to finish the whole event as soon as possible, began showing signs of impatience.

'If your client had hired you to launch a pro-war campaign,' repeated the chairman, 'what would you do?'

The executive from room 1903 moved closer to the podium, almost touching the microphone with his lips.

'Nothing,' he said. 'I would do nothing.'

#2

'I can't get no, satisfaction. I can't get no, satisfaction! Cuz' I try and I try and I try. I can't get no! I can't get no!'

'Nicholas! Nicholas!' She's pounding rhythmically on the bathroom door. He's at it again, taking his morning shower. Him and Mick Jagger.

'Baby, you're out of sync, the song has four beats...'

'There are other people in this house, you know!' she shouts, though she can't resist smiling as well. There's nothing like being married to an aging rock star. There's the singing in the bathroom, the hair that gets more attention than a bride on her wedding day, and of course, those leather pants. He might be well over forty, but one thing he'll never give up on are his leather pants. And what drives her really crazy, is that girls still recognize him on the street. Girls less than half his age come up to him for an autograph. And the leather pants only seem to excite them more.

Nick steps out of the shower, wearing nothing but a towel around his head. 'Nicholas! Why do you have to walk around like that?!'

'Because it turns you on, baby...' he answers, slapping her ass. She blushes and goes into the bathroom. The steam from his shower is still hanging in the air. She looks at the mist-covered mirror. 'You rock my world!' is written across it. He does stuff like that. Surprises her once in a while. Makes her feel like a teenager. And that's probably the reason she puts up with him.

'Daddy?'

'What's up, bro?'

'Can I get a dinosaur for my next birthday?'

'Pasquale? We talked about this before. You know that dinosaurs don't exist, don't you?'

'They don't?'

'No, they don't, and stop acting as if you don't know that. You're being silly.'

He sits down at the table and drinks his coffee. On the cover of the magazine is a shot of Madonna and Britney Spears kissing. He didn't have to kiss anybody to get on the cover of a magazine. He just had to be himself, the ravishing Nick LeGrand.

'LeGrand'. He made up that name just before they released their first record, twenty four years ago. 'Nicholas Fothergill' just didn't sound right for a rock star. He wasn't sure what 'LeGrand' actually meant when he came up to their manager with his demand to change the name on the album sleeve (even though 10,000 of them had already been printed), but no one seemed to care. As long as he delivered the goods he could call himself whatever he wanted.

'Daddy?'

'Yeah, dude?'

'Can I learn ballet?'

He drops the magazine on the table, shaking his coffee mug enough to spill its contents.

'What did you ask?'

'I asked if I could learn ballet.'

'Pasquale, what are you talking about?! Only girls learn ballet! Do you want to be a girl?!'

'No, Daddy.'

'Then stop with all this bullshit. Besides, I told you. You're going to learn some martial arts.'

'Do you get to paint in martial arts?'

'No! Martial arts is about fighting. Fighting like a man. Not dancing like a little girl.'

'Yes, Daddy.'

At some point in our life we realize that we're probably not going to make much out of ourselves, so we might as well make someone else. Then we have kids, and suddenly, the only thing we care about is how to make sure they turn out exactly like us.

She joins them at the table.

'What's going on around here?'

'Your son wants to be a girl.'

'I do not!' says Pasquale, pounding his spoon on the table.

'Pasquale, calm down. And so can you, Nicholas. Just because OUR son doesn't want to be a rock star doesn't make him a girl.'

'Whatever.'

'Don't whatever me!'

'OK, but don't come complaining to me when he'll get beaten up at school.'

'He won't get beaten up at school.'

'Not if he studies martial arts he won't.'

'Oh, won't you just drop it? When will you get it into your head that he doesn't want to learn martial arts?'

'He does and he will, won't you Pasquale?'

'Yes, Daddy.'

'That's a good boy. We'll make an Aikido master of you.'

'What's Aikido, Daddy?'

'It's the art of overcoming your enemy by using their size and energy. It's the art of knowing where they will throw you a punch or a kick, and moving before they do.'

'Something Daddy is very good at,' she adds.

The traffic is terrible as Nick makes his way to pick up Pasquale from school.

'I spread my love like a fever!!! I ain't ever comin' down!!!' He sings at the top of his voice, competing with the radio. He's late and Pasquale is waiting for him at the school gate, clearly in a foul mood.

'My man!' he tries to high-five Pasquale as he enters the car. Pasquale offers a feeble hand in return.

'Are you psyched about going to your first Aikido lesson?' he asks, showing much more enthusiasm than his son. Pasquale nods.

'Daddy?' he says after a few moments of silence.

'What?'

'Do you think Wendy knew how to fly before she and Peter Pan met Tinker Bell?'

He swerves to the right and stops the car. 'Pasquale! Stop with all this fairy tale crap! I don't want to hear any more about Peter Pan. I don't want to hear any more about Tinker Bell, and...' and here he grabs Pasquale's sweater close to his neck, '...I DON'T WANT TO HEAR ANY MORE

ABOUT FUCKING WENDY!!!'.

He lets go of Pasquale. Both of them are shaking. They spend the rest of the drive in silence, and when they reach the gym Pasquale gets out of the car and marches towards the entrance without waiting for his father.

'Pasquale,' he calls after him. 'Are you sure you still want to do this course?' Pasquale doesn't answer. He simply marches through the sliding doors. Inside it's white and quiet. A little girl, barefoot and dressed in a white uniform and a yellow belt, approaches them.

'Hello!' she says cheerfully. 'Are you a new student?' she asks Pasquale, who is moving his head around as if he's following a butterfly.

'Pasquale, the girl asked you a question. Stop acting like a retard.'

'What's your name?' the girl asks in her angelic voice.

Nick looks at Pasquale, feeling ashamed and angry at the same time.

'His name is Pasquale,' he says, looking at his son with hatred.

'Hello, Pasquale,' the girl says, holding her hand out. 'My name is Wendy.'

#3

'How many times do I have to tell you?! I'm not doing it! I'm not going into that machine again!'

'But, Eddie dear, you know it'll make you feel better', his mother says.

'How do you know?! Are you a doctor?! You're not a doctor! You're just feeding me all the shit they're feeding you!'

He's breaking down in front of us as his Mom looks to me for support. What am I supposed to say? Tell her that he's right? Tell her that the survival rate for his type of cancer is less than 15%? Tell her that it's better to have all of him for the next three months than a third of him for a year, maybe two?

Last night Abigail asked me why I do what I do. 'Why am I a doctor?' I asked her. 'No silly, I know why you're a doctor. But why did you choose to work with people you can't really help?'

I didn't have an answer for that one, something she picked on immediately. She made me a cup of hot chocolate and left me alone in the kitchen without saying a word.

Statistically, she's right. Last year I treated 86 patients. Of those, about 40 have died so far. By March of next year, a dozen or so will join them. So why do I do it?

I ask his mother to wait for us outside, and she leaves us alone in my examination room. The first month was relatively easy. Hardly any reactions. But now the nausea is kicking in, and he's losing his hair. Now he's not only feeling ill, he's looking ill. Sometimes I think we invented chemotherapy and radiation to ensure that this disease feels and looks as dramatic as its mortality rate. It's like adding a strong odour to cooking gas to ensure that if there's a gas leak, we'll notice it, even though cooking gas is odourless by nature.

It's the first time he's not looking into my eyes, which is a bad sign. He knows his eyes can't lie. Knows that if they meet mine they will tell me that he's ready to give up. That he's had enough.

I look at his baseball cap. It looks awkward and oversized.

'What do you miss most?' I ask him.

'Being normal,' he answers without raising his head.

It's funny how we spend all our lives trying to be unique, different, original. Yet when something happens, when disaster strikes, all we want is to go back to the humdrum of our regular lives. To that steady beat of boredom. What he wouldn't give up just to spend another afternoon slouching in front of the TV, knowing that tomorrow he can do exactly the same thing.

'I miss the excitement,' I say.

He looks at me as though I just made an attempt at being funny.

'You get excited watching your patients die? Some doctor I got...'

Sometimes I forget how sharp 17 year-olds can be.

'I miss the excitement of going to battle,' I tell him. 'The rush of fighting together with my patients against this thing. I miss that sometimes.'

'Don't all your patients fight anymore?'

'Some of them do. Some of them don't. It's not for me to decide.'

'What difference does it make? Either they're gonna die, or they're not. It's not like they have a choice or anything. In fact, you're probably just planting false hopes in most of them. They think they can beat it, but we all know what the survival rates are...'

'Are you going to die, Eddie?'

'What?!'

'I want to know what you're planning to do? Are you going to die?'

'Shit man, what kind of doctor are you? I should be asking you that fucking question! How the fuck should I know if I'm gonna die?!'

He's scared now. I can see the fear in his eyes. I can see the anger.

I get up from my seat and leave him in the room on his own. Outside his mother hangs her face at an angle, trying to read from my expression whether I managed to persuade him to continue his therapy.

'Will he be okay?'

I look at her. I want to tell her something good, something positive. Something that will give her the strength to make him stronger.

'I don't know.'

#4

It was simple plan. Call Igor Ilyushin and ask $1 million dollar or we kill his little boy. Ilyushin he son of son of great aero plane engineer Piotr Ilyushin. He maybe $30 million rich.

The plan was for me to make phone call and ask for money. I would be negotiator.

I came up with name. Before, I'm just little guy supposed to call Ilyushin on the phone. But after I see movie with Kevin Spacey, I say myself - me and Kevin, we look the same. I have black hair, he have black hair. I am losing my black hair, he is losing his black hair. He is cool guy, I am cool guy.

So when my boss Nikolai tell me that I am a telephoner, I say to him, 'Nyet. I am not a telephoner. I am negotiator, like Kevin Spacey.' My boss, Nikolai, he very ignorant man. He never watch American movies. He not know who Kevin Spacey. I say to him, 'Kevin Spacey he negotiator for FBI.' When my boss he hear word 'FBI', he look at me and say, 'Da. FBI is good. You can be a Kevin Space for me.'

I say to my boss Nikolai, 'No, I be negotiator, not Kevin Space.' So he say, 'Da, you be Kevin Space Negotiator.'

So I have two week to practice for my role. I watch movie maybe twenty or thirty time. I watch so well, I know what Kevin Spacey is say every minute. Like example, the bad guy who is acted by Samuel L. Jackson, say Kevin Spacey, 'You were wrong about me. What if I'm right about them?' And Kevin Spacey he answer to the Samuel L. Jackson, 'But what if you're wrong about me?' Ha! I tell you, this FBI guy is very smart.

So after one week my wife Dasha say to me, 'Tolya, you say you are working on special project. But all day you sit in front of TV and watch same movie again and again.' Dasha, bless her souls, is a patient woman. If not that Samuel L. Jackson he is acting in the film, Dasha would tell me stop watch movie many day ago. But Dasha like Samuel L. very much, so she say nothing.

After one week, even Dasha start worrying. I don't like my woman ask me question, so I think, if Kevin Spacey his wife ask him difficult question like Dasha, what would he say? And believe me, all the answers is in the film, The Negotiator. So I say to Dasha, 'Dasha, I will give you answer, but not now.' Later, after I finish watch the movie again, I come to Dasha and say, 'Dasha, I have answer for you. The answer is this: I once talked a guy out of blowing up the Sears Tower but I can't talk my wife out of the bedroom.' This is what I say, because this is what Kevin Spacey say in difficult situation in movie.

Dasha not like my answer and I had to make dinner for

my own.

But I am tough guy, and very cool, so I keep watching the movie very close. Again and again, until I feel that I becoming Kevin Spacey. I am not Kevin Spacey, because I am Anatoly Alexandrovich, but I am very like Kevin Spacey so that even my friends tell me, 'Tolya, why how much have you changed.' And this is to me signal that I am ready for job.

So I come to my boss, Nikolai, and I say, 'Nikolai, your negotiator is ready.' Nikolai, he look at me funny, but I know it is because he see in front of him not Tolya, but Kevin Spacey, negotiator FBI.

On day of mission I sit at home and wait for phone call from my boss, Nikolai. I sit for many hour, never leave the phone. My wife Dasha, she ask me, 'Why you sitting next to phone like teenage girl?' I say Dasha to be quiet. I say her that I work on very special project for FBI. Dasha, she not know what FBI is, but think maybe is like KGB. We not have KGB anymore, but Dasha think maybe better for her not to ask question. So she go kitchen to make dinner.

At 7.03 I get phone call from my boss, Nikolai. He say, 'Tolya, you have permission to call Ilyushin.' I say to my boss, 'Give me green light.' My boss, Nikolai, he not know what green light is. So he say, 'Tolya, make call now or you in trouble.' My boss, Nikolai, he dangerous man. So I say, 'OK boss, I will make call now.'

I pick up phone and call Ilyushin. His secretary ask, 'Who is this?' I say, 'The Negotiator.' She ask me wait. After one minute she come back and say, 'We not have Mr. Negotiator here.' So I say to her, 'Listen cow, I am not looking for Mr. Negotiator, I am Negotiator. I like Kevin Spacey.'

When secretary hear I say, 'I like Kevin Spacey' she begin all excited. She ask if I see K-PAX and if I see American Beauty. I say American Beauty is best movie ever. And she agree. We talk about Kevin Spacey for many many minutes and I forget why I call. After half hour I remember I suppose to negotiate with Ilyushin. So I explain secretary what happens and ask to speak with her boss. So secretary say to me, 'We no have Mr. Ilyushin here. This is office of Mr. Plotnitsky, you make mistake.' I feel bad. I feel like my boss, Nikolai, he find out, he kill me. I tell secretary I feel bad. So she tell, 'I advice for you'. I ask her, 'What advice?' She say remember what Samuel L. Jackson say to Kevin Spacey, 'When your friends betray you, sometimes the only people you can trust are strangers.' I say to her very much thanks and go and eat dinner Dasha makes me in kitchen.

#5

'I dunno, man.'

'What?'

'That thing she does. I don't know what to do.'

'The burps?'

'Yeah. Oh come on. Stop laughing. I thought I could trust you.'

'You can trust me, all right. I just think it's hilarious that your girlfriend burps.'

'Great! I'm happy my love life is providing you with entertainment.'

'Dude, what are you talking about. I'd kill for a girlfriend that burps. That's like the coolest thing ever.'

'Cut it out, man. I'm trying to tell you I have a problem with her and I don't know what to do about it.'

'Oh, poor baby. It's natural to burp you know. Everybody does it.'

'Girls don't.'

'Hello?!'

'What?'

'Of course they do.'

'What?'

'Shhhyeah! And they fart, too.'

'Get outta town! Girls don't fart!'

'Earth calling Kevin! Hello, is there anybody home?!'

'Rita doesn't fart.'

'And she's never had sex before you either.'

'Well... I didn't say that...'

'But that's what you'd prefer to believe.'

'No, I don't prefer to believe anything. I just don't care.'

'Bullshit!'

'What?!'

'You want to tell me you don't care how many sexual partners your girlfriend had before you?'

'Who said it was more than one?'

'Hello?! Kevin, the woman is 27! It's safe to assume that she's bedded anywhere between 10 and 50 guys by now.'

'You make me sick!'

'Wake up and smell the coffee, Kev, this isn't the 1930s you know.'

'Yeah, and my girlfriend isn't a nymphomaniac.'

'Man, if you prefer to live in a parallel universe where girls don't burp, fart or have multiple sexual partners, then be my guest. All I'm saying is, that chances are your girl has tried everything you can imagine by the time she hooked up with your sorry ass.'

'Wha... what do you mean "everything"?'

'Are you for real?!'

'What?!'

'What, do I look like Dr. Ruth? Everything as in EVERYTHING!'

'Rita isn't like that.'

'Oh, she isn't. Well my condolences. You must have a miserable sex life.'

'Excuse me?! We have great sex, thank you very much.'

'And where do you think little Rita knows everything she does? Do you think she was born with the knowledge?'

'What are you saying?'

'Gee, Kev, aren't we slow upstairs today. What's gotten in you? We talk about your girlfriend's past and suddenly you're all weird and shit.'

'I dunno man, that stuff freaks me out.'

'Freaks you out? How so?'

'I don't want to be thinking about all her partners when I'm with her.'

'You're thinking about her partners when you're having sex with her? Man, we've got a bigger problem on our hands than I thought...'

'No, no, it's not like that. It's just like... that I never thought of her in that way...'

'That way? as in "not the Virgin Mary" way?'

'Look, if you can't be serious, then we don't have to talk about it.'

'Kev, take it easy. I'm just trying to help.'

'I know. It's just that I prefer not to think about all this stuff.'

'Dude, you should be grateful to her partners.'

'What?'

'Yeah. Like think about the way she goes down on you.'

'Hey!'

'What?! Oh now you're going to tell me she doesn't go down on you?'

'No, no. I mean yes, yes. She does.'

'Right. Now, you know how she does this little twist in her wrist every time she moves her hand up and down?'

'Yeah?'

'Well, that's something she learned. That's a piece of experience handed over by one of her partners, a piece of experience that you, Kevin Bailey, must be enjoying tremendously.'

'Hmmm... I haven't thought about it that way. I did wonder where she... What the? What the fuck man?!'

'What?'

'How did?! How did you know about the little wrist thing?!'

'Oh that? Emmm, well, that's actually something all girls do. But you get the point. Emmm... listen... I really gotta go now. I'll talk to you later bro? Keep it real.'

#6

'We get our inspiration from African music. You know, the drums and the beats.'

'But you guys play piano.'

'Well, yes, but isn't a piano just another form of a drum?'

'No, it isn't.'

'Well, that's just an example of how the Western world is stealing our musical heritage.'

'But you're two white guys from New Jersey. Who's stealing your musical heritage?'

'See, there you go again, it's all about White supremacy. You know, there comes a time when brothers got to get together and fight.'

'Right... well, I'm afraid that's all we have time for folks. Stay tuned for Rodney Duncan's Classy Classics coming up after this announcement from our sponsors.'

He shuffles his papers together and gets up from his seat. 'Nice try, guys,' he says to his two guests, and leaves the studio. John Nolan is 42 years old. He's been working at WXBX ('Your kinda station') for 11 years and can feel each one in his ears. He never thought it to be scientifically possible, but he's actually losing his hearing, selectively. It's like his brain would shut down whenever the person he'd be interviewing would sound too new-agey or too pretentious, or too anything.

He was a DJ in college, but his father convinced him that working in a radio station had no future. So he became a lawyer and for 10 long years he wrote and rewrote contracts. Contracts that no one cared about, that no one understood. Contracts that were so boring he actually caught his secretary asleep a few times while typing them up. When his first wife left him on account of 'not being there, and when you were there you were boring as hell' he seized the opportunity to take stock and figure out what his real passion in life was.

Nolan failed miserably at that and ended up working part-time doing legal work at the local radio station. His love of music and hatred of the legal world was clear enough for the station manager to offer him a deal. He could work as a DJ as long as he kept on doing the legal bits every now and again. Nolan said yes and so began his second career. Years passed by. There was a string of failed relationships, followed by another one. John Nolan was not a happy man.

He takes the elevator down to the parking lot. Suddenly he feels a wave of cold sweat on his back. He can't remember where he parked the car. Worse than that, he can't even remember if he brought the car today, or whether he hitched a ride with Angie, his producer. A quick check in his pockets reveals a set of keys to his house. No car keys. He must have come with Angie.

This happened to him twice before. Not with car keys, though. The first time was the scariest. He woke up at 3am to find himself curled up next to the elevator of his apartment building. He had no idea how he got there, how long he had been there or whether any of the neighbours had seen him. The second time he lost himself like that was a week ago. He went out with Angie for a quick bite after work. Three hours later she called him at home, worried crazy that he was abducted by aliens or the mafia. He had no idea what she was talking about, had no recollection where they had eaten lunch, and worse, had no idea how he got home.

He takes the stairs back to the main entrance and steps out to the street. Standing on the curb he hails a yellow cab. 'How are you this afternoon?' the driver asks in a deep, raspy voice. 'I'm well, very well,' Nolan answers.

'Where can I take you, Sir?' the driver asks with a smile that exposes a neat row of white teeth, save for one golden tooth.

'I'm sorry?' asks Nolan.

'Where do you want to go?'

And then he feels it again. As if someone had turned on the air-conditioner to maximum. He closes his eyes. 'This is stupid,' he says to himself. 'Completely stupid...'

'Sorry, Sir, could you speak up please, I didn't quite get that address.'

'I don't know,' he answers to the driver. 'I don't know.'

'Is it a restaurant, Sir? I know most of them by heart.

Just try me.'

'No, no,' says Nolan. 'I need to get home. It's just that... I don't remember the address.'

The cab driver turns around and looks at him, as if making sure he's not pulling his leg. Looking at Nolan he can see that he's not joking.

'Did you just move there? Maybe if you tell me the neighbourhood I can drive there, I'm sure you'd recognize it when we get closer.'

'I've lived there for 8 years,' Nolan answers. The driver looks at him, trying to decide what to do next. Nolan reaches for the door. 'Look, I'm sorry to have taken your time...'

'No,' says the driver. 'It's OK. Stay. We can just go for a drive, right? Who knows, we might find your home on the way.'

And so it happens that John Nolan is sitting in the back of a cab that's taking him back to a home he doesn't know the address for.

'You like movies?' asks the driver after a few minutes of driving.

'Yeah, I guess,' answers Nolan, still shaking from his inability to remember where he lives.

'You ever see Deliverance?' asks the driver.

'No,' answers Nolan, 'though maybe I have and I can't remember,' he says and chuckles, as does the driver. 'Some sick humour I got...' he says to himself.

'Sometimes you have to lose yourself before you can find anything,' the driver says to Nolan, catching his eyes in the rear-view mirror.

#7

Dear Miss Eisenstein. I promised I would write you a letter when my writing gets better. So here I am writing you a letter.

I like candy. When I grow up I'm gonna work for a candy factory. I bet I could be a really good worker in a candy factory. That's what my Daddy said. He said I could be the CTO - the Chief Tasting Officer. I think that's supposed to be some kind of joke, cuz my Daddy and Mommy laughed really hard when he said that. I laughed too, but I didn't get the joke. Grownups can be strange.

Next week school is over and my summer holiday begins.

I'm a bit scared of the summer. I made all these friends at school this year, like Matt (who likes to be called Matty) and Patricia (who doesn't liked to be called Patty). Matt and Patricia are my best friends ever. Mom said I could invite them over during the summer holiday but that's not going to work because they're both going overseas. I'm not sure what that means, but I think it means they are learning to walk on water or something.

Miss Eisenstein, can you come over and visit me? I really miss you. Why did you have to move to the universe city? Was it because there are astronauts there and you want to be an astronaut? Mom told me that it's a place where people study all day so they can get smarter. But, Miss Eisenstein, you are the most smartest person I know. So what can they teach you that you don't already know?

I still have the t-shirt you gave me (the one that says 'Go Bears' on it). All the kids at school wanted to know how I got the t-shirt. I told them Mickey Bailey personally gave it to me. They asked me why I didn't have his autograph on the shirt or something like that. I told them that Mickey and I are close friends and that you don't ask close friends for autographs.

I still have the autograph notebook you gave me, except now it's a bit full. The first page I kept empty, with only your autograph on it. But the other pages have more than one autograph on each since I figured I'll have hundreds and hundreds of them in no time. So far I have the following autographs:

Mr. Wu from the corner deli.

Mrs. Spielman from the second floor.

Arnie, the doorman.

Jose, the super.

Aunt Michele and Uncle Jason.

Lakisha - who does Mommy's hair.

Art - the delivery guy.

Mr. Clarkson, my sports teacher (all the other teachers I asked said no. Maybe they don't want to be famous.)

I thought about putting my own autograph in, but I can't figure which one I should use. I spent one whole afternoon trying to copy the signature off a $20 bill, but all I got was waves and waves and waves. Besides, my name is Tom Cohen, not Reginald McKenzie III. Who gives their kid a name like that anyhow?

My friend Patricia says that names are really important. She says that people either grow into their names or they don't, but they can't escape them. I'm not sure what that means. My name never ran after me or anything like that.

And I don't understand how you can grow into your name. Anyhow, I'm sure I've already grown into mine since it's only three letters long and I'm already seven years old.

I had a big fight with Patricia over her name. She said that her name means 'Noble One' in Latin. I told her she was lying. If her name was 'Noble One' then why doesn't everyone call her that instead of calling her Patricia? And what kind of name is 'Noble One' anyhow? Patricia said that I'm miseducated and that I don't understand anything. So I got angry at her and made up a new name for her: Noble Two.

The next day at school I got all of our class to call her that. After recess, Mrs. Cunningham asked to see me. She said that it's not nice to make fun of someone's name. I wanted to tell her that I didn't make fun of her name, that I could have called her Potty or Pooty, but Mrs. Cunningham looked kind of angry, so I said nothing.

Miss Eisenstein? If Mom says it's okay, can I come and visit you in the universe city? Do I have to bring my astronaut suit? Do I have to buy an oxygen mask as well?

Thank you for reading my letter.

Your friend,

Tom Cohen.

#8

If you could avoid one mistake in your life. If you could go back in time and take a right turn instead of a left. Show up to a meeting instead of staying in bed. Say what you really wanted instead of remaining silent. What would you change?

Tariq Zawari knew the answer to that question. In fact, a day hadn't passed that Tariq hadn't prayed to wake up and discover that the death of his brother was all just a nightmare. Yet everyday, for the past 13 years, he woke up to the sad reality that was his life.

The Zawaris emigrated from Tunisia in the late 60s and opened 'Fattoush', a small traditional Tunisian bakery, shortly after their arrival. Though small and hidden in an alleyway, tales of the bakery's magnificent bread soon made their way across the community. Within two years the bakery had to be relocated to a larger building, adding Bejma and Ten-Layer bread to its selection.

Each morning, Tariq and his brother Ajmi would wake up at 3.30, make their way to the bakery on their bicycles, and begin baking the bread. At 5.30, after finishing his morning prayers, Abdul Zawari would join his two sons. Together the three would bake until the late afternoon hours. Every day at 5pm the three would sit around a heavy oak table, drink mint tea, and eat some of the day's Baklava, a traditional sweet made from chopped nuts and honey, wrapped in delicate pastry. 'This was their little treat,' says Zawari senior. 'We were never a rich family, and I always felt bad about not sending the kids to school. So this was my little way of showing them I respected their work.'

Hearing the same account of the story from his eldest son, Tariq, would lead you to believe that the two were talking about a different bakery. 'My father has no conscience. No compassion. No love. Not for his children, not for his wife, not even for himself,' says Tariq, sipping from his milk-white glass of Araq, an alcoholic beverage he became addicted to soon after his brother's death.

'This is a man who would send his children to work at 3 o'clock in the morning, every day, every year,' says Tariq. 'Do you know how it feels to see all your friends go to school, then to high school, and instead of joining them you go to work for your father? Do you know what it feels like to become stupider and stupider each year?' he adds, emptying his glass.

Aden Zawari refused to be interviewed for this story, but friends of the family report that she sides with her son, Tariq, though she would never say so in front of her husband. 'This community is still very conservative. Women here are expected to do two things - raise the children and run the household,' says Nadia Sachnin, the owner of a small beauty salon in the village centre. 'Not a lot has changed in the past 30 years.'

But a cold morning in January 1979 changed this community forever. Neither Tariq, nor his father Abdul, are willing to recount in detail what had happened that morning. People familiar with the event told me how the two brothers had hatched a plan to burn the bakery down. They would fabricate a malfunction with the bakery's large steel oven, ensuring a fire would break before their father would arrive.

'They knew Abdul had no insurance,' says a reliable source. 'They knew that if the place burned down, he would never have enough money to rebuild it.'

Police logs from the morning show that at 4.23 an unidentified member of the community called to report a loud noise. The police dispatched an officer to look into the matter. The police log then shows that at 4.45 an ambulance was ordered to arrive at the bakery (at that time, all village emergency services were handled from the same station).

'When I got to the bakery... well, it was a mess,' says Yusuf Al-Shafi, the ambulance driver who arrived at the scene that morning. 'There was Baklava everywhere. Thousands of pieces... on the walls, on the floor, even on the ceiling,' adds Al-Shafi between puffs from his Hookah. 'It was a mess, a big mess.'

The coroner's report is a concise document written in shorthand. The cause of death is listed as 'Asphyxiation'.

'The boy didn't stand a chance,' says Dr. Farouk Majid, the village doctor at the time. 'I remember this as if it were yesterday. He had eight pieces of Baklava, you know, the small cylindrical type with the pistachio on top, lodged in his pharynx,' he says, pointing at his throat. 'I've never seen a case where anyone with that amount of Baklava in their throat had made it through the night.'

Ajmi Zawari didn't make it through that night. At 21.23, as the coroner's report reads, he was declared dead. The morning after he was brought to burial.

So what really happened during those early hours of that cold January day? The villagers are vague when it comes to details. One can't escape the feeling that there is some code of silence that is strictly enforced, ensuring the real events of that day are never made public.

'It's pretty clear what happened there,' says Walid Walid, a technician for Cinelli-Esperia, the company that manufactured the oven installed in the Zawari bakery. 'The 510 could never handle long cycles...' added Walid, referring to a model similar to the one used for baking sweats at Fattoush, '...especially not with the high heat required for Baklava. The kids must have forgotten to turn the oven off and BOOM!' adds Walid, clapping his hands for dramatic effect.

Thirteen years later life seems to be back to normal in this sleepy village. Children wake up in the morning and go to school. Women, most of them at least, still stay at home and take care of the house. And men, most of them at least, gather at 5pm in the village café, for a little glass of mint tea and a puff from their Hookahs.

But no one eats Baklava.

#9

'Morris, I'm tired of all this shit. I'm tired of moving every six months. I'm tired of these trailer parks. I'm tired of working at Burger King with some 15 year-old telling me what to do.'

Morris is sprawled on the Lay-Z-Boy, watching TV. He is wearing an unbuttoned Hawaiian shirt and white underwear. On his belly are three objects: a can of beer (Miller Lite), a bowl of popcorn and the TV remote control. He's been picking his ear for the past few minutes. If he's hearing his wife, Darlene, he isn't showing it.

'Look at me when I'm talking to you! Can't you stop watching that stupid TV for one second and talk to your wife?!'

Morris flips through the channels and takes a sip from his beer. He can't feel the liquid on his lips, so he raises the can higher, but without results. He stretches his hand a bit and shakes the can, as if hoping some liquid will miraculously materialize from it. Nothing. As Darlene continues to talk in the background, Morris is caught in a dilemma. If he gets up from the sofa to get another beer he might send Darlene the message that he's actually interested in talking to her. Yet if he stays on the sofa, the alcohol's effect will soon run out and her words will become even clearer.

'...should have listened to my mother and left you a long time ago. To think that I could be married to Phil McGraw today, living in Phoenix, playing tennis in the afternoons, taking yoga classes... but no, here I am stuck with Mr. Nobody, who doesn't even understand the concept of self-fulfillment.'

Morris realizes that inaction is also a form of action, and that Darlene is treading into the dangerous territory of psychological syllogism. If he doesn't act quickly, soon after she finishes talking about Maslow's hierarchy of needs, she'll move to Freud and explain to him how his ID is stronger than his Superego. Usually, that's when all hell breaks loose and someone gets hurt. Usually, that's Morris.

'Baby?'

It takes Darlene a few more seconds to understand that

a. Morris has spoken and, possibly more importantly, b. he might have used a term of endearment.

'Baby, why are you so angry?'

'What?' Darlene answers. Obviously she's been caught off guard.

'Why are you so mad? You know I love you... don't you?'

Darlene is perplexed. Morris hasn't said anything in the past three years that would lead her to believe that he cares about whether she's angry or not. To make matters even more confusing, the word 'love' hasn't been used, as far as she can recall, for over 12 years.

Morris leans back in his recliner and pulls up the foot support, carefully balancing the popcorn bowl on his stomach. He stares at a distant point on the ceiling and takes advantage of Darlene's silence to add an air of importance and drama to his words.

'I was thinking to myself the other day: how long has it been since we took some time off? Went on a holiday, you know, just you and I? Like in the good ol' days.'

Eleven years was the answer to his question, and as far as Darlene could remember, there was nothing good about the 'ol' days' but she's interested in seeing where this is leading to.

'So the other day I called up my uncle Leo, you know, the travel agent. He said there are great deals to Florida. We could go for a week. Heck, why not two?'

'We... we're going to Florida?'

'Sure, why not? You've always said you wanted to see Miami.'

Darlene has heard enough to convince her that a miracle has happened. She takes three quick steps to Morris's recliner and embraces him.

'Whoa there, tiger,' he says as he balances the popcorn bowl. 'At this rate we won't be going anywhere.'

Which is exactly what Morris has in mind. A trip to Florida isn't really in the plan, and Morris can't afford to take Darlene to the drive-in theatre, let alone to Miami. But that's OK. Because Darlene knows that. She knows his uncle Leo isn't a travel agent, but a used car salesman. She knows Morris won't take her anywhere. But that's OK. Because right now, as she holds the man who is her husband in her arms, she can make believe for just a little bit longer.

#10

I've got a chance to be rescued, I know. I'll be able to wake one morning and speak - and someone will listen. I'll be able to wake one morning and talk - and someone will notice. I'll be able to wake one morning and walk, and someone will follow me.

But until then, there's me, and me, and me.

It's cold outside, or at least down here, three floors under the penthouse flat that's now somewhere around ground level. How I used to envy the Mazurskys for owning a penthouse flat. Now I envy them even more - they were probably the only ones who made it out alive.

When a building collapses, who's got a better chance of surviving? The folks on the first floor? The top floor? Some floor in between?

Those are the kind of things you think about when you're trapped under a ton of concrete.

But not at first. At first you spend a lot of time freaking out and trying to wake yourself up from the nightmare that happens to be your life.

'There's no way this is happening to ME,' you keep thinking.

That goes on for a few hours, maybe even a day.

Then you become angry.

In my case, I was particularly mad that I hadn't backed up my computer. I had just gotten a lot of work done on my book, and at least half of it, the only existing half of it, was on that stupid laptop.

Not everything was bad, though - I was also lucky enough to have Lowenstein as a target for my anger. Lowenstein was the only neighbour in our building who refused the building committee's plan to replace the gas unit which fed our central heating system.

'The chutzpah of these people! Two hundred shekels for a gas valve?! I bet you I can make one of these valves for twenty shekels, if not less.'

So he did. And now most of the people who lived in this building are dead, or injured, their life course altered by some idiot pensioner who used to be an orthodontist before he retired twenty years ago.

Or maybe Lowenstein has nothing to do with it. Maybe it was the Hamas avenging the death of their leader. Mind you, why they would choose a building such as ours, which houses no one of any importance, was beyond me.

Lowenstein dissented, of course. 'Ask yourself for a second,' he shouted during the first and only conversation we had after the building's collapse, 'if you wanted to hurt a people, I mean really hit them where it hurts - wouldn't you take out all the orthodontists?'

'Yes, Lowenstein,' I yelled back, not unhappy that I had someone to direct my anger at. 'I can't think of a more painful way to hurt the spirit of a nation than having its children grow with crooked teeth!'

Lowenstein muttered something that sounded like, 'Here goes another one with an ugly smile,' but I didn't have time to ask him to repeat his words. A block of concrete or steel must have come loose and crushed him. From then on I was on my own.

On my own. That's something I thought I'd never be again. We'd been together for five months now, going on twenty years, and I knew she was the one, forever. Now all this shit happens and the only positive thing about it is that she's not here. Thank God for nieces that need babysitting.

'Remember all those things I promised I'd do? All those great plans for the business - that stuff that was just on the bottom of my to-do list? Those things that somehow got delayed for month after month? Well I'll do them now!

Straight after I get out of here. Even... even in the hospital!'
I was talking to no one in particular, as if negotiation was
an effective technique for getting rescued.

'I promise, I'll change! I will!'

'Yeah, right,' the voice in my head answered. I didn't
know if I should laugh or cry. Here I am, trapped without
food, water or light for, what is it, two days now? Yet I still
have full capacity for treating myself like shit. As if now
was the time.

The third day was the worst. I know it was the third day
because someone's alarm clock (Lowenstein's?) had gone
on for the third time. This time I didn't care when it rang
for an eternity before it stopped. On day one I amused myself
with the thought that someone might actually reach over
and turn it off - and they did. But by now everyone is dead.

So why aren't I?

'Give it time,' I say to myself. 'All things come in due time,
and your time seems to be more and more due.'

Nothing is going on in my head. I've gone through it all:
past, present and future plans. And I have to admit, most of
it wasn't that exciting. Sure, there was that time when I
learned how to windsurf, or the time I won my first customer,
but you know, all that seems a bit, well, insignificant. Except
for one thing...

'So, when are we going to kiss?' she says, two hours into our first date.

'How about now?' I ask. How about now.

#11

'Anyway, you'll get what you want.'

'Oh, yeah - how do you know what I want?'

'What do men want? It's not that difficult.'

'Humph.

'What are you doing?'

'Taking my clothes off.'

'Why?'

'OK, so I won't take them off.'

'No... I mean, yes... I mean... just... just wait a second... I need to think.'

'That'll be a first.'

'What?'

'A man who needs to think, let alone capable of doing so.'

'What's your problem?'

'My problem?'

'Yes, what's your problem with men? Why... why do you think... well, why the attitude?'

'Excuse me?'

'Yeah, I'm tired of hearing you complaining all the time!'

'You're the one who kidnapped me, remember? What did you expect? Moral support?'

'Shut up!'

'Typical...'

'What's typical?!'

'You talk back to a man and he thinks you've critiqued his sexual prowess.'

'What? Huh? How did you get from here to there?'

'It's new to you?'

'What's new to me?'

'That men are obsessed with their sexual capabilities?'

'I'm not obsessed...'

'Oh, yeah? Well, tell me, what's more important, a big penis or a great technique?'

'Great technique of course.'

'Ahhh, there goes another one with a small dick...'

'Hey! Shut up! My dick isn't small, OK. If you don't shut up I'll...I'll...'

'You'll what? Prove it?'

'Yeah, I'll prove it!'

'Fine. Suit yourself. But unless you've got 14 inches on you, don't expect any ooohing or ahhhing from me.'

'That's bullshit.'

'What is?'

'No one's got a 14-inch dick.'

'How would you know?'

'How would YOU know?'

'Darling, I may seem young, but I've been around.'

'And you've seen a guy who had a 14-inch dick?'

'Up close.'

'Shit. That's fucked up.'

'I'd say that sums it up nicely.'

'Shit...'

'Did... did...'

'Did I enjoy it?'

'Yeah.'

'Oh, so now you're my sexologist?'

'Forget about it. Keep your mouth shut or I'll shoot you.'

'Classic.'

'What's classic?'

'Your reaction. You can't impress me with the gun in your trousers, so you opt for the one in your holster. You seem perplexed?'

'I don't understand the words you're using, lady. Not all of us went to some fancy shmancy language school, you know.'

'What I meant was that you seem confused, puzzled.'

'It's just that... well...'

'That dick?'

'Yeah, I... I can't get it out of my head.'

'Well, you're lucky, I could hardly get it out of my mouth. Or in it, for that matter.'

'You're sick!'

'And you're desperate.'

'Desperate?! For what?'

'For approval.'

'Approval? Approval of what?'

'Of your manhood.'

'My what? What are you talking about?'

'Oh, didn't they teach you anything in school? You're ashamed of your sexual abilities and you want me to confirm that you're capable of pleasing any woman in the world.'

'I'm not ashamed of anything.'

'Suit yourself. But denying it won't make it go away, you know.'

'Won't make what go away?'

'The knowledge that somewhere out there is a guy with a dick that's a lot bigger than yours.'

'Tell me, lady, is that all you care about? Someone's dick size?'

'What else should a girl care about?'

'What about his manners? What about his sense of humour? What about whether he takes good care of you or not? What about all those things?'

'Amazing!'

'What is?'

'You have a brain?! For a minute there I actually thought you were incapable of real emotions.'

'I'm capable of emotions.'

'Oh, really? Well, how do you feel now?'

'Listen, I don't like the way this is going. I think I'm going to let you go.'

'Already? But you haven't even made the ransom call to my parents.'

'Yeah, well, I'll do it some other time... I... I mean, I'll find someone else to kidnap... Em...'

'Look, you don't have to explain to me. I understand.'

'You do?'

'Yes. Now come here and I'll give you a hug. See, that feels better already, right?'

'I... I guess...'

'There we go... that's a good boy.'

#12

Ten years later and I'm not sure why I'm on my way back home. There's something unidirectional about leaving home in anger. Something about shutting the door behind you with the knowledge that you'll never re-open it again.

Until today.

I hated my father, but I detested My Mom. Dad was the devil and Mom was the devil's accomplice. I think it was 5 years ago, maybe 6, when she wrote me a letter. Tried to explain how she let him do what he did to me.

'I don't expect you to start loving me again,' she wrote, 'but there are some things you won't understand until you have children of your own. Things you won't understand until you get married and seal your fate with that of another man.'

The letter sat on the kitchen counter for days. My first reflex was to throw it away. But something inside stopped me. Maybe it was curiosity, maybe it was anger, or maybe it was my deep desire for there to be an explanation for everything that happened.

'I know you'll find it hard to believe, but your father did

love you.

What he did, he did out of love.'

I could kill her for saying that.

'You may not remember this, Anthea, but you weren't exactly an easy child. God only knows the number of times we'd stay up - both your father and I - not knowing when you'd be back. Not knowing who you were with, whether you were OK. When you did come back, you always had this look of despise on your face. As though it was disrespectful of us to worry about you, to care for you.'

She was right about that. 'Despise' pretty much captured what I felt for my parents back then. Of course, after what he did to me, 'despise' had to be retired and 'hatred' promoted in its place.

'I know that nothing I say will make you forgive me. I thought long and hard about writing this letter in the first place. But I want you to know that I had no idea he was going to do what he did. I knew how much your behavior bothered him. But his anger all came from a good place, Anthea. From a place that cared and worried about you.'

Oh yeah, lot's of care. Calling me a 'slut' every time I went out dressed a little too sexy. Telling me that if I 'like fucking so much I might as well turn it into a full time occupation and help pay the bills'.

I remember the night it happened. Mom was away and I was getting ready to go out. Dad had been drinking since noon, just like the day before, and the day before. He'd been fired from the paper mill two months earlier and drowned his sorrow with booze. Lots of booze.

As I passed the living room, I could see him sitting in front of the TV, watching the game his team was losing. You could hear him curse for miles.

'Where the hell do you think you're going?' He asked me with a slur.

'None of your business,' I answered. It had been more than three years since I cared giving any of them details about my whereabouts.

'You bet your ass it's my business. I'm you're goddamn father and I make it my business to know where my fucking daughter is going to!'

'A friend,' I answered, walking towards the kitchen to grab a drink.

'A friend?! You mean a client?! You're going to see one of your clients, right?!'

'Fuck you!' I fired at him and walked towards the door with a can of 7UP in my hand.

The rest is still vivid, even ten years after. I recall the speed in which he got up from the sofa. That surprised me and I remember that for a few seconds it was the only thing I could think about - how could someone so drunk move so swiftly?

He came up to me and held me by the throat. I'd been called pretty bad things by him before, but aside from the occasional slap on the face, he had never hit me. He turned my face and pinned it to the door. 7UP spilled all over the floor.

'What's this one paying you to do?! Huh?! What's he paying you to do?!'

I couldn't speak. For one, he had his fingers closed on my throat. Aside from that I was so terrified I thought I was going to pee in my pants.

'You don't want to tell me, huh?! You don't want to tell me what you do with your clients?!'

He inched closer and pressed his body to mine. I could smell the alcohol on his breath.

'You want to play games with me?! Want to play games with your father?!

'Want me to guess what you do to them?! OK, let's play a game. Let's see what you're wearing underneath that skirt of yours. I bet you're not even wearing any underpants, you little slut.'

I was, but that didn't stop him from ripping them off. He then pushed me to the three-seater we had had for ages, bent me over and entered me from behind. I'm not sure what was more painful, the physical violation of my body or the fact that it was my father who was raping me. When he was done there was blood everywhere, on the sofa, on me, on his clothes.

'Now look what you've done you little whore. Where did all this blood come from?!'

I couldn't speak. Couldn't say a word. Couldn't tell him I was a virgin until 10 minutes ago.

Later that night my mother came into my room, pale as snow. I had told her what happened. She accused me of lying. Accused me of trying to distance my father even further from her. She kept on talking and talking after that, but I shut her off. I shut everything off. By morning I was on a Greyhound to New Mexico.

And now he's dead. The drinking and the depression had finally gotten to him. Or maybe it was the guilt. I'm not sure why I even decided to go to his funeral. Maybe I wanted to make sure they put him deep enough in the ground.

#13

'Tee tee tee! Tee tee tee! Look, Mommy! Look how I can twirl!'

'Where do they get that, Harold? It's amazing! She's hardly three and she can twirl. How do these kids do it?'

'What? Huh?'

'Honey, you're not paying attention. Mila is dancing her little dance. Look!'

'Yes, look, Daddy! I'm doing my little dance! Tee tee tee! Tee tee tee!'

'Ooops! Darling, are you OK? No, no, there's no need to cry, you were doing great, you just tripped on the third twirl that's all.

'Yes, of course Daddy would like to see you try the dance again. Go on... why, of course he's looking.'

'Ouch! What did you do that for?!'

'So you'd put down the paper for a second and look at your daughter dance!'

'But... but they're talking about hiking the interest rates up again... OK, OK, I'm looking, I'm looking. Do your little dance for Daddy, honey.'

'Ooops! Darling, are you OK? Mila, you're fine darling, just fine. Yes, yes I know it hurts. Here... Mommy will give it a kiss. See, it doesn't hurt anymore, does it? Well, OK, but it'll pass in a few seconds, OK? No, darling, you're not scarred for life, you're going to be fine.'

'"Scarred for life"? Harold, where on earth did she learn that from?'

'Oprah?'

'Oh, Harold, do be serious for a second, will you. And put down that paper for a second! Really, I don't understand you!'

'What's there to understand? I'm just... I'm... OK, I'm sorry. Mila, darling, why don't you try and do the dance one more time? Daddy would really love to see you twirl again.'

'I don't want to do the dance!'

'But honey, Daddy really wants to see you dance.'

'No he doesn't.'

'Great! I hope you're proud of yourself, Harold. Now she's starting to doubt herself, just when we started dealing with the twirl issue.

'Honey, no, please, honey, don't throw your dancing shoes like that, no, NO! Mila! We don't throw shoes into the fireplace! Harold! Do something!'

'What do you want me to do, leap into the flames?'

'I can't believe you just did that!'

'What?'

'Just let those shoes burn!'

'What are you talking about?! What did you want me to do?'

'What did I want you to do?! Your daughter's ballet shoes are burning in the fire and you're asking "what did you want me to do"?!'

'Why are you all upset with me, then? It's not like I threw them into the fire, she did...'

'Mila, Mila honey don't cry, please don't cry! Daddy didn't mean to offend you, right Daddy? RIGHT DADDY?!'

'Rrrright...'

'You see, Mila, Daddy didn't mean to hurt your feelings. It's just that he can behave very silly sometimes... can't you Daddy?!'

'I guess...'

'Daddy?'

'Yes Mila?'

'Can you show me how you twirl?'

'What?'

'Show me how you do the twirl. I want to see you do the twirl.'

'What? Why are you looking at me like that?!'

'Well, you heard the child, Harold. She wants you to do the twirl?'

'The twirl?! What's "the twirl"? Are you out of your mind?!'

'Mila, don't cry honey, Daddy didn't say you were out of your mind... calm down honey...

'Harold!'

'What?!'

'Just do the fuckin' twirl!'

'Yes Daddy, just do the fucking twirl!'

#14

I think I'm going to die.

I can see it. I mean, literally. I can see how I'm walking on the street. I see Jes and Alek on the other side of the road, you know, passing Benjy's to make fun of that Korean woman who works there. They see me, signal me to come over and join them, which I do. I cross the street and this Porsche, this slick black Porsche which belongs to that faggot who's fucking my sister, comes running down the street and slams into me straight on. The impact throws me up in the air so hard that my shoes, my Puma Sacramento shoes, fly off my feet, even though they're the special edition with Velcro on them. And even though I'm flying in the air, I have time to look at Jes and Alek, and they look back at me in this totally surreal way, like they're both smiling or something, like I've done something really cool.

'Mr. Bovington! I'm glad to see that you are taking the time to finesse your literary skills!' the history teacher says in his loud, authoritative voice.

'Give me back my notebook,' Nathan says.

'How unfortunate it is that you are using my history class to do so...'

He continues to read out of the notebook: 'And just before I hit the ground, I see that my girlfriend is looking at me from inside the Porsche.

'An expensive taste in cars, Mr. Bovington?' continues the history teacher, holding Nathan's notebook high up. As he does so, three small colour pictures fall out. Nathan bolts to the floor, but the history teacher bends down and picks them up before he reaches them. The pictures are of Samantha, his girlfriend. In the pictures she is naked.

'Aha, a true Renaissance man, Mr. Bovington, a writer and... how shall I say, a photographer of sorts.'

Nathan, all five feet of him, is standing close, perhaps closer than he'd like, to the history teacher. Though he's not looking in their direction, he knows all the class is looking at him, waiting to see how he reacts to this double invasion of his privacy.

At this point a few things could have happened. Nathan

could have tried to grab the notebook from the history teacher's clutch. He could have tried to grab the pictures of his girlfriend in the buff.

But he didn't.

Nathan could have yelled back at the history teacher. He might have called him 'stupid' or 'idiot' or even an 'arse'.

But he didn't.

What instead happened was that Samantha, Nathan's girlfriend, got up from her chair and walked very slowly towards Nathan and the history teacher. When she reached them, she moved Nathan aside, stood silently for a few seconds in front of the history teacher, who looked at her intently, and gave him a hard, forceful slap on the face.

The slap was so hard that the history teacher, 55 and heavy-framed, lost his balance and had to use his desk to stop himself from falling. In the process he dropped Nathan's notebook and pictures to the floor, where all eyes were now focused.

Samantha leaned down and picked up the notebook and photos. With a face lacking emotion she went through the photos, putting them side by side on the teacher's desk. She then took the notebook and placed it next to the photos. With that, she turned around, opened the classroom door and left without closing it behind her.

Nathan looked at the history teacher, who kept rubbing his hand on his face, which was now adorned with the surprisingly clear outline of a palm.

'I... I can explain, sir,' said Nathan. Not sure whether he really could.

'You see... we... she... we had this argument about how I said she shouldn't let people boss her around and... and I told her... I told her she has to take a stand, you know, fight for what's hers and...' and by now the history teacher wasn't looking at Nathan, nor was the class. By now everyone was looking at the entrance to the classroom, through which Samantha had just re-entered the room. In her hand she was holding a small pistol, the type that could fit in a woman's purse.

And then she used it.

#15

'This feels like walking on moonlight!' she says.

'Yeah, it's pretty good, isn't it?'

She looks at me and smiles. She's got many smiles, my girl. This one is the life-can-be-so-good! smile.

We're walking on water. Well, almost. We're wading through 10 inches of water, enough to cover this muddy reservoir with a thin sheet of silver. That's how it looks if we don't move - like a sheet of silver stretching from one end of the reservoir to the other, with the moon providing the special effects. When we walk, our feet sink into the shallow soil as the water breaks into little dances of light and darkness.

'How far in can we go?' she asks, leaning to waggle her hand in the water, as if to test whether it's real water or not.

'How far do you want to go?' I answer.

'Can we go there?' she asks, pointing her hand to the little island located in the middle of the reservoir.

I don't answer. For a second I forget why we came here in the first place - to talk about the future, or lack of it. She notices that I'm lost in my thoughts and takes my silence as an affirmation. 'Yes,' she says, 'let's go there.'

I snap out of my reverie to find that she's quite far away from me. Though it's well after midnight, the moon is shining so brightly that I have no problem noticing her looking back at me. I start running, and catch up with her as she giggles. 'Someone's in bad shape here...' she says. 'Yeah, I wonder who,' I answer, before realizing the sarcasm in my comment.

The words are floating in my head: '...results from an acquired genetic injury to the DNA of a single cell... blockage in the production of normal marrow cells, leading to a deficiency of platelets... long and painful process... no guarantee that it will work...'

Cancer is a quiet disease. It's whispered. 'S h e ' s g o t c a n c e r...' kids would explain to their friends when they asked why the girl they had just seen in the cafeteria had no hair. Heart problems are in a different category - they're loud diseases. You never hear anyone whisper 'h e h a s h i g h b l o o d p r e s s u r e...' No. It's always 'HE'S GOT HIGH BLOOD PRESSURE!'

I'm not sure why cancer is such a hushed disease. After all, you don't catch it from other people like AIDS, and it doesn't mess with your head, like Alzheimer's does. Then again, maybe that's the reason it gets the silent treatment. We're scared of what we don't know, and no one really knows anything about cancer.

'What are you thinking about?' she asks me as we sit on the wet soil of the island in the middle of the reservoir.

'I'm thinking about how no one really knows anything about anything. How it's all a matter of belief. How there's no way to prove anything.'

She doesn't answer, just smiles. This time it's her I-like-to-hear-you-talk-complete-nonsense smile. She takes my hand in hers, gives me a kiss on each finger, and looks at the moon.

'Do you think they'll ever make it?' she asks, referring to the three astronauts who had taken off into space earlier that day.

They did, but she didn't. Three days later, as all of my family was huddled around the TV set, I'm huddled around her hospital bed. Two teenagers lying together in a hospital bed. The nurses didn't even try to stop us from lying next to each other. They knew she was dying.

That was more than 30 years ago. Now they're thinking about putting up a resort on the moon, giving rich people a chance to touch the sky. I'm married now, with kids of my own. I love my family. But somewhere inside there's a little part that misses her. A little part that lights up every once in a blue moon. And when that happens, whenever I want to touch the sky, I just head over to the old reservoir and walk on some moonlight.

#16

36

72

84

91

3

For the untrained eye these are just numbers. Numerical representations of a series, at most. A few enthusiasts would try to deduce whether there's an order in these numbers - some form of pattern, perhaps.

But though he's been called 'The Numerical Engine', all Panjit Bajaj sees are flowers. Bright pink flowers. Those who have seen his work are forever changed. Those who have studied it claim that he is the greatest mathematician-cum-painter of his time, if not of all times.

Panjit Bajaj was born one humid August afternoon to a well-to-do family in the state of Kerala, India. His father began his career as the keeper of the cricket grounds in Thiruvananthapuram, the state capital. Bajaj senior's deep understanding of the human psyche, coupled with his fondness for the game of cricket, soon bought him a place on the state team as a psychologist of sorts. Bajaj's 'positive thinking' sessions were so effective, that the great Balan Pandit, who's record of 262 is still unbroken 45 years after it was set, once said that, 'without Bajaj I'd still be sulking in the dressing room'.

Bajaj junior was destined to follow his father's footsteps and practically grew up on the cricket fields. But instead of tending for the delicate souls of Kerala's up-and-coming cricket players, Panjit found more interest in numbers. He had a photographic memory and could recite all the exact scores that his state, Kerala, had ever achieved against any other cricket team since the state was founded.

Bajaj's way with numbers did not go unnoticed and his father sent him to read mathematics under the great M.K. Rajasekharan. Math however, it was soon found out, was not the right department for Bajaj junior. Though his understanding of the subject was on a par, if not greater than that of his teachers, his patience for conducting research and writing essays left much to be desired. 'Academia,' Professor Rajasekharan told Panjit's father, 'was not set up for the brightest stars, but for those who are willing to stay in orbit.'

After leaving Kerala university, Bajaj decided to move to Kodaikanal, one of India's most picturesque hill stations. Bajaj's choice of Kodaikanal turned out to be a watershed in art history. Unbeknownst to Bajaj, his pilgrimage to Kodaikanal had intersected with an event that happens only once in 12 years - the blossoming of the Kurinji flower.

Bajaj, who had never drawn in his life before reaching Kodaikanal, was immediately mesmerised by the town's serenity. Yet it wasn't until a local guide took him to see the Kurinji blossom, that Bajaj took brush in hand and begin painting.

'The effect was sudden and complete,' he wrote in his autobiography 'Petals' (Scribner 1987). 'Here I was, 2,000 meters above sea level, and I had found God. Not "God" in the sense most of us use, but the representation of "Perfection." Mathematics deals a lot with issues of perfection. But it wasn't until I'd seen this flower, this perfect pink creation, that I understood the true meaning of the word.'

It has been the topic of many a theory what would have happened had Bajaj been inspired by a different flower, such as the rose, or even the daffodil. The pundits remain split. 'This question is simply of no value,' claims R.M. Viraswami, chairman emeritus of the Indian Art Foundation. 'Bajaj is Kurinji. It's that simple. Bajaj could never be associated with, or inspired by, a different flower. The connection here is one-to-one.'

Others are less convinced. 'It's not as if the man had never seen a flower before the Kurinji,' said N. Raghavan, artist and author of some 20 books on modern Indian art. 'Bajaj was certainly exposed to flowers before he saw the Kurinji. To think that this flower is the only one that ever inspired him is to take the Kurinji incident out of its context.'

Bajaj's style is not easy to define. 'A cross between Monet and Raja Ravi Varma (Kerala's greatest painter - NZ)' said the Kerala Herald in its special cover edition dedicated solely to Bajaj on the first anniversary of his death. The New York Magazine called him 'Picasso without the mistakes'.

But perhaps our inability to pin down Bajaj's style is a testament to his greatness. For true greatness can never be appreciated in its time.

'I am not a painter,' Bajaj is claimed to have said on his deathbed. 'The painting comes through me'.

#17

It was the last good day of the year.

The sun was falling hard on the pavement, leaving the air hot and humid. Angel had been in intensive care for over two weeks and we were all waiting for Stella to bring back the good news that would tell us she's coming back.

The residents of 109 Waverly were all out on the front stairs. There was Alexei, the Polish artist from the top floor and Anka, his girlfriend who never spoke. There was José, who was from Puerto Rico, but kept insisting he was from L.A. ('Los Angeles baby, and I don't mean maybe!').

There were Peter and Tom, the gay couple who'd been arguing with each other since they moved into the brownstone in 1969. Then there was me and Mateo, our Haitian landlord. All waiting.

'It's not "stupa",' said Tom in his didactic voice. 'It's "stoop". It's in Dutch.'

'Stoop? What the hell is stoop?' said Peter, wiping his brow with a blue bandana.

'It's in Dutch,' answered Tom, impatiently.

'Mateo - stoop or stupa?' asked Peter.

'Both. Technically you can call these stairs a stoop. But I call them "stupa".'

'You see!' jumped Peter. 'I told you so!'

Tom, ignoring Peter's festive mood, turned to Mateo,

who was handing out mint iced tea in tall glasses.

'Why "stupa"?' asked Tom.

'You ever heard of Buddha?' asked Mateo.

'Buddha? Isn't he the black dealer from Fourth street?' asked José.

'Of course I've heard of Buddha,' answered Tom, ignoring José.

'"Stupa" means "mound" in Sanskrit. In the Buddhist religion, a stupa is a holy place, a monument.'

'See, I told you it wasn't in Dutch!' said Peter, smirking at Tom.

'A holy place!' said José, taking off his shirt and using it to wipe his forehead. 'Like Bethlehem?'

'More like Mount Moriah,' said Mateo.

Alexei and Anka whispered to each other.

'Mount Moriah? Is that in Vermont?' asked José.

'No. It's in Bible,' said Alexei. 'It is where Abraham sacrificed his son Isaac to God.'

'I'm confused,' said Tom.

'What else is new?' fired Peter.

'Tom, you remember when you guys first moved in here?'

'Yeah. It was the day Judy Garland died.'

'Judy Garland? Isn't she that actress from the Wizard of Oz?' asked José, to the amazement of all.

'Ten points, José!' said Tom.

'A week before you guys moved in I went down to Brooklyn to buy a car. It was a second-hand El Camino. A real beauty. I drove it back home and parked it over there,' Mateo said, pointing up the street. 'I opened the door and slammed it straight into the fire hydrant. "Some luck," I thought to myself. I buy a new car and the minute I get home, I hit the door on a fire hydrant.

'I remember stepping out of the car and looking at the door, trying to figure out how much it would cost me to fix, wondering why I didn't look for a better spot to park, when I heard someone crying. I turned my head and saw a crowd of people on the steps.'

'What ha happened?' asked Alexei, adding the 'ha' to the 'happened' in a way that made you unsure whether it was due to his poor English or to his rich sense of humor.

'I ran towards the steps. There, amongst the crowd, I saw Angel holding my boy in her arms. He was dead.'

'Your boy?!' interrupted Tom. 'I... we never knew you had a boy, Mateo.'

'Before I left he begged me to let him play out on the street. I figured it was too hot to stay indoors anyhow, so I let him play. When I came back he was dead.'

No one said a word. Half of us were probably in shock from the story. The other half in shock that Mateo never told them he had had a son.

'You couldn't tell he was ever hit by a car,' said Mateo after a long silence. In the background a phone rang.

'He had this perfect smile on his face, as if he was only sleeping in Angel's lap.'

Tom and Peter looked at each other. Anka wiped a tear. José scratched his neck.

Stella, Mateo's wife, came out of the front door, cordless phone in hand.

'She didn't make it,' she said with a sad voice. 'I just spoke to the doctor. She died an hour ago, peacefully.'

Mateo got up and walked back in to the house.

It was the last good day of the year.

#18

'Yeah, well I'll tell you how I'm going to feel. I'm going to feel like someone just pulled the rug from under my feet. That's how I'm going to feel.'

He slams the door behind and leaves. He won't return. Not tomorrow, not the day after. Not ever. In about 30 seconds his life will end. Freak accident, that's what they'll call it. An elevator door opens, a guy steps in, and falls twenty floors to his death. A malfunction of some sort. No one is really sure how it happened. Maybe a fuse blew, maybe a regulator was faulty. That's not the point, though. The point is that now he's dead, and he isn't coming back.

Which is kind of what she hoped for, but not really. Not for good. Only for a bit.

They were having dinner at her place. He cooked. She made dessert. They watched a video. Something with Sean Penn playing a retard. Then, she isn't really sure when, he asked her that question. That question he ends up asking her now and then...

'So, would you say I'm a good lover?'

'Of course you are, baby! You're MY lover, aren't you?'

'Yeah, I know that. But am I a GOOD lover?'

'Not just GOOD, baby - you're GREAT!'

He takes a swig from his beer and looks at the TV without paying too much attention to it. He's at a different movie now.

'But last night, yeah, you didn't really come, did you?'

'Of course I did, baby! I was coming so hard the neighbours could hear me!'

'Yeah, but that doesn't say anything, does it? You women do that stuff all the time, don't you? The oooh-ing and ahhh-ing. Like in that movie, you know, when Mary met...'

'...When Harry met Sally,' she interjects.

'Yeah... yeah... see, you know what I'm talking about.'

'But baby, you always make me come.'

'But how can I know? How can I really be sure that I make you come?'

'Well, because I'm telling you that you do. That's why.'

He gets up from the sofa and starts walking around. He's scratching his right shoulder, trying to get at an itch that just won't let go.

'Would you be happier if I had a bigger dick?'

'Of course not baby, I love your dick just the way it is.'

'But you'd prefer if it was a bit bigger. You know, a few inches longer.'

'Baby, I'm really happy with your dick. I love your dick. Besides, it's not like I have endless space there.'

'Yes, but you wouldn't be against the idea of doing it with someone who has a bigger dick, right? And you have, right? I mean, even if my dick isn't small, I'm sure you've seen bigger ones, right?'

She doesn't answer. She knows where this is heading, and it's not a good place. 'Just let him get it out of his system,' she repeats to herself. 'This is not about you, it's about him. And we all know that you can't change him. Only he can change himself.'

'Darling, why don't I get you another beer?' she offers.

'No! Why don't you answer my fucking question instead. Have you had someone with a bigger dick?'

She stays silent.

'Have you?!' he asks again, moving closer to her.

'Yes. OK? But I didn't even enjoy it that much.'

'Who was he?!'

'What difference does it make?'

'Who was he?!?!'

'Alan.'

'Alan? Alan?! Alan's got a bigger dick than I do?!'

'Honey, I told you, it doesn't matter to me. I don't want Alan and I don't want Alan's dick. I want your dick. Only your dick, baby.'

'I can't believe this. I can't fuckin' believe this. Now every time I see Alan at work I have to think about his dick and how you... how you... Oh, for Christ's sake Sheila, did you have to tell me who it was?!'

'But... you asked me...' she says, tears running down her throat.

'This is great! This is just fucking great! How... how do you think all this makes me feel?! Huh?! How do you think I'm going to feel every morning when I walk into the office?!'

He picks up his jacket and looks for his keys.

'Please don't, baby... please don't go. I'm sorry.'

'Yeah, well I'll tell you how I'm going to feel. I'm going to feel like someone just pulled the rug from under my feet. That's how I'm going to feel.'

He slams the door behind and leaves.

#19

The road to Angemustash runs for 645 kilometres. One shouldn't really call it a road, considering the fact that 643 of these kilometres are unpaved gravel. We were lucky enough to get an old Land Rover from the Belgian Embassy, which was the least they could do considering it was one of their men we were going to rescue. The car came with a driver - a mountain of a man named Assif, whose language skills proved to be only slightly better than his driving.

Ivan, my partner on this assignment, was an old dog at this game. You could tell that by the way he popped two sleeping pills immediately when we pulled out of the city. At the age of 50, Ivan had seen more recoveries than anyone else in the service. He also knew that the key to staying sane in this business is to use every opportunity you have to sleep.

Most people who join the service do so because they're adrenalin junkies. 'Emergency Incident-Response Services' sounds like such a sexy career, that it attracts over two thousand applications each year - and this is just with our company. Of those two thousand, only ten or so become agents. Five make it through their first year, and two or three to their second. Most people think that agents leave this job because it's too stressful. The truth is they leave it because it's not stressful enough.

Take this assignment, for example. Two weeks ago we get a call from the Belgian embassy that one of their agents had failed to make his weekly contact. 'Could you send some of your men to check if he's OK?' they asked. Our firm said yes, of course. And so Ivan and I have been on the road for the past 72 hours, with absolutely nothing to do but solve crossword puzzles, or in Ivan's case, sleep.

To be quite frank, I was getting bored as well at this point, and the thought of being driven by a mute driver on a gravel road for over 12 hours didn't add to my excitement. The fact that the scenery outside hadn't changed for the past four hours didn't make things any better. The only traffic we'd seen since we left the city was a dog, and even he was lying dead on the road.

The only reason I did stay awake was that a. I didn't trust our driver not to fall asleep, and b. I didn't even trust him to, well, drive.

After six hours of non-stop driving I needed to relieve myself. And so I asked, or rather signalled, our driver to stop. He looked at me and shook his head.

'No good,' he said, surprising me that he a. spoke and b. spoke English.

'Listen, old chap, I really need to go and it doesn't look like there's a lavatory in this car, so could we please stop for a second and have a quick loo break?'

Assif looked at me and shook his head. This time he didn't even bother speaking.

There was no sense arguing with a man who's twice your size and happens to hold the wheel of the car you're being driven in. I made a simple calculation that as large as his bladder might be, he too will eventually heed nature's call.

I was wrong.

Nine hours into our drive and we still hadn't had a break. I pleaded with Assif one final time. This time he didn't even bother looking at me. It was only when I began opening my trousers with one hand, and positioning the empty water bottle near my fly with the other, that he took notice and brought the car to a halt. I leapt out of the car and dropped my pants just in time. A minute later and I'd have wet myself.

'You have permit?' I heard a voice behind me.

At first, I was sure it was Ivan, trying to provide some comic relief.

'You have permit?' the voice said again.

'Oh, bugger off, Ivan!' I shouted.

Suddenly, I felt a blunt object pushed into my back. I turned around. Behind me was a soldier of some sort, his head wrapped with a massive scarf. Behind him, aiming straight at me, was another soldier. The car was surrounded with at least ten more.

Where on earth did they come from?

The soldiers took Assif and Ivan out of the car and forced them to lie on the ground.

'Excuse me,' I began saying. 'We are British nationals. We have a permit to drive to Angemustash. Please calm down. Ivan! Show them the permit,' I yelled.

The solider behind me must have understood at least some of what I was saying, as he moved his gun away from my back. He barked some orders to the soldiers next to the car. One of them took the permit out of Ivan's pocket and brought it to the solider behind me who examined it briefly.

'Permit not good,' he said, returning the gun to my back.

'Not good?' I pleaded. 'But it's an official permit by the Ministry of Interior.'

'Yes, it permit by Ministry of Interior,' the soldier said.

'And it permits us to drive to Angemustash.'

'Yes, permit permits you to drive to Angemustash.'

'So what seems to be the problem?' I asked the soldier, who was now getting restless.

'Permit not good for peeing in the middle of the road.'

#20

It's almost midnight and I'm standing on the wooden porch, naked. There's hardly any wind, but I know it'll come soon. I can feel it. I close the door behind me quickly - the less light that comes from inside, the less the mosquitoes will notice I'm here.

I can hear the water kissing the sand, like a dog sipping from his bowl. All else is quiet. I close my eyes and try to imagine the wind, still a few miles away, blowing closer and closer. The moon is partially covered, but I can already see the heavy clouds moving in our direction. They've been waiting all day, hanging in the sky, barely able to delay their arrival.

I walk down the wooden steps till I feel the ground, pine needles under my feet. Every now and then an acorn reminds me to watch my step. I walk thirty steps or so and reach another flight of stairs. These are heavier, made from old crossties that were used for a now defunct railroad track. Fifty years later, you can still smell the diesel they were soaked in.

From here I can see the lake stretching in front of me. It's calm right now, but there's a tension about it. As if the water knows a storm is rising. I close my eyes and take a deep breath. Soon.

The beach is deserted. During the day there are hardly any people here; during the night, it's empty. Even the dogs are too tired to take a stroll, having spent the better part of the day chasing each other in the sand.

There's a flash in the sky. No sound yet. That means the storm hasn't arrived. But it will come. It always does.

I can feel the sand under my feet. I take a few steps and let them sink in the silky texture. As they break the outer layer and dig deeper, I can feel the warmth of the afternoon sun still trapped inside. A shiver passes through me. The temperature is dropping and I can feel the wind picking up. Tiny wingtips are starting to form in the water. It's coming.

Then I feel something else. It's her. I know it. Don't ask me how. Her house is too far down the beach to hear a door slam, or the stairs of her wooden porch creak. No, this is something you hear from the inside.

I take a few steps and stand on the water's edge. The wind is blowing stronger. I feel something behind me move, but I don't turn around. Instead, I let the water wet my feet. It's always warmer than I remember.

A flash lights up the sky. This time thunder follows, slowly rolling towards us. It's moving.

I kneel and dip my hands in the water. I pull them out. I hold them above my face, letting the drops fall on my skin, feeling the tingle. I take a few more steps forward, til I'm knee-deep in the water. I can feel drops on my face, only this time they're coming from the sky. It's raining.

She'll be here any minute now. She'll come from behind. Though I'll hear her wading in the water, I won't turn around.

The water is up to my waist now and I fold my hands to warm myself. I turn my head down and lick the raindrops from my shoulder. She's in the water too. Getting closer.

Now she's behind me. It's been a year since I saw her last. A year since I felt her body cling to mine.

Lightning strikes again, lighting up the lake. The rain is falling hard and for a second it seems to be dangling from the sky, like some kind of beaded curtain.

Her tongue is on my neck. A jolt of electricity passes through my body. I can feel every single nerve ending. She takes her hands and glides them over my shoulders, down towards my arms. Her nipples are hard against my back. I turn around and hardly get a chance to look at her before our mouths lock into each other. We kiss hard, drinking each other. As though we've been walking in the desert for years without water. We stop for a moment and look into each others' eyes. The rain makes it difficult to keep them open, so we bring our heads as close as possible together, till our lips almost touch.

She keeps her gaze fixed on mine as her hand moves lower and lower. She holds me in her hand, squeezing, caressing. She keeps looking at me as my fingers glide over her mound. I move them up and down, slowly. She lets out a gasp. We kiss again, and as the sky is lit once more, there's a look in her eyes. Craving.

I move my hand away from her and bend my knees. She moves in unison with me, putting her arms around my neck as her legs lock around my waist. With one hand under her, and the other guiding myself into her, I lower her slowly. As I enter her, I wait. In, then out a little, then in again. I can feel the weight of her body buoyed by the water. I move her up again, then down, in one swift move. She lets out a little yelp.

I am in her now. Or is it her that's in me? There's no telling the difference.

And there, in the eye of the storm, nothing else matters, nothing else exists, but us.

#21

We are in a small TV studio. On the main stage, the set is ready for another live recording of 'Cogito Ergo', a one-time highly rated talk show that has since fallen from grace. Two comfortable-looking leather sofas are positioned at 45 degrees to each other. Between them is a simple glass table. On it is a pitcher of water and two tall glasses.

The wall behind the two sofas is covered with illustrations of famous philosophers: Aristotle, Socrates, Sartre, Descartes, Hume and many others. A brainchild of Ron Harris, a high school dropout, the show has been running for over thirty years. Miraculously, Harris managed to do what hundreds of others before him failed: bring philosophy to the family dinner table.

The secret to the show's appeal is its host's ability to burrow deep into the psyche of his guests, and Harris had the gift of getting even the most enigmatic guest to expose his deepest secrets.

But tonight is the last show and we now join Harris in his dressing room. May, the makeup artist, has left the room, and for the next 30 minutes, Harris will do what he's done for the past 30 years before he goes on air - meditate.

Except that tonight Harris is troubled. What was supposed to be a festive closing show is now turning out to be a major headache. The focal point of this headache is Professor Augustus Black. Widely considered the most important philosopher of the century, Black had repeatedly refused Harris's invitations to the show. After the fifth rejection, Harris decided to give up.

That was five years ago.

Yesterday, Black's agent contacted Harris and informed him that, 'Professor Black might be able to set aside some time for an interview.' The fact that Black was the only university professor, not to mention the only philosophy professor to have an agent, didn't escape Harris. With all his contempt for his elitist behaviour, Harris couldn't resist admiring Black's ability to market himself and his ideas.

'Beware what you wish for,' his wife used to tell him. Now Harris is feeling the burden of her words. What do you do when the most important living member of your field is in your studio? What do you ask him that no one else has asked?

/Opening Music/

'Good evening, ladies and gentlemen, and welcome to the final show of "Cogito Ergo". Our program tonight promises, even more than usual, to be thought-provoking and intriguing. It will not leave you unmoved.

'Every generation has its geniuses. The men and women upon whose shoulders we stand. Tonight we are fortunate enough to have one of those geniuses with us in the studio.

'Born in Boston, Massachusetts in 1913, he graduated from Princeton at the ripe age of 16 and took a professorship position at Yale at the age of 21, the youngest man ever to do so. In 1938 he volunteered to the US Army, where he built the first Psychological Warfare department and in 1945 became special aide to President Truman, a role he continued to keep up until the end of the Clinton administration. Along the way he wrote more than 40 books and has won every possible award in his field, as well as in other, less-obvious fields such as Finance, Law and Chemistry.

'Ladies and gentlemen, please join me in giving a warm welcome to Professor Augustus Black!'

/Wild applause from the audience/

The camera pans and focuses on Black. Despite his years there's a certain intensity about him which hasn't faded at all. If anything, he can be described as glowing. Harris is looking through his notes now. Early that morning he and his production crew assembled a list of questions, many taken from a makeshift assortment of experts in the field, who were interviewed only hours earlier in a last-minute attempt to provide Black with a battery of challenging questions.

There's an extended silence as the camera focuses back on Harris. He looks at his notes, but is drawn to the face of the towering genius sitting next to him. Almost a minute passes by and Harris is speechless. Black moves in his chair, showing the first signs of discomfort.

And then, just before the show's director is about to cut to a commercial, Harris stands up, carefully removes the microphone from his lapel, placing it on the glass table next to Black. He folds his notes neatly, tucks them into the inner pocket of his suit, and leaves.

#22

'That she managed to show complete disrespect for my request is one thing, but to mock me in front of my family and friends is something altogether different. I'm afraid, Jeeves, that there's no turning back from here.'

'And what will you do with the engagement, sire?'

'The engagement? Yes. I'm afraid you're right. 'Tis time to deal with this thorny issue here and now. The engagement, Jeeves, is off. You shall notify Lady Devonshire tomorrow morning. Tomorrow evening you will begin communicating the news to the rest of the family.'

'But what about the wedding plans?'

'Jeeves, have you been listening to a single word I've said all evening? The engagement is off. Hence, the wedding is off. Hence, there are no plans.'

'Yes, sire.'

I send Jeeves away. Sometimes I ask myself how my parents managed to get anything done with that sorry excuse for a butler. I sit on my sofa and watch the fire burn. Amazing things they are, fires. No two flames are alike, yet even a child can recognise a fire when he sees one. This thought made a profound impact on me. How do we know the chairs from which all other are spawned? My thoughts then led me to a more disturbing query. How do I know that Lady Devonshire really is who she is? I can see her beauty in my eyes. I can smell the sweet scent of lilac of her skin. I can touch her warm hand. And when I do so, I know that it is her. But do I really know her? Does anyone? Can we truly know what one feels, thinks, hopes or dreams?

Perhaps it was all an illusion? Perhaps my infatuation with Lady Devonshire had nothing to do with any deception on her behalf? Perhaps it was me who preferred constructing an image of her, an image that did not exist in reality, other than in my head?

'Jeeves?! Jeeves?!'

'You called, Sire?'

'Yes, I called. Jeeves, come here and take a close look.'

'Sire?'

'Closer, Jeeves, closer. Take a close look at me. Do I remind you of anyone?'

'Sire?'

'Jeeves, will you please stop saying "Sire" all the time and answer my question?'

'Yes.'

'Who?'

'Who?'

'Yes, Jeeves, who do I remind you of? Who do I look like? How do you know that it is me you're speaking to?'

'Why Sire... I'm sorry, milord, emmm, I have known you all my life.'

'Yes, but how can you prove that I am me?'

'You and not...'

'Someone else, Jeeves, someone else. How can you be certain, absolutely certain that I am who I am?'

'Well, milord, I suppose you have a point there. I don't think I can be absolutely sure.'

'Then how, for heaven's sake, can you call me your master, your Lord, if you're not sure who I am?'

'I'm not sure why, Sire, but I've always found life a bit easier that way.'

'Jeeves, you are playing with my temper and avoiding the issue altogether. Can't you see what I'm dealing with here?'

'How can I help, milord?'

'Punch me.'

'Milord?'

'Punch me, Jeeves. If I feel the pain then at least one of us knows that I am who I am.'

'Ahhh!!! Jeeves!!! What on earth were you thinking?!'

'I... I'm so sorry, milord. Please forgive me. I simply

wanted to please you.'

'Please me? By punching me so hard my nose is dislocated?! How on earth do you think that Lady Devonshire will react when she sees this injury?!'

'Milord? I... I thought...'

'You thought what?!'

'The engagement... The, the wedding... I...'

'Jeeves, will you please stop worrying about the wedding! The pain will disappear by the wedding.'

'Let's just hope you don't...' said Jeeves without being heard.

#23

You could tell by the weight of the envelope that she chose an expensive firm.

Opening the envelope and pulling its contents was like a journey into the world of paper supermodels. Inside there are no more than thirty sheets. Their silky texture was cool and inviting, and as I began easing them out of the envelope they made a soft noise, not unlike the sound of the palm of my hand caressing her arm.

The cover letter was short and to the point. I had been expecting this for quite some time, and having a fairly clear idea of what it would read like, I chose to focus on the top part of the sheet, where the name of her law firm was written in majestic letters. They used a somewhat rare copperplate typeface called Young Baroque, developed by Doyald Young, the renowned West Coast designer.

'Debevoise, Dupuy & Declercq'

I wonder what it takes to have a name like that? How far back into French aristocracy would you have to go? Who would you have to marry?

The paper is really magnificent. I hold it in front of the light to see the watermark. That it's Monarch is no surprise. But it seems that it belongs to a limited edition. The serifs of the 'M' are somewhat pointier than the standard, top of the line, Monarch stationary. The sheet I'm holding must retail at more than two dollars a page. That is, assuming you could buy this at retail. Which you wouldn't, because Monarch stopped accepting new customers to its special edition stationary paper five years ago.

I put the cover page on the side and thumb through the

remaining papers. Though they were printed out on an Indigo machine (no doubt the firm's own) each sheet of paper is individually numbered by hand. I take each sheet, glide my fingers over it and fold it over, placing it in a pile on my desk.

14 years summed up neatly in 28 sheets of paper (not including the cover page). That puts it at 2 sheets per year. One sheet for every six months. An average of one paragraph every two weeks. About 10 words per day. That's the total of our relationship. Ten words per day.

The phone rings, startling me. It's my agent. She wants to know when my fifth and final draft will be ready. Before she gives me a chance to tell her that it will take at least another month, she slips into a diatribe about how she's convinced that Andrew St. James, who was almost short-listed for last year's Booker award, penned his own 5 star review in the New York Book Review.

The last page of the stack has her signature on it. Her handwriting is so perfect, that for a second I actually contemplate calling her and asking her to reconsider our divorce.

Is it so crazy to stay married to someone just because they have impeccable handwriting?

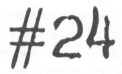

#24

Switch off the phone, close the door.

If anyone calls - simply ignore.

Say you're not in. Better yet, stay at home.

Sit in front of the fire. Make sure you're alone.

Take the day off, put everything aside.

It's OK to feel scared and it's OK to hide.

It's been a while since you knew what was real.

What was true, what was not, and how it all made you feel.

Shed a tear, don't be shy.

There's no one here that's hearing you cry.

Why all the sadness, why all the fear?

Read a bit further, where it all becomes clear.

You don't like to be sad. You could do without the sorrow.

And that's fine with me, as long as you wait til tomorrow.

For today I ask for a favour. Today I ask for despair.

I'm afraid that I've got some news, you may find hard to bear.

I lived a long life, full of wonder and awe.

I could fill a whole library with all that I saw.

Snow leopards in India, wild orchids in Spain.

Three thousand flamingos, the winter in Maine.

I wanted to tell you, I wanted to try.

To say how I feel, to explain to you why.

Please forgive me for saying, to you I can't lie.

For tomorrow, my friend, I'm going to die.

If I ask for some sorrow, if I ask for some tears.

It isn't for me, for I'm done with my fears.

The sadness, my friend, is a little reminder.

To open your eyes, and take off those blinders.

So look at yourself and all that you've got.

Look at who you are, not who you're not.

And do what you dream of, cease all you hate.

Before you too find, that it's a little too late.

#25

Strassman is an evil bastard. He's a devil worshipper. He's Beelzebub himself.

Strassman is my dentist.

I know you might find it hard to believe, but when I was young, up until the age of 16, I liked dentists. I liked Strassman. Strassman was cool back then. He was the same age as my Dad, but he knew that Aerosmith was not the name of a refrigerator. He knew that Lotus isn't just the name of a flower. Strassman knew what being a teenager was like.

I trusted Strassman. I didn't get to talk much when I visited him. That's kind of hard to do when you're lying down with a pneumatic drill in your mouth. Still, I liked the way he thought. Here was a grownup who gave me hope that there was a way to turn 40 without turning old. But I was 16 back then. That's what you do when you're 16. You hope.

Now I was hoping death would come quickly. Strassman is excavating my second molar. I can feel the pressure of his whole body on me. The pain is excruciating. Even Eva, Strassman's assistant, has stepped out of the room, no doubt unable to witness my suffering. I'm about to pass out when Strassman says, 'I heard from Nelly this weekend. She and Edward are going to Acapulco next week. Just like that! Things were different back in my time. I had to work like a dog to put food on the table. But Nelly's got it made. She says Edward is the highest-paid partner in his firm...'

This is Strassman's gift. He's the only man I know who can inflict both physical and emotional pain at the same time. Driving a drill down my nerve while ripping my heart out. And for what? For one blowjob?

We never planned to get caught. Who ever does when they're having sex? But we were young and reckless and drunk. The Strassman's were away for the weekend and I decided to invite myself over to Nelly's. I finagled an invitation to come and see her by claiming that I knew how to cook Italian food. Nelly knew I'd never been as much as close to Little Italy, let alone the country itself. But that didn't seem to stop her from fantasizing that a bona-fide Sicilian was going to cook her dinner.

Of course we didn't get past the appetizer. In fact, there was no appetizer, just a bottle of Chianti and copious amounts of groping. I didn't know how far I was going to get with Nelly. We'd only been dating for a few weeks and frankly, our generation wasn't the most sexually active. So it was quite surprising that half-way through the bottle Nelly moved her hand to my pants. Her mouth didn't take much time to follow.

Seeing Nelly going down on me in Mr and Mrs Strassman's kitchen was the most amazing scene I had seen up to that point in my life. That is, if you don't take into account the scene that immediately followed, in which Mr. and Mrs. Strassman suddenly materialized in the kitchen. I'm not sure where they came from. Neither of us had heard them come into the house a good four hours after they were supposed to be well on their way to the Catskills.

I saw them first. The look on Mr Strassman's face was one of hope. I could see how, despite his surprise, he genuinely hoped that this wasn't his daughter kneeling in front of me. The fact Nelly noticed that something was wrong and pulled away from me, turning her head towards her parents and exposing my fully erect penis for all to see, sealed my fate for years to come.

Not a lot was said between Mr Strassman and myself after that incident. In fact, we never talked about it. But from that day on I learned about pain.

When I think about it, there's no good explanation why I continued to see Strassman as my dentist. I guess I felt bad about what happened and figured it would be awkward if I suddenly switched dentists. It did take me two years before I returned to his clinic. But by then I was 18 and out of school, and I had almost forgotten about the incident with his daughter. Strassman, as I soon discovered, had the memory of an elephant. He also had the mind of a strategist. Which explains why I've been coming back to Strassman every other month for the past 20 years. Every treatment plants the seed for the next one, in a series of non-ending oral complications.

'That's what I say to all the kids I treat. Right, Eva?'

'Right, Dr Strassman!' Eva yells from the room next door. 'Watch what you put in your mouth.'

Strassman smiles and leans harder on me.

#26

What was I thinking, coming to the Shi'va with cream-coloured cords and a black turtleneck, looking more like a struggling film student than a nice Jewish boy?

Still, I think she would have been glad to see me here.

So many people. Laughter, sadness, joy and pain, all mixed up in one small room. 'And this is the drawing room, I just had it painted,' I remember her telling me once, many years ago, long before I knew what a drawing room was. Long before the concept of death became more than a concept.

Most of the people here look the same. In their 50s and 60s, not dressed too well, though they could afford to. I'd call them old, but at my age you gotta watch the categories you create.

First in line is a woman I've never seen before. She could be her sister, though I'm not sure. It would be rude to pass over her without saying something. I don't kiss her, though. Just hold her hand in both of mine. There's something quite amazing about holding someone's hand. Even a stranger's. When you hold their hand with both of yours, if you linger for just a few seconds, you can feel their hand warming up.

It's as if by extending this basic gesture, by opening your heart just a little to a complete stranger, something opens in them as well.

Next in line is Thaddeus, the oil magnate. He made his fortune in women's undergarments, but could never boast about it. So he bought himself an oil tanker and a few oil fields in Texas. Then he started introducing himself as being in 'the oil business'. It took twenty years for people to stop referring to him as the King of Underwear. Eventually they started calling him The Tycoon, even though by then he had lost most of his money when his tanker sank off the Gulf of Mexico.

I shake his hands and he looks into my eyes. Does he recognise me? It was ten years ago when he last saw me. Practically sat me on his lap to tell me all about how I should become a self-made man. Never mind that he inherited the underwear business from his father.

I must be the hundredth person that shook his hands this evening, yet something in his eyes changes when he sees me. A hint of a tear starts showing up in the corner, and he turns away.

Mustn't cry.

I move on to kiss and embrace her two children. Having not seen them for many years, we were all reacquainted on her death bed, only a few days ago. And though she had already signed a pact with death ('let me tie all the loose ends and you can have me forever'), she never lost that air of royalty around her. Later her son would tell me that she died as she lived: like a lady.

I shake some more hands of people I do not know. All of this must not really register with the kids. There is no way they are comprehending that she is gone. That all these people will go back to their very much alive husbands, wives and children, but they, they will be without her for the first time in their lives. It must be that we're all here to suspend their grief for just a little bit longer.

Or maybe we're not here for them. Maybe we're not even here for her. Maybe we're here for ourselves, to remind us how fragile life is. How we can't really afford to wait 'just a little bit longer'. How we can't really 'wait till the time is right'. How there's never going to be a 'better time to say it'. It's now, or never.

I don't know anyone else here. I could walk out the door and leave. But I feel I should stay a bit longer. I walk around the room, trying not to look too suspicious. No one else here looks like a film student. On the little Chinese tables are bilingual prayer books. I pick up one and flip through the pages. I make a point of holding it at an angle, to show that I can read the text in God's own language. As if anyone is looking. As if anyone cares.

I read the words, and they pass me by, like leaves falling

from a tree. 'Blessed is our Lord... He is thy only...'. I search for a word, a phrase, something to hang on to. Something I can take back with me. Something to explain, to calm, to heal.

But instead, something else grabs my attention. It's a portrait on the wall opposite me. I put down the book, careful not to knock over an old couple gossiping about someone's triple bypass operation, and approach the painting. The painting is beautiful, stunning, really. She must be in her early thirties here. Pretty as a doll. She looks at me with a mixture of confidence and fear. Yes, there is fear in her eyes. Or maybe I'm mistaken. Maybe the fear is in my eyes. The fear that one day someone will be staring at my portrait, wondering, just like I am right now, what I was thinking about when it was being painted. Whether, sitting in front of the painter, I am thinking that one day I too will die, and people will come to my home to bid farewell to myself, my family, and their own hopes for immortality.

Yeah, she would be happy to see me here. Even though I am the only one wearing cream-coloured corduroys and a black turtleneck.

#27

'Are you joking? Do I still remember how Emma and I split up? I remember every single word, man. I can still hear the sound of the door slam behind her.'

'And what happened?'

'I don't know, man. I'm not really sure I want to go into this. It was a long time ago.'

'Sorry, buddy. I thought you wanted to talk about it. It's cool. We can talk about something else.'

'And what a past...'

'Huh?'

'That's how it ended. We were talking about something, something about Emma having a past. I think we might have been joking about it. I blurted out that line about her having a past. I might have been joking, I'm not sure. Anyway, it hit a nerve. She got upset. Really upset. She asked me if I'd never done something I'm not proud of. Something I'd never do again.'

'Did you?'

'Of course. A lot. Didn't we all? But instead of telling her that, I just went straight for the jugular and told her that I'd never done something like "that". Then she really let me have it.'

'What did she say?'

'She said, "Fuck you". Only very loudly. She screamed, in fact. I didn't know Emma was capable of screaming. She asked me what gave me the right to judge her. Said it was her life I was talking about, not one of the movies I critique for my "stupid paper".'

'Did you answer her?'

'Yeah, with a real smart one. I told her the Boston Globe was not a stupid paper.'

'Ouch!'

'Yeah, I guess I was so surprised at how she reacted I felt cornered.'

'I hear ya.'

'Wait, it gets worse. When I made that comment about the paper, she told me that I should do the right thing instead of trying to be right'.

'That's a good one.'

'Whad'ya mean it's a good one? Whose side are you on?'

'Yours, as always. But she did have a point.'

'A point? You haven't even heard the end of the story.'

'No, but you do have a tendency to try and come clean out of any situation, irrespective of what that means for others.'

'I do not!'

'You do too. You know how back in college everyone had a nickname?'

'Yeah. And?'

'Teflon.'

'What?'

'Teflon. We used to call you Teflon. Not to your face, that is. But that's what we called you behind your back. Teflon. Nothing would stick to you, Mark. Look, I'm sorry, I didn't mean to cut you off like that. Go on.'

'I'm not sure I want to.'

'OK, but I'm here to listen, not to judge you. And I'll be your friend whether you tell me the rest of the story or not.

It's up to you.'

'Yeah, OK. Anyway, where was I?'

'You being righter than right.'

'Yeah, well, that really pissed me off. So I let her have it. Said something about her giving blowjobs to the whole football team... and all that... Well?'

'Well what?'

'Aren't you gonna ask me?'

'Ask you what?'

'You know what. Aren't you gonna ask me if she did it?'

'Do you want me to ask you?'

'Man, would you stop playing games?! I know that's what you want to ask, so go ahead and ask it!'

'Look, Mark, if you've got something you want to tell me, tell me. But right now, you're the only one playing games, and I'm not having much fun.'

'Yeah, OK, I'm sorry. I guess, well, I guess that pretty much explains it. I couldn't deal with it back then. Can't deal with it now. I mean, I don't know. I never even asked her, so she never really told me what happened, if it happened. It was a story that kept running around college. Something about her in the locker room after a big game, ten guys standing in a row. I... I... look, I don't want to talk about it. Shit! Shit! Shit! Why can't I let this go?!'

'Maybe you're afraid?'

'Of what?! I already lost the girl? What else can I lose?'

'Your innocence? Your vision of a perfect world? Your need to control everything, including what someone else did, or didn't do, 15 years ago? I don't know, Mark, sounds to me like there are plenty of reasons you can't let go of this.'

'OK, Freud, thanks for the psychoanalysis.'

'I'm sorry if this isn't what you wanted.'

'I don't know what I want. I don't know much about anything anymore. I just wish I could change things. Wish I could go back to that evening. Wish I could go back to college and, I don't know, stop her from being used like that. I know, it sounds childish. And maybe you're right. Maybe I am crazy.'

'I don't think you're crazy, Mark, but I do think you need to learn about the difference between what you can do and what you can't.'

'And what might that be, oh wise one?'

'You can't change the past, Mark. But you can change the way the past changes you.'

#28

It's not every day that you get to see a life taken in front of your eyes. Today was such a day.

I promised Henry to stop by the 7-11 and get him some Reese's peanut butter cups. We all have weird addictions, and the peanut-butter-coated-milk-chocolate-artery-cloggers are Henry's. 'Can I offer you a different product from the same manufacturer?' asks Raj from behind the counter. 'Perhaps some Reese's pieces or even a Nutrageous?'

'Thanks Raj, but you know...'

'Mr Davis likes his peanut butter cups,' he says, completing my sentence. I smile and a young woman comes in. Raj and I both look at her. Normally, I don't notice people around me. Call me a space cadet, but I'm usually so caught up in what I'm doing that I just don't see much of what goes around me. Henry calls it 'Tunnel Vision', but I prefer to think of it as simply being in the moment... all the time.

But this woman, there's something special about her. You can sense it immediately. She looks at Raj, then looks at me, and smiles. It's a gentle smile, almost non-existent, like she's hiding a secret. Which makes it all the more noticeable. Raj leans closer to me and whispers 'L-O-V-E'.

'How do you know?' I ask him, though it's clear that he's right.

'Raj knows,' he answers.

Raj knows.

'Let me call Rikesh on Mulberry Lane,' Raj says and calls up his brother or his uncle or some relative. Mulberry is somewhere I'm not too happy to drive to. Brunswick Avenue, where this 7-11 is located, isn't exactly the safest place in the world, but it's closest to our house and I wouldn't think twice about going there at any hour of the day. Mulberry Lane... well, that's something else. It's as if there's an imaginary line that was drawn from north to south, passing through Brunswick Avenue. Everything to the West is wholesome and pretty, and everything to the East is, well, not.

'Acha... acha... no, not the peanut butter bites. Madam needs the peanut butter cups.'

Raj covers the receiver with one hand and whispers to

me, 'He's gone to check. Everyone is low on stock today...'

The lady in love walks up to the counter and puts one single Hershey Kiss on it. 'Will that be all?' asks Raj. 'No chocolate milk? No Hillside cookies?' The woman looks at me and blushes. Her face flushes lightly with a salmon-like hue which spreads down to her chest. She sees me looking at her, which only intensifies the blush. She giggles and I giggle back. I want to say, 'I know,' but I'm not really sure. I know how she feels. I felt the same when Henry and I first met. But there's more than just infatuation behind her blush. There's a certain guilt of finally finding that thing you've been looking for.

Raj, still on the phone, winks at me and smiles. 'Rikesh is keeping the last pack for you, but I suggest you go there now. It seems like the market for peanut butter cups is heating up.'

I laugh and walk to the door. 'It's waiting for you,' Raj says. I thank him and step outside, not quite knowing what he meant by that.

The ride to Mulberry Lane feels like a time warp. Imagine a street where someone arbitrarily announced that from this point onwards people must stop caring. Stop caring about the way they drove, the way they looked, the houses they lived in, everything. Even the kids here look different. Dressed in their tribal clothes, sweatpants with one leg pulled up, baggy pants which reveal their underwear completely, gold chains that look heavy enough to cause back problems. Oddly enough, it's here that I start noticing little things, as if I were watching a movie.

There's a white Nissan standing next to mine. Four kids inside, all wearing those black nylon head covers everyone seems to be wearing these days. We've stopped at a red light and suddenly they start driving. I release the brakes, only to realize that they've skipped the light, that it's still red. I brake and scowl at myself.

And then I see him. Hanging onto the passenger door. I do a double take, trying to fully register what I'm seeing. It's clear - there's another kid, outside of the car, being dragged by it. I slam my foot on the gas pedal. The light is green now, or maybe it's not. Something draws me and I accelerate. I hear a group of girls screaming as I drive by them. Following this Nissan is not a good idea, but like drivers slowing down near a car crash, I simply have to watch, to get a better look, to take the front seat.

We must be going 40 miles per hour now. I'm driving next to the Nissan, without really being sure what exactly it is I'm planning on doing. Through the car's windows I can just about catch the expression on the face of the kid that's being dragged. It's one of complete and utter horror. And then I notice that the kid sitting in the passenger seat is holding the other kid's arm. Holding so hard that the kid can't free himself.

A few more seconds pass by and I feel I am about to throw up. Then something really strange happens. The driver, who until now hadn't even noticed I was driving next to him, turns and looks at me. And he gives me this look, this mixture of pride and male machismo. And just before I look away, just before I turn my sight off to watch the road, he blows me a kiss.

#29

I wasn't always like this. Really. When I was younger, I could carry on a conversation for hours. I mean, I remember Mom coming up to our bedroom in the middle of the night and telling Donny and I to stop talking. What did we talk about? Things brothers talk about. Action heroes. Baseball. Cars.

Donny was an expert on cars. His specialty was German car manufacturers. God knows how he got interested in German cars. After all, the most exotic car we ever saw in our neighbourhood was a Cadillac Eldorado. But Donny had this thing with the Mercedes, Audis and Porsches of the world. He could tell you that Audi merged with NSU in 1969 or that the Carrera RS 3.0 sports version had a breaking power of 230. He even knew Mercedes would be the first company to come out with a five-cylinder diesel engine, a full six months before the story broke in AutoMotiv.

Like most dads in our neighbourhood, ours worked at Boeing. Our Mom was a supply teacher, which meant that she knew a lot of stuff about a lot of things. It also meant that every now and then Donny and I would get her as a teacher. All the kids thought it was really cool for us to have our Mom teach at the same school we went to. They thought it meant we could do whatever we wanted during class, and still get good grades. But the truth is, Donny and I hated it. It's one thing having your Mom work as a school secretary, or counsellor. But when your Mom is a teacher, that means all bets are off.

When you're a kid, grownups are the enemy. And if grownups are the enemy, then teachers are the arch-enemy. It's as if a mad professor created a special breed of grownups who, unlike some grownups, had no understanding of what it means to be a kid, nor any wish to do so.

My Mom, of course, was different. Unfortunately, none of the other kids knew that. This meant that I had the dubious honour of knowing exactly what kids in my class (and other classes) thought about my Mom.

Top five nicknames my Mom had in 1974:

1. Ddddddddiana (my mother had a very slight stutter)

2. DIE ANA

3. DooDoo

4. Dodo

5. Reynolds wrap (on account that our last name was Reynolds and the fact that she always brought with her sandwiches wrapped in Reynolds Wrap).

No one actually called my Mom by her first name (Diana, if you haven't guessed by now), but behind her back, that was a different story.

Donny and I never talked about how much it sucked to hear all your friends make fun of your Mom. That was the only thing we didn't talk about. That and his tumour.

In the summer of 1976, Donny collapsed during softball practice. The coach told my mother it was heat exhaustion. But when Donny didn't wake up for three days and had to be hospitalised in intensive care, it was pretty much clear that heat and exhaustion had nothing to do with it.

I wasn't allowed to visit Donny in the hospital. Things were different back then, and letting a kid see his older brother lying in intensive care was considered an 'unnecessary burden'.

Three weeks later, when Donny came back home, things

between us were different. It wasn't so much that Donny was angry at me or anything. It was just that he seemed disinterested. I would try and get him talking about why he thought Joaquin Andujar signed up with the Houston Astros or whether he thought Captain America got beaten up when he was in school. I even went to McKinley's to buy the latest issue of AutoMotiv, and rushed to tell Donny that Mercedes was about to come out with a coupe version of the 123 in next year's Geneva Motor Show.

But Donny didn't care. And being a kid, I hadn't really realized that Donny had stopped caring about most things, me being only one of them. So I stopped trying.

This went on for two weeks. Then, one night, I was lying in bed. It was 10 o'clock already, but when you're used to falling asleep after midnight, being in bed for two hours with nothing to do can be a nightmare.

'Donny?'

'What.'

'You asleep?'

'No.

'Donny?'

'What?'

'Did I do something wrong?'

'No.'

'Are you angry at me?'

'No.'

'Did Mom and Dad do something wrong?'

'Look, what's your problem?'

'I just want to know what happened. You don't talk to me anymore. You're not interested in baseball. You don't want to talk about Captain America. You don't even read AutoMotiv anymore.'

Donny didn't answer. The next morning I woke up and he wasn't there. At first it seemed no one else was home either. But then I saw Grandma sitting in front of the TV with the sound turned down. When she saw me, she got up and hugged me. She was crying.

I asked her why she was crying.

'It's all over,' she said, between tears.

When school started in September, Mom decided not to return. And no one ever made up nicknames for her ever again.

#30

'Once we hit the interstate again we can... what the fuck was that?! I almost broke an axle on that bump... Man, I can hardly see a thing in this rain.'

Robbie was sitting close to the wheel, like old people do when they drive. As if getting closer to the windshield would give them better control of the car.

'Robbie. Stop the car,' said Adrian, after a long silence.

'Fuck off, dude, it's not THAT bad. If I drive slow enough I can pretty much see the...'

'Robbie. Stop the car.'

'Are you fucking mad? It's pouring buckets out there. I'm not stopping here, in the middle of...'

'Robbie! Stop the motherfuckin' car!'

'OK, OK. Jesus. Aid, what the fuck has gotten into you?!'

'I think we hit something.'

'You fucking what?!'

'I think we hit something.'

'I didn't see us hitting any fucking thing,' he said to Adrian, though he wasn't really sure. That was quite a big bump, and the road was fine until now.

'Aid, where the hell are you... Dude... Fuck, dude... don't get out of the car here...'

But Adrian was already out. It took him seconds to be completely drenched in water. The rain was falling so hard and he began walking to where they heard something go THUMP.

They had been on the road for over ten hours, with only one pit stop in a little trucker's café on the way. 'It's amazing,' Adrian remembered telling Robbie earlier, 'how these truck joints make the same disgusting concoction they call coffee. It's as if they all signed up for the same program for spreading really bad coffee. How else can you explain the uniformity of it across this country?'

For all he knew, they might have just hit a bump in the road, though something deep in his gut was telling him something completely different.

He could hear Robbie calling from behind. He was having trouble restarting the engine and he cursed constantly. Robbie cursed more than any person Adrian had ever met. But the rain, coupled with his growing distance from the car, meant that soon he could hear nothing but water falling on asphalt.

And there it was. Lying on the side of the road. A deer. A baby deer. A fawn. It lay there, body motionless, but eyes still very much alive.

'My God... you poor little thing,' he said, as he leaned down closer to the animal. 'It's.... a... ummm... Robbie! Robbie! Come over here! You hit a deer, man! You hit a deer!'

The little fawn tried moving its head, but it was clear that it had broken something. Maybe its neck.

'Don't... Don't try to move,' Adrian whispered. 'She... She's just a fawn... Robbie! Come here, man! Quickly!'

Adrian couldn't see Robbie, but he could hear the engine being revved.

'Here, little baby, here, I'll help you,' he said, as he lowered his hand to touch the animal on its head. 'Don't be afraid... OUCH!!!'

The bite was sharp and sudden. The surprise of it all meant there was no pain at first. But as blood started flowing from his hand, some trigger in his brain flipped, and the pain came gushing in.

'Dude, what did you do?'

'I... I was trying to stroke her on the head... You know... Make her feel better... and she just bit me. Just like that.'

'Dude, that looks nasty. We should get you checked for rabies or somethin',' said Robbie. 'Let's go get a coffee or something and wash you up.'

'How can you think about that right now?! We have to take her to the hospital!'

'What?! How you gonna get it to the hospital?'

'In the car. How else did you think about taking her to the hospital?!'

'I wasn't. And there ain't no fuckin' way that thing is getting in my car.'

'"That thing" was alive and kicking before you hit it.'

'Before I hit it? Since when is all this MY fucking fault?!'

'I'm not getting into the car if she's not coming with us.'

'Dude, you're fuckin' nuts. You can stay here for all I care. I'm not ruining my Mom's car for some stupid deer... what?'

Adrian was looking at the other side of the road. The rain was falling softly now and hardly made a noise.

On the other side of the road, they could see quite clearly now, the fawn's mother looking at them with two wide, brown eyes.

#31

The archives of Langdon County Sheriff contain a transcript of an obscure conversation conducted between Frank Desdemondes, the local bank manager, and one Leroy Michaels, who took hold of the bank at gunpoint. The conversation was recorded using a security system the bank had installed only weeks earlier, and it provides the only known account for the events that occurred on July 24th, 1983. Due to a malfunction, the security system only began recording five hours after the ordeal had begun, by which time Mr Michaels had released all remaining hostages save for Mr. Desdemondes.

--BEGIN--

FD: 'Let's imagine for a second that I do give you this job. Let's imagine for a second that tomorrow morning you wake up and find yourself running this bank. What would be the first thing you'd do?'

LM: 'Snacks.'

FD: 'Snacks?'

LM: 'M&Ms. I'd make sure each counter has a bowl of M&Ms next to it, so when people are waiting in line they can munch on something.'

FD: 'Emmm, OK. What else?'

LM: 'I'd get rid of the lines.'

FD: 'And how, exactly, would you do that?'

LM: 'I'd get rid of the (INAUDIBLE). I'd set up a lounge where your staff can sit and conduct business with your customers in a relaxed atmosphere.'

FD: 'Don't you think customers will find it a bit awkward doing business with a bank that looks like a lounge?'

LM: 'Don't you think your customers find it awkward doing business with a bank that looks like a morgue?'

FD: 'Obviously you've never run a business before...'

(SHORT SILENCE)

FD: 'I'm... I'm sorry. It's... it's just that you've had me tied up here for over (INAUDIBLE). I just want to go back home.'

LM: 'All in due course.'

(SILENCE EXTENDS FOR A FEW MINUTES)

FD (HUMMING):

To everything - turn, turn, turn

There is a season - turn, turn, turn

And a time for every purpose under heaven

LM: 'Ecclesiastes 3:1-8.'

FD: 'Excuse me?'

LM: 'That's were they stole it from.'

FD: 'Who? Stole what?'

LM: 'The Byrds. That song you're humming. They stole it from the Bible. Ecclesiastes 3:1-8:

To everything there is a season

And a time to every purpose under the heaven:

A time to be born, and a time to die;

A time to plant, and a time to pluck up that which is planted;

A time to kill, and a time to heal;

A time to break down, and a time to build up;

A time to weep, and a time to laugh;

A time to mourn, and a time to dance;

A time to cast away stones, and a time to gather stones together;

A time to embrace, and a time to refrain from embracing;

A time to seek, and a time to lose;

A time to keep, and a time to cast away;

A time to rend, and a time to sew;

A time to keep silence, and a time to speak;

A time to love, and a time to hate;

A time for war, and a time for peace.

FD: (VERY QUIETLY) 'Great, just what I needed, a Bible fanatic.'

LM: 'What did you say?'

FD: 'Nothing.'

LM: 'Maybe it's time for you now...'

FD: (INAUDIBLE)

LM: 'And those now dead, I declared more fortunate in death than are the living to be still alive.'

(A LOUD BANG GOES OFF THREE TIMES. NOISES OF BREAKING GLASS AND VARIOUS SHOUTS FROM THE POLICE.)

--END OF RECORDING--

#32

'My name is Jamila. I am thirteen years old. Tomorrow I will be a real woman. Tomorrow I will be married to my husband. I am the youngest of my parents' 12 children, and the only girl. They say that my mother prayed for my arrival since the day she was born. They say that my mother could not sleep for more than two hours at night before I was born. My mother says that after tomorrow, after I am married, she can die in peace. I do not understand many things. I know I will, one day. But now, all that I care about is looking beautiful for my husband. To make him, and my parents, the proudest people in the world. My girlfriends envy me. They look at all the dresses that I am to wear tomorrow (four in total), and tell me, "Jamila, you are the luckiest girl in the world". And I agree. I am the luckiest girl in the world. After all, I am marrying the son of our Imam, our spiritual leader. My parents love me very much and my father had to give away half of his livestock as dowry. How many thirteen-year-olds can say that about their father?'

I look back at this letter I wrote to no one in particular. Thirteen years old! My goodness! That's so young. I knew nothing when I was thirteen. Nothing, and everything. And that wedding! Oh, how excited I was at the wedding. I think I went through it in a constant state of ecstasy. And though it's been more than 70 years since, I remember every detail. Every single detail.

'Tell me, Uma, tell me more about the wedding. Were you all dressed up and pretty?'

'Was I pretty?! Why, child, I was the talk of the town. My father had three of the country's best artists come and paint me. You know these paintings - the ones in our dining room?'

'That's you in those paintings?!'

'Why, of course, child, who did you think it was?'

'I don't know, some princess...'

'That's exactly what your great-grandfather called me when he first saw me. "My little princess". Still calls me the same till this day,' I say and chuckle. It's true. I've been married to the same man for over 70 years, and he still calls me 'my little princess'. How many 83 year-olds can say that of their husbands?

'Tell me about your dresses, Uma. I want to hear all about them.'

'Well, the first dress was the one I wore on the morning of the wedding. It was blue as the sky, with white little flowers scattered all around. I wore special matching sandals, they were blue too. Even my toenails were painted blue. "Daughter of the sky", my mother said when she saw me in that outfit. I remember wanting to run out to the street and show off my dress to all my girlfriends, but mother forbade me. She said to me, "Jamila, today is the day when you become a woman. Yesterday you were a child, with the worries of a child. But today, today you join the family of women, and that means that you have to stop running around in the streets." Of course,' I said, winking to my little Usha, 'I still went ahead and ran out of the house to meet my friends.'

She giggles, the little one. It's my giggle. I remember that laugh from when I was her age. My goodness, how could I have been so carefree back then? Sometimes I wonder. I look at Usha, she's fourteen now, but really she's just a little girl. She dresses like a grown woman, but really she's still a little girl. And worried. She's always worried, that girl. Worried about this boy or about that girl or about that outfit, or her hair, or her skin.

Goodness, life used to be so much simpler back then. Hardly any decisions to make. I didn't choose my husband. I didn't choose to get married, to have eight kids, to work at home all day. Yet I was happy. Yes, there were difficult times. But frankly, I would never want to switch places with Usha. My little Usha. I look at her and I see myself.

'Uma, how long did you and Grandpa go out before you got married?'

'Go out?! Why child, what are you talking about? Back then, no one "went out" with anyone.'

'They didn't?!'

'Of course not.'

'Then how long before you married Grandpa did you first

meet him?'

'Oh, about two or three hours.'

I can see the wheels in her brain coming to a halt. She looks at me in complete disbelief, hoping to hear it was all a joke.

'But... but how did you know he was The One?' she asks me. So young, so innocent this little one.

'The One? What is The One, my dear?'

'The One, you know. The one you fall in love with.'

'Oh, you mean that. That fleeting moment. That thing that knocks you down one moment and blows over you as if nothing happened the other? I know this doesn't make much sense to you, and I know that you'll think I'm just a silly old woman. But all this; finding The One, falling in love; all this is transient, my child. It passes.'

'It passes? It... Then, then what stays?'

'What stays? Friendship stays. Compassion stays. Duty stays.'

'Duty?' she asks, incredulously.

'Yes, duty. Duty to your husband. Duty to your children.

Duty to God.'

She is so naive, this little girl. I can't expect her to understand. Her life is so full of opportunities. She can do whatever she wants. Yet her life will be more difficult than the one I had. She will have to make decisions at every single step and turn. And with each decision she will have to do 'the right thing'. There will be no one who can help her, no one who will force their wisdom upon her. Sometimes I fear for her. Fear that she will grow old and will not be able to look back and know. Know that she has lived her life in full. Know that she has given all that she could give, and is a better person for it.

#33

'Sometimes you set something in motion, and there's just no stoppin' it. That's all I can say.'

'Did you think they would end up in jail?'

'I don't know. I wanted them to pay for what they did. I wanted them to hurt. I guess you could say I wanted them to feel what I felt like... to be humiliated like I was. But no, I didn't think they would go to jail.'

'Three years, right?'

'The two guys got three years each. The girl ended up in a psychiatric ward for six months of observation.'

'Are you sorry you went to the police?'

'No. It wasn't me who called them, though. The farmer that found me in his field, naked and half frozen to death did. But when they showed up, all I could think of was how much I wanted to nail the bastards.'

'Do you know why they did it?'

'I don't think like that. My mind doesn't work like that.'

'What do you mean?'

'I mean I don't care why they did it. Would it have made a difference if they grew up in broken homes? Or whether they were abused when they were children? No. Not to me. Whatever these kids did, it didn't matter to me why. See, I was brought up with a simple rule. You lay in the bed you make. Why you chose not to make the bed in the first place is an irrelevant question, as far as I'm concerned.'

'Tell me more about the farmer who found you.'

'Not much to tell, really. Some little farm in Cumbria. The guy was woken up at 3am by his dog. Well, really by his wife. The dog wouldn't stop barking. The farmer's wife is a light sleeper and she pushed him out of bed to see what all the commotion was about. He followed his dog and found me. That was pretty much it.'

'Did he ask you any questions when he found you?'

'Well, not at first. I mean he could see that I was in a bad way, you know, naked and freezing and all. But after he took me in and gave me some clothes to wear and something warm to drink, after he saw that I wasn't crazy or on drugs or anything, he asked me what happened.'

'And what did you tell him?'

'What I told you. That two guys and a gal stopped their car next to me as I was walking back home. They forced me into the car and threatened to kill me if I tried to escape. Then they drove their car for about 20 minutes on some dirt road, had me take all my clothes off, and left me.'

'Were they drunk?'

'Not particularly. I don't think they were on drugs, either. They just wanted to have a bit of excitement, I suppose.'

'So you understand how a group of teenagers can do something like that for kicks?'

'I told you I don't. Don't understand, and don't care. All

I know is that if you kidnap an old man, take him to a field in the middle of the night, and leave him there naked when the temperature is five degrees below zero, then you should be punished.'

'Did you ever meet their families?'

'The father of the girl contacted me at the beginning of the investigation. It's kind of against the law, but I didn't mind hearing him out. But all he wanted was for me to speak to the police so they would drop the charges. You see, all he cared about was that his little girl wouldn't go to jail. I told him I couldn't. Not in the moral sense of the word, but in the legal sense. Once the police decided to take action, there was nothing for me to do.'

'But if you did have control over the situation, would you have dropped the charges?'

'Look, what these kids did was wrong. The police know it, their parents know it, and even the kids know it.'

'Would you have dropped them?'

'No. I wouldn't. Young people these days think that everything is reversible. You say you're sorry and the game starts over again. Well, life simply ain't like that. You start a fire, something's gonna get burnt. And there ain't no changing that.'

#34

It's been like this for the past week. She's having sex with some guy upstairs and I can't sleep. At first it was actually cool. You know, I love to see other people having sex as much as the other guy. But there comes a point, and with me it was the third night, that hearing someone gettin' on, gets on my nerves.

So I wrote her a letter. It read:

Dear Ms Capabianca,

Unfortunately the builders behind 54 Ashton Park did not have access to very fine materials. Often, I ask myself if they had access to any building supplies at all. The end result is that more often than not, your nightly excursions around your flat transform my bedroom into a somewhat inhospitable place in which to sleep. I would therefore request that you either reschedule you carnal activities, or install some sort of muffler contraption that will increase the isolation properties of your floor.

Yours,

T.S. Reese

As often happens in inter-apartmental relationships, my request fell on deaf ears. In fact, judging by the events of the night that followed, my request fell on antisocial ears. Later that night I could hear that gone were the soft, velvety oooohing and ahhhings of the previous nights, and in came the do-me-like-you've-never-done-me-before school of verbal lovemaking.

Naively I convinced myself that Ms Capabianca simply didn't have time to read my note, so I decided to give her the benefit of the doubt and simply wait another night. Alas, things got worse shortly afterwards. At approximately 1.30am the following night, an array of sounds not unlike those you hear in certain hospital wards began to emit from above. Due to the lack of coherent words or sentences, I find these hard to reproduce in writing. But suffice to say that one of the more alarming sounds produced from above was that of extensive choking.

I admit that the events of last night caused me some distress. To start off with, it was the sixth night in a row in which I hadn't slept properly. Then there was the issue of Capabianca's complete and utter disrespect for my needs. Last but not least, I felt guilty for not going upstairs and offering my help, should last night's events have actually been some form of occupational accident of one sort or the other.

On the seventh day, which happened to be a Saturday, I decided to fight back. I disassembled the stereo system and brought it into my bedroom. I pulled out the tall ladder that the painters left behind three years ago (one has to wonder what happened to their business following the loss of what one might argue is their most important tool. Who knows, perhaps they don't do ceilings anymore), and secured the 300W subwoofer to the top rung. I then went for a short trip to the local video store and picked up a copy of 'The Best of Dirty Debutantes'. For those of you who have never seen Dirty Debutantes, and are therefore clueless about what the 'Best Of' might look like, I can only say that it is a concept series, the focus of which is the successful attempts of the hero to copulate with first time movie stars (first time as in 'first time on camera'). As I hadn't watched the final 34 chapters of the series I decided to play it safe and use the 'Best Of' to fight the enemy.

Around 1.15am, as I heard the footsteps of my arch-enemy make their way towards her bedroom, I hit the play button and sat back in my director's chair. In the first scene, our host interviewed not one, but two 'debutantes'. The two were apparently twins, though upon closer inspection it became clear that they did not share the same mother. The two 'twins' then went on to describe their lives ('we're athletic and love sports'), their hobbies ('Megan loves to go to the movies while I love making out') and their experience in the matters of intimacy (Megan had done it with four guys and one girl and Leonie had never been with a girl but had been with 'many' guys).

It was hard to keep my focus on the screen for more than

a few minutes. At the end of the day, with or without clothing, Megan and Leonie were as boring as you can get, though I must admit that watching them without clothes wasn't as painful as I thought it would be.

But the most intriguing aspect of the whole event, was that the clock had already passed the 1.30 mark and there was no sign from my upstairs co-star. Either last night's events left her handicapped, or something else was preoccupying her.

By the time our three 'actors' had finished their business I was getting a bit worried. Not that I expected her to call the police or anything, but a long session of banging on the door, or even a few taps on her floor would have appeased me. But from upstairs there was nothing but silence.

I stayed awake till 2.45am, just to be on the safe side, but all I could hear was my own breathing and the static from my 300W subwoofer which I forgot to turn off.

The next morning I awoke somewhat confused. Here I am, supposed to be happy that I fought back (and won?) with my enemy's own weapon. Yet I could not shake off the feeling that my victory wasn't as sweet as it should have been.

I decided to go out for an early cup of coffee and discuss the matter with Bruno, the video clerk. Perhaps my inability to bring my neighbour to an extreme rage attack had to do with the selection of my film material? Perhaps I was using the wrong speakers?

I stepped out the door and turned around to lock it when a sudden panic attack hit me. I am not sure how I had not seen her first, but standing directly next to me now was my neighbour, on her way to work. I desperately wanted to run back into my apartment, but the door had already been slammed. I kept facing it, hoping that she would pass me by as quickly as possible, preferably without stabbing me.

And though I was terrorized and quite shaky at the time, it was quite clear to me that as she passed behind me, she uttered one word in my direction:

'Stud!'

#35

When they built this place, it was the largest sports stadium in the world. People said it would never be finished, or that they would never be able to fill it. But last night there were over 80,000 people here, and I gotta tell you, it was a sight to be seen.

Normally, I'm not what you call an emotional guy. I believe what will be, will be. Why get all tangled with emotions? But when this place fills up with people, thousands and thousands of people, I feel something inside.

I started working here 45 years ago. I never dreamed that I would still be here 45 years later, doing the same job. Many people have a problem with cleaning. I don't. I like to keep things in order. I like to keep things clean. And if that gives the thousands of people who come here every weekend a better experience, then I've left this world in a better shape than I found it.

I wear a uniform nowadays. It took me three years to convince the club management that the cleaners need a uniform of their own. What didn't I say to convince them? I told them it's not fair that we have to damage our own personal clothing. I told them that some of the other clubs give their cleaners uniforms as well. I even said that if they gave the cleaning staff uniforms, it would improve productivity and decrease turnover. Yeah, I guess that was a bit hyping it. No one bought that.

But at the end it was Marjorie who came up with the winning argument. We were having dinner one night. Marj was in her eighth month and the baby's weight was starting to be a real burden. I came back home and found her sprawled on the sofa like a beached whale. She looked so tired that the only thing I could do was offer to cook her dinner. I'm not a big cook myself. I always think that women do the home work better than the men. But I figured Marj here was working overtime, so I decided to give her a break.

'You know, Andy?' she said, after we had eaten and after I finished washing the dishes (only one wine glass broken!). 'You and I make a pretty good team.'

Later that night I thought about what she said. And I realized that she was right. That at the end of the day it doesn't matter which role you play, as long as you feel that you're part of the team.

The next time the stadium's management committee got together I asked to have a word with them. 'Fine,' they said, 'as long as we don't talk about the uniforms.' I knew they were joking, but I also knew there was an element of truth in it. There's only this many times you can come back to the same subject again and again.

So there I was, wearing a suit that Marj got me on sale a few months before, and a blue tie (Marj says blue makes other people comfortable in your presence). I knew everyone on the committee, so it's not like I was in front of strangers or anything like that. Still, these people are very powerful and I... Well, I'm just the head cleaner of the stadium.

'And to finish off our meeting, I'd like to ask Andy Armitage, who asked to address the committee for a few minutes, to come up here and say a few words. Andy, take it away.'

'Thanks, gents. I appreciate you giving me the stage again. I recognise everyone here around the table. I don't see you guys often, but I've met you all before. You're all fine people. My crew and I have a lot of respect for the way you run things. I guess that's why all of us have jobs here, jobs we're proud of.

'You know, I was talking to the others a few days ago, sort of giving them a pep talk, you know, checking out what's going on in the trenches. And I hear people moan about this and gripe about that. And that's fine, because that's what people do in life. So I ask them a straight question. I ask them, "If you could go back in time, to the day you started working here at the club. Would you do it again?"

'They were silent for a few seconds, you know, didn't really know what to say. Some of them held their heads a bit low, as if they felt bad about what they said earlier, you know, complaining and all. But then some smiles started to appear. Little smiles, at first. The kind that start at the edge of the mouth. But then I looked around and, I tell you folks, people were smiling. There are 42 people on my crew. Some have been working here for longer than I have. It's not often you see a group of people, all of whom are doing exactly what they want to be doing.

'I appreciate you gentleman have a tight ship to run. But there's something I'd like to tell you, because I was surprised to find out about it. I asked the guys another question. I asked them, "If you like it here so much, then what's the main reason for it?"

'I knew it wasn't the pay. Heck, anyone of us would get paid more if we worked in the city parks department and... and I'm not saying this to make you feel bad or ask for more money. So I ask the question and the room goes silent. No one really had an answer, or wanted to give one. Either way, I just waited and waited. Frankly, I wasn't sure what the answer was either.

'Then Tom Winter, you know, the quiet young guy who cleans the toilets, raises his hand and says: "I can't really speak for any of the others... emmmm, this is just my opinion here... And I don't want you to think that I'm a softie or something like that..." and by now everyone is like, "Come on Tom, spill it out..." And then he just said something that almost brought tears to my eyes. He said: "I'm here because of you guys. I don't come to work every day to clean toilets, or to empty garbage cans. I don't even come here to watch the games for free. I come here because I'm part of the team."

'Tom Winter, gentlemen, cleans the toilets in this stadium, yet he feels part of the team.

'We're not asking for a raise. We're not asking for more

flexible hours. All we're asking for is our own uniform. Just like any team.'

Once upon a time, in a land far, far away, lived a king. The king was good and wise, and his people loved him. The king's wife died young, leaving him with three sons to take care of. The king loved his sons very much, and brought them up to be good princes.

When the king entered his 70th year, he summoned his closest advisor to his private chambers. 'I am an old man now,' said the king to his advisor, 'and I have depended on your wise words for many years. Now, as I reach the twilight of my life, it is time for me to choose my heir.'

'Will it be your eldest?' asked the advisor.

'No,' answered the king. 'My eldest son is very wise and cautious. I know that he will think through every decision and choose the most sensible one. But I am wary that in an emergency, he will deliberate too long for fear of making the wrong choice.'

'Will it be your middle son?' asked the advisor.

'No. My middle son is strong and courageous. I know that in time of war he can lead my army and conquer any enemy. But I am wary that he will forget that the sole objective of war is to achieve peace for our people.'

'So you have chosen your youngest son to take your place?'

'No. My youngest son has a big heart. I know that if he will be king, our people will love him very much. But he is young and inexperienced, and I am wary that if he ever needs to go to war, he will not be strong enough to fight an enemy.'

The advisor remained silent, realizing the weight the decision bore on his king.

'My trusted advisor. What would you do in my place? Which son should I choose to become king when I die?'

'My dear king. I cannot decide for you. But I can help you devise a test to find out which one of your sons is worthy of being king.'

The king leaned forward as his eyes opened wider. 'Tell me then, what is this test you speak of?'

'Far, far away, beyond the dark mountains, deep in the

EverForest, hides a special flower: the golden-hearted flower. There is only one golden-hearted flower in the whole kingdom. The man who finds the flower, and returns with it back to the palace, is the one worthy of being king.'

The king leaned back in his throne and pondered on the advisor's advice. The dark mountains were a treacherous place, occupied by a demon who created terrible storms. The EverForest stretched as far as the eyes could see, and there were rumours about ogres and wild beasts hiding in it. Even if one of his sons did find the golden-hearted flower, the two others would surely die on the way back.

'Is there no other test I could use?' asked the king.

'I'm afraid not, your majesty. This is the only test that will show you who is worthy of being king.'

The king was tormented. On the one hand it was his duty to choose an heir. On the other, by giving this test to his sons he ran the risk of losing them all. What was the right thing to do? The king could not decide. And for seven sleepless nights he twisted and turned, agonized by his predicament.

On the eighth night, the king could not fall asleep again. He got up from his bed and slowly made his way to a special room in the palace. The room was dedicated to the gods, and the king entered it only on special occasions. Tonight was a special occasion. The king, tired from endless nights of twisting and turning, could barely walk. But as he entered the special room and closed the door behind him he could feel the presence of the gods immediately.

'I am here to seek your help,' cried the king. 'I am here to ask your assistance. What should I do?'

The gods did not answer. Instead, there was a deep silence all around him. The only sound he could hear was the chirping of a little mouse, nibbling at his foot. The king, tired and exhausted, did not even have enough strength to kick the mouse away. And so he looked at the mouse, nibbling softly. 'Little mouse,' asked the king, 'what should I do?'

'Do as you need to do,' answered the mouse to the surprised king, and ran into a hole in the wall.

The next morning the king summoned his three sons to his private chambers.

'My dear sons. I am old, and my days are numbered. It is my duty to choose an heir before I die. I love you all dearly, but I cannot choose which one of you will be king. I must therefore put you all to a test.'

The three princes looked at each other, and then at their father.

'Far, far away, beyond the dark mountains, lies the

EverForest. Deep in the EverForest hides a special flower, one of its kind. He who finds the golden-hearted flower and brings it back to the palace will be king. But beware. The journey is long and hard. And if any of you wishes to spare himself from this ordeal, you will not be punished. But by staying here, you will be deemed unworthy of being king.'

The three princes looked at each other. They had heard stories of the dark mountains and the storm-raising demon that guarded them. They knew how few people ever returned from the EverForest. And all three of them knew that no one had ever found the golden-hearted flower and lived to tell the story.

The princes worked for seven days in preparation for their mission. They chose the best horses from the king's stable and assembled the best armour in the kingdom. On the morning of the eighth day, they bade their father farewell and galloped towards the dark mountains.

The dark mountains were a horrible place indeed. Thunder storms constantly covered the sky, casting permanent darkness. The terrain was treacherous and the air thin. After three days of constant travel and lack of sleep, the sun suddenly peeked from behind the clouds. When light began spreading around them, the three princes saw an awesome site: an EverForest, deeper and wider than they had ever seen in their lives, lay in front of them. The EverForest was so wide and immense that none of the three could see where it ended. It seemed to go on forever.

'Let's rest here for a while before we head off for the EverForest,' said the youngest brother. 'No,' said the middle one, 'we do not have much time. Let's split up. That way we can cover more of the forest in less time.' The oldest brother did not say a word. He looked at the forest stretching in front of him and pondered for a long time. Finally, he broke his silence. 'We should not rest, for time is short. We should not split up, for the forest is dangerous. We should ride to this clearing I can see, deep in the forest. There seems to be some smoke rising from it. Perhaps there is someone there who can help us find the golden-hearted flower.'

The two brothers listened to his wise words and agreed to travel together to the clearing, deep in the heart of the forest.

For seven days and seven nights the princes struggled to make their way. Their horses had difficulties passing through the dense trees and the princes had to make most of their way on foot. Twice they were attacked by hordes of ogres and for twelve long hours they had to battle with the three-headed wolf, a fierce beast the size of an elephant.

On the evening of the eighth day, the youngest brother spotted a clearing in the forest. In the middle of the clearing stood a rickety old wooden cabin, with smoke coming out of its chimney.

The three princes dismounted from their tired horses. The young brother took the horses to the animal shed and gave them water to drink. The oldest brother began exploring the surroundings of the cabin. The middle brother walked to the cabin's entrance and knocked forcefully on the door.

'Bang bang bang,' he knocked.

Silence.

'Bang bang bang,' he knocked again, harder this time, drawing the attention of his two brothers.

Just as he was about to knock for the third time the door suddenly opened. The three princes all let out a gasp. In front of them stood the most beautiful princess they had ever seen. Her hair was long and golden. Her skin was pure as snow and her lips were red as blood. 'You look tired and weary,' said the princess. 'Why don't you come in and I will prepare you something to eat?'

The princes, still speechless, followed the princess into the small wooden cabin. There she fed them a rich and wholesome soup, fresh vegetables and the finest beef stew they had ever tasted.

'What brings you to the EverForest?' asked the princess after the three had finished their meal.

'We are in search of the golden-hearted flower,' said the youngest. 'He who finds the flower and brings it back to the palace will be crowned king,' said the middle brother. 'But even if one of us manages to bring the flower back to the castle, the two others will not make it alive through the dark mountains,' said the eldest, as his face and the faces of his brothers became sad and serious.

'You have travelled long and hard,' said the princess. 'The simple fact that all three of you made it this far as a group is something to be proud of. Why don't you stay here for the night and tomorrow morning I will show you where to find the golden-hearted flower?'

The three princes looked at each other, nodded and went upstairs to sleep.

But sleep they could not find. The thought of one of them crowned as king, while the two others perished in the dark mountains was too heavy to bear. Without speaking, all threre felt the same: they had been given an impossible test.

In the morning, the brothers were woken by the sweet smell of fresh bread. As they made their way downstairs they were welcomed by a magnificent breakfast laid out on the table. The three sat silently and ate their food without saying a word. The princess, they noticed, was nowhere to be found.

When they finished eating the brothers waited around the table for the princess. And waited. And waited. When they started their adventure, each one thought about how he would be the lucky one who would find the golden-hearted flower. Now they all dreaded the thought.

After three long, silent hours, the princess finally appeared.

'Do you want me to show you where to find the golden-hearted flower?' she asked.

The brothers were silent for a long time, until the youngest opened his mouth: 'I think we've already found the golden-hearted flower.'

'We've decided it should stay here,' said the middle brother.

'As should we,' added the eldest.

And ever since then, the golden-hearted flower can be found in a land far, far away, beyond the dark mountains and deep inside the EverForest. And guarding the flower are three wise, loving, courageous princes.

#37

'Thank you, Dr. Enrique. Ladies and gentlemen, we'll be back after the break with a special guest who teaches chicken how to speak in... Spanish.'

[commercial]

'And we're back to our final guest for tonight. Over the years here at "The Wonderful World of Animals" we've had our fair share of surprises. We've had dancing bears, parakeets that do back flips and pigeons that count. But tonight we have a real treat for the audience in the studio and all you folks at home. With us, from Catalonia, Spain, is Dr. Maria Estephan. Dr. Estephan is a world expert in animal communication and is a pioneer in the field of chicken linguistics.

'Dr. Estephan, good evening. I must admit that even our research staff was a bit sceptical when they first heard about your experiments with chicken. Do you find this a common reaction?'

'Oh yes, absolutely. The field of chicken linguistics has been underfunded and underappreciated for years. In fact, my university has been running the only active research lab in the field.'

'Could it be that one of the reasons for this scepticism is that most of us have never seen a talking chicken, let alone one that speaks Spanish?'

'Well, let me first correct you. My chicken do not speak Spanish.'

'They don't?'

'No, they speak Catalan, which is a local dialect here in Spain.'

'I see. And how do you get the chickens to speak? After all, don't they lack the developed vocal cords us humans have?'

'I'm sorry, but that's simply racist.'

'I'm sorry - did you say racist?'

'Yes. There's nothing wrong with their vocal cords. In fact, anyone who's ever lived on a farm knows that chickens have a very wide repertoire of sounds that they are capable of producing. For example, the "Kookooreeko" is basically synonymous with high-level communication, and the "baaak baaaak baaaak" is a universal phrase - found in chickens around the globe.'

'Yes, but isn't this more of a communication mechanism between chickens and themselves? Perhaps the reason most people react somewhat suspiciously to your claims is that none of us has ever heard a chicken talk.'

'Just like Galileo.'

'Excuse me?'

'No one thought the world was round until Galileo proved them wrong.'

'Ummm, yes...'

'And no one thought chickens could talk until we began our research some ten years ago.'

'Yes, tell me please, how did your research get started? Did you receive a special grant from the farmer's association?'

'Oh, no. The farmers have a vested interest in keeping the chickens quiet.'

'Why is that?'

'Farmers are not very developed animals. They rule by ensuring none of their animals can communicate with each other. We tried to convince them that productivity will only rise if their animals are communicative. But the farmers? All they worry about is unions. They are afraid that once they started to talk, the animals will form their own union and demand better treatment.'

'So other animals can talk as well?'

'Why yes. All farm animals have an inherent capability to talk. But humans have suppressed these natural capabilities for so many years, that most animals need to go through intensive training to regain their speech skills.'

'So what do the animals talk about?'

'Which animals?'

'The ones you teach how to talk. The chickens, for example. What do chickens talk about?'

'Oh, you know how chickens are. They nag about this, nag about that. "Where are all the worms today?" you know, that kind of stuff.'

'I see you've brought one of your chickens with you today.'

'Yes, this is Vicky. One of our best chickens.'

'Does Vicky talk?'

'Does Vicky talk? Vicky, heh heh, the gentleman wants to know if you talk. Of course she talks. She talks all day.'

'Baaaaak!'

'Yes, that sounded like a regular chicken.'

'No, it didn't.'

'Baaaak!'

'Yes, she sounds just like any other chicken.'

'No, she doesn't. She just said good evening and asked what your name was.'

'Baaaaak!'

'She wants to know if you're married.'

'That's ridiculous. She's not talking. She's just, she's just making chicken sounds.'

'Baaaaak!'

'Vicky says that she doesn't like the way you're talking to us.'

'Baaaaak!'

'I'm sorry, Vicky. You can't say that on TV.'

'Baaaaak!'

'What is she saying?'

'She said she doesn't have to take this shit from anyone and she wants to leave.'

'Baaaaak!'

#38

His hands are very white. More than usual. He holds them in front of the fire, watching the reddish outline around his fingers. 'Fingers of an old man,' he thinks to himself, though he's barely fifty.

He turns his hands so they're facing him and notices the faded blue dot at the base of his index finger. He smiles in that sad way people smile when they realize that time moves in only one direction. When he was six, his brother pounced on him and drove a pencil into the hand he held up to defend himself. The tip of the pencil broke off, waiting in his flesh year after year.

The sound of crackling wood in the fireplace is the only solace he can find in this cold, empty house. Though it's only five in the afternoon, there are no other sounds to be heard. No birds singing, no animals making whatever noises animals make, no baby crying. No Amanda preparing something in the kitchen.

No baby. No Amanda.

Not long after they met, when the realization that he had found the woman of his dreams had begun settling in, he began tormenting himself with a series of 'what if?' questions. What if she would leave him? What if she would fall out of love with the same ease she fell into it? What if she found someone else more attractive/interesting/funny/challenging than him?

All these questions forced him to imagine what 'the day after' would feel like. And 'Death' was the only word he could think of back then. And even though he knew that he wouldn't simply drop dead if she left him, that always remained the feeling.

Only it's her that ended up dead. Her and the baby. And now he's standing with his hands too close to the fire, trying to see whether her departure, her most final departure from his life, had left some kind of mark on his hands. Surely it must show somewhere?

He sits on the wooden floor. It's covered in ashes. He had no patience in lighting a proper fire earlier and ended up throwing all the newspapers and magazines he could find in the house into the fireplace. Now the floor is a tapestry of burnt news and photographs.

His eyes hurt. The temperature outside was well below zero and he refused to take a ride back from the cemetery. The 40 minute walk back home was silent and cold. He felt like staying out there, in the field leading to their, no, not to 'their' house anymore. Now it was only his. He felt like staying out there in the field and... and what? That's when he felt the weight of things to come. The unbearable lightness of being.

He gets up and takes his clothes off. The thick wool sweater that smells from his sweat. The mud-stained trousers, his underwear and socks. He inspects his body: the white skin that covers his flesh. The patches of hair on his chest. His flaccid penis, that looks tired and sad at least as much as he does. His feet, with their unkempt toenails.

He leans down, picks up the bundle of clothes, and throws them in the fire.

The fire dies instantly. A few seconds later smoke begins rising. He turns the flue to the right, stopping the smoke from flowing up the chimney. A thick, grey curtain makes its way out of the fireplace, enveloping him and causing tears to run down his cheeks. He raises his hands in the air and lets the smoke glide over his skin.

He's finding it hard to breathe now. He steps back a bit and tries to fight the urge to cough. He fails and coughs dryly. He wipes the tears from his eyes, only to fill them with smoke particles that had stuck to his palm. He can't keep his eyes open any longer.

He lies down on the floor. The wood is cold and unresponsive. He used to love lying on this floor before. He would play with the baby for hours and hours as Amanda would write, occasionally turning her head to look at the two of them, smile, then return to her writing. It all seemed like such a long time had passed since she went away.

There's a knock on the door. He looks around, confused. He can't recall inviting anyone after the funeral. All he wants is to be left alone. He shouts for them to go away, but they open the door anyhow. The couple enters the room. She covers him with a blanket, he opens the chimney, then the window.

It doesn't happen often. Only when the winter sets in and the sky is grey. Then, he sometimes forgets that she and the baby have been gone for more than thirty years.

'Look, I can just leave and...'

'And?'

'And you can return to being what you are.'

'Which is?'

'A bastard. A self-hating, gutless, spineless bastard.'

'Oooh, I love it when you talk like that baby.'

'Idiot.'

And then we freeze the scene.

Alex, in his green Army surplus Parka, is sitting on a small metal stool next to the kitchen table. In his right hand is a cigarette in the final stages of consumption. On the table (a cheap, thrift-store one), sits a makeshift ashtray made from a cap of a beer bottle. There are several of those caps tossed around the table, neighboring the eight or so bottles of beer, all of which are empty. At some point during the evening both Alex and Karen were sober and cool. But that was a few hours ago, long before the eight bottles of beer and the bottle of vodka were consumed.

Karen is dressed up tonight as at some point in the recent past she was expecting to go for a show. Her make-up shows she took her time in front of the mirror. She is leaning against a SMEG fridge, the only item of luxury the couple own. Technically, they don't even own it, as the owner of the apartment left it there when he moved to bigger and better fridges (Sub Zero, if you want to know). She too is smoking, but for some reason she stopped using the ashtray long ago, and every now and again simply taps her cigarette and lets the ashes fall to the floor.

We're not really sure what's going to happen now. There are a number of possibilities. We could have the situation escalate. Alex could say that he's tired of being treated like shit. Karen could answer that Alex should know very well what that would look like as he practically wrote the book on the subject. It could also be that instead of a verbal confrontation, things could get physical. If that happens, the amount of beer bottles on the table and in his bloodstream pretty much ensure that Alex will do something they'll all regret later. Then again, something completely different might happen.

'Mom! Dad! I'm home!'

There's no answer from the kitchen. Heather, 13, knows that means her parents are having another one of their 'moments'. She's not really sure where she gets the energy to enter the house each time with such a cheerful manner, given the fact that nine times out of ten her parents make her feel like she was all just a big mistake. Heather walks into the kitchen and stands at the entrance, looking at her parents. There is no way she's going to let them spoil her mood. No way.

'Excuse me.'

Heather is standing next to the fridge her mother is still leaning on. The tension between her parents is strong enough to be suspended over hours, but finally Karen realizes she's blocking her daughter's way and moves away from the fridge, though not enough so that Heather doesn't need to lean behind her mother to grab a can of coke.

'Aren't you going to ask your father if he wants one as well?' asks Karen.

Heather doesn't answer. Instead, she simply closes the fridge door and, as she opens the can, walks towards the sink, where she stops, puts down the can and uses her two hands to leap up and sit on the counter.

'Your mother asked you a question Heather,' Alex says to his daughter, though his eyes haven't left Karen for a second.

'Yes, I heard her question, Daddy. Thank you very much. I'm not deaf, you know.'

Neither of them are looking at Heather. She's seen this technique time and time again. Boxing each other, then using her to draw the last pint of blood.

'Though sometimes I wish I were.'

She's testing the water. If they look at her, that means there's a good chance her Dad won't hit her Mom. If her Mom looks at her, there's a good chance she'll get a slap in the face for talking back to her Dad.

At this point we freeze the scene.

Several things could happen now. Not all of them are nice and convenient for us readers. Not all of them will leave room for a happy ending. In fact, the chances of that are quite slim. But it's still possible.

Heather's phone rings with an old Britney Spears tune. That means it's Alice, her best friend, calling her. Her phone is hanging around her neck and as she takes it in her right hand, she stares at her parents, giving them permission to keep on saying absolutely nothing.

'A, Baby? How you doin' darling?'

That's the last thing we'll hear Heather saying to her friend. From here on her face will tell the story. Lisa's sister died two hours ago. Technically she killed herself. Hanging. We don't know more than that, though suffice it to say, that some part of Heather's world is falling apart. She lowers the phone slowly, as if enacting a slo-mo scene. And 'scene' is really what she's thinking about right now. It's simply all too surreal to act naturally, so she acts like in the movies, suddenly dropping her phone on the floor and all.

Which finally catches her parents' attention. Whatever silly conversations their daughter normally has with Alice, this was not one of them. Something very bad happened, bad enough to snap both Alex and Karen from their favorite pastime of hating each other, themselves and the rest of the world.

Karen is first to reach Heather.

'Alice's sister... She killed herself.... Her sister.... She's dead.'

Heather isn't sure whether she should cry, scream, faint or anything else. If she's ever seen a similar scene in the movies, it escapes her memory.

And now it's Alex's turn to approach her. He, unlike Karen, does not embrace Heather. Alex is not the embracing type and it's not so much that he'll be out of character for doing so, but he simply lacks the capacity to hug, especially his own daughter.

But Heather isn't thinking about what her Dad's capacity for expressing emotion is right now. She needs him, as much, if not more than she needs her Mom. And so she looks beyond her mother's face and into Alex's. She's not crying, hardly even shaking. She's simply looking him straight in the eye, asking him, without words, whether he's willing to let go of her forever.

At this point we freeze the scene.

I know, a number of things could happen. We could list them all out here. But frankly, I'm tired of all these futures being all tangled and messed up. Heather will, by no means, have an easy, or even a happy life. But one thing I can promise you will happen. From this moment, her father will, every once in a while, hug her. Her mother will, every once in a while, tell her that she loves her. And her parents will, every once in a while, stop hating each other, themselves and the rest of the world.

Because sometimes, all you really need to keep on going, is to freeze the scene, and do the right thing.

#40

'Yes, there really is something there. Looks more like a blister than anything else. Well, I can ask Irina next door if she can take a look at it. Do you want Irina to look at it?'

I came here for a simple blood test and now I have to go and see Irina. I don't know who Irina is, but from the sound of his voice, I have a feeling she is not the most hospitable person on earth.

'Emmm, yeah, why not.' Why not? I can think of ten reasons why I should go home right now.

He picks up the phone and punches a few numbers. 'Irina? Hi, this is Dr. Frenkel. I have someone here I want you to see. Nothing serious,' he looks at me and winks. Does that mean it is? 'Great, then I'll send him right over.'

'Now?' I ask him, totally unprepared. I thought I would have some time to contemplate on what would happen if 'it' is serious.

'Sure, since you're already here.'

The waiting room is the size of a small toilet. The secretary alone, a woman of massive proportions, fills half of it. In the next five minutes I will find out that:

1. It was easier than she thought.

2. She's already lost 48 kilograms.

3. Her skin is slightly orange because of the carrots. No, she's allowed to eat broccoli as well, but broccoli doesn't transfer colour pigments that easily.

With me in the waiting room are two men. They are obviously here for Irina's second profession - Sexually Transmitted Diseases. There is something slightly humbling in a waiting room full of people who are:

1. Sexually active.

2. Highly promiscuous.

3. Might die in the next three months.

I, of course, am here for her other expertise: 'Dermatology and Skin Disorders'.

A large, red-headed woman enters the waiting room and immediately begins a conversation with the secretary.

'So, how is it going?' she asks the blob.

I am tempted to give her a full account, as I have heard the secretary describing her trials and tribulations over the phone at least four times since I arrived. I decide, however, to remain silent and not risk being bumped back to the end of the line. Instead, I check her consistency, as in the former reports I overheard her relay, she had lost anywhere between 14 and 64 kilograms and her diet had ranged from carrots only, to carrots and broccoli, to everything but carrots and broccoli.

'And what's with you?' the secretary asks the redhead.

'Last night...' she answers.

'Really?! How did it go?'

'I'm telling you, Dr. Jekyll and Mr. Hyde. Once I told him I won't see him anymore, he turned into a different person. I'm still shaking. Here,' she says, and stretches her arm forward, 'look how I'm shaking.' Her arm is really shaking.

The doctor's door opens and out comes a tall, skinny woman in a white lab coat. She has pointy glasses that fit perfectly with her pointed body. Now there are eight of us cramped in the waiting room. She scans all of us, and for some reason her gaze freezes on me. 'You. Blondie. You're next'.

I try to signal that there are at least three other people in front of me, but that fails to make an impression on her.

I enter the examination room which looks more like an inquisition chamber than anything else. On her desk is what looks like a small blow torch, the kind used for searing the coating on a Crème Brûlé. This cannot be a good sign.

'Yes,' she says to me, looking intently at my face. 'What seems to be the problem?'

'There's this thing on my lip,' I say. 'I think I'm biting my lower lip too much.'

'How do you know?' she asks.

'How do I know what?' I respond.

She fails to answer and gets up from her seat abruptly. 'Yes, I see,' she says as she scans my lip with a big magnifying glass. 'We will have to burn it off.'

It?! Burn?! Off?!

'No?' she asks. 'You don't want to burn it off?' she says in a tone full of disappointment. 'Well, maybe I can give you some lotion and see if it goes away.'

She returns to her chair, struggling with the aftermath of this patient who promised so much, yet failed to deliver.

'There is one more thing,' I say.

Was this my voice?

'Yes?' she answers, her eyes opening wide with anticipation.

'I've got this blister on my thumb. It's been here for quite a while. I'm not sure if there's anything you can do about it.'

She leaps from her chair and makes her way towards me, caressing the blow torch as she makes her way around her desk. 'Yes, I see the problem,' she says, holding my thumb in her cold hand. 'This, we will have to burn. Burn deep. Now.'

I am about to faint when I realize that things are actually about to get worse. She picks up the blow torch. It turns out it's not a blow torch after all.

'This is liquid nitrogen. Burns the skin very efficiently.'

And with this, she begins spraying my thumb. 'It'll feel like a cigarette burn. It will swell as well.'

For a second I am baffled by how anyone normal would know what a cigarette burn would feel like. But then the pain turns from massive to catastrophic. My thumb is held in her hand like a vice-grip. And all the while, I can't help but notice that she's not looking at my thumb at all, but staring deep into my eyes, smiling.

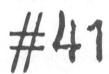

#41

'Will it always be like this?' she asks him.

'Be like what?' he answers, though I have a feeling he knows exactly what she means.

'You know what I mean,' she says.

'Us. Will we always be like this?'

'Be like what?' he asks.

She gets up from her chair and walks towards the bathroom. He turns around, following her with his eyes. It's the first time he's noticed me. He looks at me for a split second, comparing me with some profiling system he's got in his head. I guess my profile matches because now he's giving me the 'can't live with them, can't live without them' look. I nod back.

'I used to be sensitive,' he says, turning his chair a bit closer to me. 'I used to put all my cards on the table, you know, say everything I felt and that shit. God, what a fool I was,' he says after a brief pause between sentences. 'But you know what they say.'

I don't, but we're doing this male instant-bonding thing, so I nod my head as if I do.

'She's a cute girl, she really is. Great in bed as well. Really gives it all she's got. But I know that if I let her get too close, she'll freak out and run away.

'Take yesterday, for example. She comes back from the hairdresser. Looks like she stepped out of Vogue or something. I mean, I could hardly breathe when I saw her coming in. Do you think I said anything about her new hairdo?' He looks at me, waiting for an answer. I shake my head. 'Of course not,' he says.

He picks up a pack of cigarettes and taps it on the table a few times. Before he takes one out he gestures towards me. 'No thanks, I'm trying to quit,' I lie. I've never smoked in my life.

'She gave me hell for two hours. You know, the silent treatment. But then I came up to her from behind, cupped her breasts in my hands and told her that if she keeps on avoiding me I'll hang myself in the basement. Then I told her she's got the best pair of tits in the world.'

He sits back in his chair and blows three perfect smoke rings.

'So I'm massaging her from behind and she's not saying a word. Not stopping me or anything, but not saying a word. Finally, she speaks. "What about my hair?" she asks me.'

A tall blond just entered the bar and my new-found friend is scanning her, no doubt comparing her to another, albeit different, profiling system.

'Your hair is great, baby,' he says to me, catching me off guard, till I realize he's talking about his girlfriend.

'"You've got the best hair in the world," I tell her. She turns around to me and says, "you really think so?" I tell her that I don't only think so, I know so. And that's it, man.

I'm home-free.'

I contemplate asking him how long they've been together, or where they met, but the guy is on a roll, and I don't think he needs my encouragement to keep talking.

'Best sex we ever had,' he blurts. 'Fucked like rabbits,' he says. 'Like rabbits I tell you,' and with this he looks into my eyes, ensuring I understood the full magnitude of his metaphor.

'The first rule with women is not to pay too much attention to what they say.'

His girlfriend is back from the bathroom. She returns to her seat and he adjusts his to face her.

'I want a divorce,' she says.

'I'm sorry, what did you say?' he asks.

'You heard me. I want a divorce.'

He chuckles once, twice, then turns silent again.

'YOU want to divorce ME?!'

'Yes.'

'And when did you come up with this... this crazy idea?'

'In the bathroom.'

'In the bathroom. In the bathroom. What? Just now?'

'Yes. Just now.'

'And what do you expect me to do?' he asks her, in a tone that was meant to be forceful, but lost steam somewhere on the way.

'You can do whatever you want. I'm getting a divorce.'

'You can't get a divorce!' he says, raising his voice high enough to grab the attention of the adjacent tables.

She stretches her long white arm and takes the cigarette pack in her hand. She pulls one out and lights it. She leans back in her chair, blows a long stream of smoke in his direction and says, 'Why not?'

'Because... because... you can't. Because I love you.' At this she lets out a short laugh.

'Johnny, the only person you ever loved was yourself. You don't love me. You're afraid of me. Don't confuse the two.'

He takes a final puff from his cigarette, examines it and flicks it out on the floor. He turns around to me, winks, and says, 'The second rule with women is not to pay too much attention to what they say.'

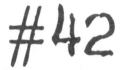

I don't know how to start this letter. It must be the third or fourth time I'm trying to write the opening line but something keeps distracting me, causing me to lift my eyes from the screen and engage in something else. When I return my eyes to the screen, what I wrote simply doesn't seem right.

How could anything I am about to say seem right? You gave me everything I could ever ask for. You brought me into your heart, and your home, without asking, even once, for anything in exchange. But now, 12 months, three days and 22 hours later, I have to leave you, Nathan.

Do you remember the first night we met? Not the first night we went out, but the first time we saw each other? It was at the documentary at the Lighthouse. We were both stuck in the front row, sitting next to each other. We couldn't help but look at each other after, for about a dozen times, we started laughing at exactly the same second. It was a good movie, but it was hard to pay attention to what was happening on the screen. I had my left hand locked in

Jacob's - that guy I was going out with at the time. But that didn't seem to bother you. I remember how, when you sat down next to me, you didn't waste a second. You turned around to me, looked me in the eyes and said, 'Hello'. It felt like I'd known you forever.

Now that I think of it, I should have known this would end in tears. Just look at how it all started. On my left, I'm holding hands with Jacob. On my right, unbeknownst to him, I'm holding your hand. I don't think I was ever excited like I was that night.

And the many nights that followed.

But now, I feel exhausted, Nathan. I feel tired. I feel spent.

I'm stuck again.

I almost deleted this letter and started again. I wish I could tell you this face to face, but I can't find the courage to do so. They say you can't hear or see anything around you. But knowing you, that's probably not true. You're probably lying there in room number nine, the life support machine pumping air into your lungs, up and down, up and down. And all that while you're probably playing dead, getting everyone to believe you can't hear a thing, so they'll feel comfortable to say everything and anything about you. All the things you've never heard. All the things you've never known. And when you've heard enough, you'll just open one eye, look at us, and grin.

What would be the first thing you'd say? 'I forgive you,' or 'Fuck you all'? Nah, knowing you, you'll just ask if we can turn ESPN back on and get you some beer.

Shit. I'm crying now. How is it that the things I hated most about you are the things I miss most now? All your stupid little idiosyncrasies. The way you'd constantly say 'hmmm' when someone was talking with you. The way your eyes would race across the room every three seconds, even when we were having the deepest conversation in the world. Those silly tiger-print underwear you'd take with you on a trip.

I stop and read what I wrote. It's a crap obituary, Nathan. It's a crap goodbye letter too. It's crap by any standard and measure. But then anything I'd produce would always be crap compared to you. You wrote better than me, expressed yourself better than me, cooked better than me. Heck, you even looked better than I do. But now all that doesn't matter. Now all you can do is, well, crap. Hah hah. Such a funny girl I am.

Anyway, I'm ditching this letter. This won't be the version that I'll leave under your pillow. This one's going straight for recycling. Not that it matters. It's not as if you'll be reading any letters soon. You're almost dead, aren't you? Nathan? Where are you, Nathan? Are you still with us, just taking a bit of a snooze in that hospital bed? Or have you left a long time ago, letting us make fools of ourselves by waiting for you to reappear?

I'm going now. For real. I won't come and visit you again. I won't write, I won't call your mother and ask how your day was. I won't even think about you.

Yeah, right.

I just want you to know, Nathan, that I'll never forget. I'll never forget that first time you looked at me and said hello. I'll never forget how I cried that night, in bed with Jacob, thinking about you, knowing that one day I would have to lose you.

So this is it, Nathan. Goodbye.

'Bueno. Bueno, Hermano.'

We're walking downstairs, haven't even entered the club. Sadik turns and looks at me, smirking. We pass two models on the way down. I'm biting my lip.

Down below it's impossible to move. There are three girls here for each man. Most of them aren't wearing much.

'Ahhh, the Kremlin!' our driver commented knowingly earlier. 'Where the money meets the honey'.

Sadik was too busy chopping up another line of cocaine in the back seat to pay any attention to his remark. Cutting lines in transit isn't a wise thing to do. A sudden slam on the brakes or a tight left turn can end with your trousers being covered by angel dust. But when you are as rich as Sadik, that really doesn't mean much. A bit of an inconvenience in having to change your pants, perhaps.

Sadik passes the silver box to me and I tell him I'm staying clean tonight. He looks at me as if I were a small child.

'Suit yourself, Hermano. Suit yourself,' he says to me in a fake Spanish accent that doesn't quite fit with the fact that he is Egyptian with a heavy accent. 'Just don't come to me later begging for some.'

I don't respond. I'm not sure coming here was a good idea, but when you're entertaining Sadik, you try not to think too hard about what you want. He is, after all, my most important client. I'll do whatever it takes to keep this guy happy. God knows I've done so in the past.

The head waiter recognises us instantly. Thank God for

that. He leads us through the impossible mass of people to the main dining room. The place is surreal. Rococo style architecture with the main theme being gold. It is a hideous sight to the eyes.

The night's already well under way and some girls are dancing on the tables. Most of them aren't wearing any underwear. No one seems to have any problems with that.

The age group, even on the female side, is too broad to make sense. There are women here who could easily be my mother's age, side by side with what seem to be a group of 14-year-old nymphs. I doubt if they are actually any older than that.

Sadik and I sit down at our table. There are six empty seats around it. These will fill within three minutes. No one passes on an opportunity in this place, and the women here are as ruthless as the men are rich. Two Iranian twins sit down next to me. One of them already has her hand on the back of my neck, caressing. Sadik has some young girl with endless legs sitting on his lap, opening the buttons of his shirt. She acts as if she's known him for all her life. Though she hasn't, it makes not much difference to Sadik.

This is the Serengeti of the human race. Some are here to be eaten, some are here to eat. Sadik Maroush is here to be fed, and tonight there seems to be no shortage of livestock.

'I should see more than one Doctor, man! With all the stuff that's in my head, I should see two, or maybe three Doctors!' Half an hour later I'm in the bathroom, and there's a middle-eastern looking guy getting his hand washed by a black attendant. He takes out a $50 bill from his pocket and hands it over to the attendant. He grabs him by the shoulders and, lowering his voice, says: 'I might be out of my head man, but damn do we have hot bitches at our table tonight!'

I walk out of the bathroom and decide to take a peek at the dance floor. People here are partying as if there's no tomorrow. The odd thing is that most of them will actually be here tomorrow, and the day after, and the day after. They will party until their bodies shut down. They will rest for a few days, and then they will party again. It's their natural cycle.

I know that if I switch my brain to 'engage' I could have an OK time tonight. I would get laid, at least with one girl, maybe two. Possibly three. Possibly all of them at the same time. But something is missing tonight. Something that's been missing for a long time.

I return to the dining room. I could sit at the table and signal one of the waiters to do so, but I decide to stand at the bar and order a drink. I scan the scene around me. I don't belong here. I want to go home. I want to call her up and tell her I'm sorry and that I want to come back. Tell her I'm ready to leave this place and go back to the country.

'Hermano! Que Pasa?!'

Sadik elbows me and I lose my breath for a second. I look into his empty eyes. Sadik is somewhere else. He hugs me and gives me a kiss on the cheek. And for a second there, I think I can make out the first signs of a teardrop forming on the corner of his eye.

'Mummy?'

'Yes, darling?'

'Is Booboo dead?'

'No, darling, Booboo's only sleeping.'

So much for Extra-Power Duracell batteries.

'Mummy?'

'Yes, dear?'

'Does Booboo love me?'

'Of course he loves you, pumpkin! Booboo's your best friend!'

'Mummy?'

'Yes, dear?'

'Is Daddy your best friend?'

He's three years old. How can a three-year-old throw me off balance that easily? I look at him. He's sitting on his little toy tractor, the one we got him for his second birthday. He played with it for three, maybe four days before it found its place in the garden shed, along with the other collection of Fisher-Price toys.

I kneel down next to him, but he seems to be more interested in the tractor's dashboard and avoids my eyes. He's been like that since Pete died. Reaching out, only to retract when I come close.

'Of course Daddy is my best friend. Daddy is my best friend ever.'

I try hard to block the tears in my throat. Remind myself what my mother told me; that I need to be strong enough for both of us. I stand up and return to the sink. I'm done washing the dishes but I turn the water on again, just to engage in some kind of activity. Maybe if I let the water run long enough I won't have to cry.

I look outside to our garden. Pete loved this garden. I used to taunt him, used to tell him he should spend more time nurturing his son than his sunflowers. Now all that's left of him is this garden. The garden, of course, and Timothy.

'Mom?'

He never calls me Mom.

I cringe, fearing what will come next.

'Yes, Tim?'

'Is Daddy dead?'

My gut reaction is to say 'no'. At first because saying 'yes' doesn't sound right, then because I don't want to make him more anxious. I've already had numerous complaints from his teachers. The hitting, the refusal to eat, the elaborate stories he makes up about what 'really' happened to his father.

I turn around to face him, leaning back on the kitchen sink. He's sitting quietly on his tractor, close to my feet, looking into my eyes. I hold the counter with my two hands behind my back for support. I can't say a word, but my lips are moving.

'Yes, baby. Daddy's dead.'

How do you explain death to a three-year-old? You go to work one morning and come back in the evening and your husband's dead. Your high-school sweetheart, the father of your only child, your best friend. Dead. The fact that some 17-year-old without a licence cut him off on the interstate makes it all the more surreal. The younger generation is taking over by any means necessary.

Tim gets off the tractor and puts his head on my lap. I kneel down and hug him. Hug him harder than I should. Hug him as if he's the last thing I've got left.

I whisper in his ear. Whisper all the lies I grew up on. Whisper that I'll never leave him, that Daddy's looking over us from above, that one day we'll all be together again.

He raises his head and pushes away from my embrace as though he's had enough of my attention. I stand upright, feeling his embrace was meant more for me than for him. He turns around and heads towards the back door, dragging his tractor behind him with one hand. He walks over to the garden shed and emerges two minutes later, hands empty.

#45

1. 'If only we had more time together' (55 percent)

2. 'I wonder if s/he is cold' (22 percent)

3. 'Why him/her and not me?' (13 percent)

You gotta have a streak of masochism to do this job. After all, if you're like me, straight out of college, then all you really care about is getting laid and, well, getting laid. You live each day as if so many more will follow. And why wouldn't you? Most people my age have at least fifty, if not sixty years to look for. So I guess it does merit some explaining as to why I'm doing this.

I do field research. I go and interview people who's significant other has just died. It's a longitudinal study, which means that it's scheduled to go on for about 20 years or so. My boss, Professor Shenk, runs the psychology department at North Western. He wants to know whether our attitudes towards losing our loved ones change across generations. Personally, I got more interesting questions bugging me. Like whether Jana, his lab assistant, wears any underwear. Or whether I'll have acne till the day I die. But I don't judge other people, so when my friend Tyron, who's in Shenk's seminar on Aging and Death, told me about this gig, I jumped for it.

Not that I'm into all that morbid shit. Take Tyron, for example. He and I have been buddies since high school. But he's got this thing with dying and grieving that freaks me out. I mean, it's not as if anyone in Tyron's family has died in the past fifty years. For Christ's sake, the guy even has a dog that's been in the family for over two decades. So if anyone has no justification enrolling in a seminar on Death and Dying, it's my man Tyron. But I don't judge people. What's good for Tyron is good by me. I guess someone has to support the black turtleneck sweater manufacturers.

Anyway, I'm digressing here. The point is that when Tyron told me about how he's bummed out because he doesn't have the balls to do this field project for his professor, I said I'd do it. I didn't want to make Tyron feel bad or anything, but the pay is good and the hours are flexible. After all, people can die at any time.

Then there are the perks. I get to carry around a beeper that can go off at any minute. This used to freak out my Mom. She was convinced I turned into a drug dealer or something, and it wasn't till I showed her an official letter from Professor Shenk that she got off my case. I also get to have a rental 24 hours a day. This has turned me into quite an item with the ladies. The way it works is I made a deal with Ricky at Rent-A-Wreck. I give him 20% of the daily rent, and he hooks me up with a convertible, or a beamer. Once he set me up for a whole week with a limo. Mind you, it was a bit weird showing up in people's driveways with a limo, especially considering they just lost a loved one.

Professor Shenk and I get along well. He took a lot of time preparing me for the job. Said that it's important to keep talking about what you go through. At first I was like, cool, if you want to know how an interview with someone whose wife kicked the bucket went, I'll tell you. But Shenk started asking me weird shit about my mother and my childhood and whether I was toilet trained and stuff like that. That's when I told him that if he wants me to keep doing the job, we have to stop having these talks about my ego and superego and shit.

Shenk was right, though. Nothing really prepares you for meeting these people whose world has changed by 180 degrees in a split second. The most difficult ones are the old people who've been married for fifty, sometimes sixty years. I ask them to rate ten statements about their feelings, and put them in ascending order. Personally, I think that's a bit crazy. I mean, how can you ask someone who's just lost their wife of fifty years whether he feels more alone than angry? But like I said, I'm not judging anyone. And I guess that if Shenk runs a department, then he must be doing something right.

Take last weekend, for example. I'm chillin' in my crib with Darlene, the chick with the fat ass who works at the checkout counter at Bed, Bath and Beyond. We're watching Jackass, high as kites, when my beeper goes on. At first, we couldn't hear it on account of Johnny Knoxville getting thrown naked into this room with about a million mouse traps. But the beeper kept on going. I'm not sure who was first, but at some point we just started laughing our asses off. Anyway, it took me like a whole hour to get dressed and step into the car (a Jaguar, no less). I arrived on location a good 45 minutes late, which if Shenk knew, would nullify the interview on account that it has to happen within sixty minutes of the spouse learning about their partner's death. That's another thing that freaks me out with these guys. They use words like 'nullify' and 'zero hypothesis' and shit no one in their right mind actually understands.

Anyway, so I park my Jag in front of this shabby old house and make it through the front door, which is open. In the living room sits a woman. She must be at least eighty if not more. She's dressed, all fancy, and with makeup. She's sitting real still on the sofa, and next to her are two brown suitcases. The kind you'd imagine people from the Mayflower used when they came over from England or Amsterdam or wherever.

So I knock on the door, just because that's being polite. She looks at me and says, 'Oh, you must be the driver. I'm ready to go.' And I'm like just about to say to her that I'm not the driver, that I'm the field researcher. But something makes me answer, 'Yes.' So I take her luggage and show her to my Jag. I feel a bit guilty for a second, but then I remind myself that the interview is technically nullified anyway, so fuck it, right?

So we drive around town for like half an hour, all the time she's talking about her husband. How Charlie did this and Charlie did that. And she's all calm and stuff, like she didn't hear less than three hours ago that her husband died. So she tells me that yesterday she and Charlie celebrated their fifty seventh anniversary. Fifty seventh anniversary man, did you get that?

And I'm thinking to myself, shit, I ain't even had a relationship with a women for more than fifty seven days. How the fuck do they do it? So I ask her. I say, 'Ma'am, pardon me for being nosy and all that, but what's the secret to such a long relationship?'

So she answers me. Get this, she says to me, 'Son, the secret to a long-term relationship is frequent separations. Frequent separations and a growing loss of hearing.'

#46

'Let's go do this, let's go do that. Can't you stop for a second and slow down? Why can't we stay in and watch the game?'

That was definitely a bad idea. I can see the smile

disappear from her face as fast as lightning.

'No, no, baby, I didn't mean it that way, it's just that...'

'Don't you baby me! I work my butt off all week and come Saturday I don't want to stay in this ugly apartment and watch TV! I want to go out! I want to have fun! I want to meet people! And I want YOU to get off your ass and treat me right!'

'Treat you right? Sugar, you know I always treat you right...'

'Don't you sugar me! You never treat me right! You never buy me things! You never take me places! Why can't you be more like Lashanda's man?'

'Baby, Lashanda's husband owns a record label. I own a few records. Come on, you know that I ain't got that kind of money. This ain't fair.'

'Ain't fair?! Ain't fair?! Let me tell you what ain't fair. What ain't fair is you spending all that money on the ugly bitch you was seeing before you wised up and moved in with me. You want fair? Fair is treating me like the woman I am.'

And with this she turns and marches to the other end of the living room.

That little scene, that little 60-second drama, that just cost me mucho bucks. And all because of what? Because last night that evil friend of hers, Janelle, told her that she saw me in a bar with another woman. I swear to God, these women must have some kind of intelligence agency working for them. This city is big. There must be three, maybe four thousand bars in it. So how come I get spotted on the one time I'm having drinks with another woman?

She's still standing in the corner, her arms wrapped around her. From behind it looks as if someone else is hugging her. My blood is rushing. Damn, that girl has a fine ass. A big fine ass. God I love that ass of hers. So why do I gotta fool around with other women? Man, sometimes I feel so stupid I'm surprised my mother didn't leave me on someone else's doorstep.

'Baby?'

She cringes as I try to put my hands on her shoulders. This is gonna be a tough one.

'Sugar? You know I only care about you... sugar. You know that you're the only one who rocks my world... Baby? Baby, look at me. Baby, don't be angry with me no more. I couldn't live with myself if you were angry with me, baby. Baby?'

'What?'

'Come on, baby, let's kiss and make up.'

'Why don't you go kiss your girlfriend's ass?'

'Baby, you know I ain't got no one but you.'

'Did you tell that to the bitch from last night?'

'Baby, that woman ain't mean nothin' to me. I was just thirsty, so I stop on my way home for a quick beer. She just sat next to me. I swear, I don't know that woman.'

We're making progress here. I'm holding her from behind. At least she didn't smack me again on my face. Man, that hurt. The woman's arm has the velocity of a football making its way to the end zone. I need to figure out what to do next. If I kiss her on the neck she might think I'm trying to seduce her. If I flick my tongue over her ear, she'll think the same. It's a lose-lose situation.

'I got a surprise for you, baby.'

Now why did I say that?

She turns around and looks at me, her face is still angry, but her eyes are considering forgiveness. IF...

'Did you get me something?'

No.

'Yes, baby. I got you something real special.'

'What? What is it?'

Now she's getting excited. Damn, I am such a fool. Now what?

'It's a necklace.'

A necklace?

'A necklace? What kind of necklace?'

'A diamond necklace, baby. From diamonds.'

A diamond necklace, from diamonds. Nice move, genius. And what do you do when she asks you where the necklace you never bought her is?

Her eyes are glimmering now.

'Baby!' she holds my head in her hands, kissing me. 'A diamond necklace?! For me?! Oh, baby, I knew you had a surprise for me. Oh baby, I'm so excited. I can't wait to see it. Where, where is it?'

Where is it? Now that's a good question.

'It's... It's at the shop, baby...'

'What shop?'

'Tiffany's.'

TIFFANY'S?! ARE YOU MAD?! What has gotten into your head? There ain't no way I can afford that necklace.

'BABY!!! You remembered! You remembered I showed you that necklace when we walked down on Fifth Avenue! Oh, my God! I'm so happy! I can't wait to see the look on Lashanda's face when she sees me in that 14 carat necklace!'

14 carat necklace? Rrrright.

She's giving me a huge hug now, but that's not the reason I find it hard breathing. Man, I knew I should have listened to my dad.

'Son,' he said to me when I turned 18, 'when it comes to women, silence is golden'.

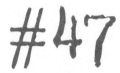

#47

I'm running down the street with my clothes off. Technically I'm naked, though Josh would later argue that wearing my boots disqualified me. It's 3am in Dublin and I'm running naked down O'Connell street. Bad idea. The concierge at the Best Western has already called the police after I stopped to hug two Japanese tourists who were on their way to the airport. I guess he was hurt that I didn't hug him too. Envy does that to people.

Twenty four hours later, I'm still trying to recover from the worst hangover ever. They say that after you hit 18 your brain cells start dying. I'm 17, but after last night, I feel like I've started the process prematurely.

Josh and Teddy and Lisa and Alice and me were all at the Barge by the Canal. By beer standards, the Barge isn't the best pub in the world. But it does have something going for it that always wins me over. Clean, nice smelling toilets. Small, but clean. Did I say they smell great? Yeah, I know I'm a bit anal in that department (pardon the pun), but a girl's gotta have at least one quirky thing about her.

So there we were at the Barge, playing Devil's Six. For those of you foreign to the drinking games of the North, the objective of Devil's Six is to get up on a chair and sing a popular Irish song. Last night it was the Pogue's 'Dirty Old Town'. Whoever gives the worst performance loses.

Oh, and I forgot to mention that you have to do it after drinking a bit, which, where I come from, means quite a lot more than in most places. The version of Devil's Six we play involves consumption of the following liquids:

6 shots of Vodka

6 shots of Tequila

6 Pints of Guinness

6 glasses of water (optional)

The glasses of water were introduced by Lisa last month after her liver had collapsed. Or so she says. My suspicion is that it's just an excuse to reduce the amount of alcohol in her blood, thus increasing her chances of winning. In any case, by the end of the first round, when all the drinking had been done and Josh and Teddy performed Dirty Old Town to standing ovations, it was my turn. I got up on a stool, supported by Lisa, who claimed that she didn't trust me enough not to fall off the chair and bust my head as a cheap way to disqualify myself, and started to sing:

I met my laaaav by de gaaaaaas works waaaaall

Dreamed a dream by de ol' caaaaaanaaaaaal

Kissed a gal by the factory waaaaall

Dirty ol' town!

Dirdy old town.

Anyway, that's as long as I lasted. The crowd booed widely and when a can of Heineken hit my head I knew it was all over.

And so, five minutes later, there was no option but to obey Josh's command. Josh, who lost last week, was this week's Devil and was allowed complete freedom to humiliate me. Given the fact that last week his task was to French kiss the ugliest, drunkest bastard at the Barge (which was my idea), letting me run naked down the most famous street in Dublin only seemed fair. My own hunch was that more than humiliate me, Josh just wanted to see me without my clothes. But that's another story altogether.

I can take off my clothes real quick. That didn't come out right. I can disrobe really quickly. And so by the time Josh and the others spill out of the pub, I'm already running. I pass the taxi stand and get wild cheers from the red-eyed cabbies. One of them actually tries to outrun me, at which point I make a break to the left, running into the concierge at the Best Western. He's trying to order a cab for an old Japanese couple and I slam right into him and he drops to the ground. The cabby running behind me is in such shock that he stumbles and falls as well. At which point the

Japanese couple, jumping up and down in glee, ask me if they can take a picture with me. We help the cabby up, give him the camera, and I pose, naked, in between two Japanese who could be my grandparents' age. The concierge is now on his feet so it's time to dash back to the Barge. I'm running like a mad woman. It's cold and freezing and I don't feel any part of my body expect my nipples which feel as if they're about to pop off.

And then I spot Josh, who's running towards me ahead of the group. Could it be he's trying to cover me with his long coat before the others see me in my birthday suit? Or maybe he just wants to have a better look? Josh puts his coat around me as I shiver, breathless. He takes my face in his hands and looks in my eyes. I smile a stupid smile of someone who's just done something really foolish. He smiles back and says, 'I love you.'

#48

'If you run out of wine, look to the right and borrow from the person to your left... And if you run out of water, look to the left and borrow from the person on your right.'

I'm standing in the doorway, looking at her, amazed at

so many things, that I feel overwhelmed. Amazed that this girl, this wonderful, smart, funny little four-year-old is actually my girl. That something this good could have come out of me. Amazed how she was the one who kept Mitch and I together, against all odds. Amazed at how bright she is, ordering her little dolls around the miniature dining table we got her after Molly died.

Her teacher asked to speak with me today after school. 'The kids are making fun of her, Mrs. Li. She's the only one in class that can't hold a pencil correctly. She can't even draw like the other kids. She... she just scribbles.'

I wanted to slap her teacher there and then. Instead I promised we'd look into it and left with my tail between my legs.

'Can't draw, my ass!' I shout later, telling Mitch on the phone what had happened. 'For Christ's sake, Mitch, she's barely four. What did we know when we were four?!'

Mitch tells me to calm down. Mitch always tells me to calm down. When my Mom called to tell me that my Dad had left her after 30 years of marriage to shack up with some bimbo from headquarters, and I told my Mom I would kill him next time I saw him, Mitch told me to calm down. When our neighbour took down a fifty-year-old tree that was making too much shade on his side of the lawn and I threatened to sue, Mitch told me to calm down. When Molly was killed after a car slammed into the car that I was driving, and I couldn't stop tearing hair out of my head, Mitch told me to calm down.

I'm tired of calming down. That's what's always been the trouble with us. Mitch needs to control, even when all I want him to do is let me cry and act like a lunatic and hold me and tell me that everything is gonna be all right. But he doesn't, and so it never will be all right.

Emily knows that. She was only three when her baby sister died, but already then she knew that 'Mommy and Daddy are feeling bad'. God bless her soul, that little angel. If not for her, I'm not sure which one of us, Mitch or I, would have left. Left, or worse.

And now she's sitting on the floor, playing with her dolls, locked in her imaginary world. She looks at me in that funny look of hers. It's as if she's looking through me, seeing what's really inside me and reacting to what I really feel. She predicts me, this girl.

'Mommy?'

'Yes, angel?'

'Are you and Daddy going to bring me another baby sister?'

'I don't know honey,' I answer, more to blurt out a quick response that would precede the tears I can feel building down my throat, than anything else. 'It depends on the storks.'

I can see she doesn't appreciate my attempt at humour. She's organizing the main course on her little dinner table. She's doing an excellent job of laying out the dishes, and an equally excellent job of disregarding me. There are four plates on the table. One on each side. Next to each pink plate are matching forks and knives. Tiny pieces of Kleenex have been cut out to serve as napkins. There's a salt shaker and two bottles. One apparently for water, the other for wine. Askew, on chairs too small to fit them, sit four dolls. Two big dolls and two little ones. Where she got the smallest doll, the one dressed up in diapers, I do not know.

'Tonight we'll be having beef stew with potatoes. Daddy, I want you to serve the wine. Mommy, I want you to serve the water. Emily, if you run out of wine, look to the right and borrow from the person to your left. And if you run out of water, look to the left and borrow from the person on your right.'

It's only now that I notice what she said.

She's four. She's only four.

#49

'They come from small villages and big cities. Dressed in rags and handovers, they are the people no one notices, the people for whom no one cares. They come to see one woman who experts say is behind one of the most important forces in social development. It's called Hug Therapy and it's coming to a town near you. And with me tonight in the studio is Praveena Chilan, who is known to her followers as Mother Earth.

'Miss Chilan, thank you for joining us in the studio tonight. Could you tell us a bit about the origins of your movement?'

'Good evening, Charles. It is a true pleasure to be here tonight. This "movement" as you call it, is as old as mankind, or shall I say, womankind. Hugging is one of the oldest, innate forms of human communication. It is cross-cultural, cross-racial and is not limited by geographical boundaries. So one could say that it is the oldest form of social behaviour in the world.'

'Last year you and your followers organized a 20 country tour across Africa. In the process, you claim to have personally hugged over a million people. What's it like to be so close to people you've never met, and will probably never meet again?'

'It's like being in a dream state, Charles. It's as if there is a wave of energy flowing from you to all these people. An endless wave of energy. And with each person you hug, with each person who is courageous enough to shed behind their social misconceptions and basic mistrust of strangers, with each new hug I feel recharged again and again. It is truly one of God's wonders.'

'In doing research for our program tonight, we interviewed numerous people who received one of your hugs. All of them describe it as a life-transforming experience. Let's take a look at some scenes from your recent visit in Ghana.'

NARRATOR: 'They stand silently in line, in perfect order. To a bystander they simply seem as if they're waiting to buy supplies, or receive medical treatment. But their eyes are what make them stand out. It is the look of people who have nothing to lose. People whose life, in one way or another, let them down. And now they are here to receive a blessing, an infusion of hope. Watching these people emerge from Mother Earth's embrace is like watching a set of "Before and After" pictures. Some of them look so different, even their relatives find it hard to recognise them. Others are so moved by the experience they have to lie down to recover.'

'Miss Chilan, it's clear that your hugs have an intense impact on people, but I wonder if it lasts?'

'What lasts, Charles? Does life last? Does death last? When a loved one dies, how long does that last? One person would say it takes a few seconds for a person to die. Another would say that dealing with the death of a loved one can last a lifetime.'

'I understand that, but some of your critics say that your hugs simply provide a "Quick Fix"; that they don't really solve the significant problems that people, such as those we saw a few minutes ago, really need to deal with.'

'Charles, some people in the West find it hard to believe, to believe in anything really. If something takes too long then it's not worth the effort. If it doesn't take long enough then they label it quackery. I am not omnipotent, I don't know if what I do has any lasting effect or not. I'm a normal woman who gives hugs in a world where we find it hard to talk to family members we've known all our life. If my hugs make someone happy for only one minute, helping them forget their hardships and sorrows for only a blink of an eye, then I have done my work.'

'Tell me a bit about how you got started. I read in my production notes that you grew up in a small village in Bihar, the poorest state in India. Your parents were farmers and did not have enough money to pay for your education. In fact, I believe that you never even learned how to read and write. How do you explain that a woman from such humble beginnings becomes what Time Magazine calls in a recent cover story, "Our Hero"?'

'It is true, Charles, that I never knew how to read a book or write on paper. But my parents, my mother especially, taught me something far more valuable. When I was six, Bihar experienced one of the worst floods in its history. A year of crops was rendered useless. Most of our livestock had drowned. Two of my brothers had disappeared. I remember the family gathering around a makeshift fire my father made after the water had settled. We were all silent, too stunned and tired to talk. Suddenly, my father, who I had never seen express any emotion of any kind, began crying, in front of us all. Here was a man who never had much, but took great pride in his ability to provide for his family. And now he had lost even that. My mother said nothing. She simply knelt beside him and hugged him. She hugged him as if nothing else mattered.

'My father never talked about what happened that day again. But from then onwards, he looked differently at that woman. She had saved his and our lives on that day.

'Sometimes, Charles, all we need to keep going on is a little hug.'

#50

It was exactly a month ago when he started with this crazy adventure. 30 days, 720 hours, 43,200 minutes. Two tubes run from his transparent box. One brings in water, the other takes it out. A box and two tubes. This will be his home for another two weeks. And then, his work will be done. Then he can go back to Emma and the kids. Then he won't have to prove anything to anyone.

Until next time.

I asked him once what drives him. What attracts him about making all his stunts, those death-defying feats he undertakes. He didn't answer for a while. For a minute, I thought he never would. At the core, he is a very private man. Ask him about tricks, illusions or magic, he'll talk for hours. But ask him something personal, and chances are he'll get up and leave. Not this time. He looks at me with his penetrating eyes, as if he's judging whether I really care about the question I've just asked.

'Some people are driven towards something. Some people look ahead and see the destination. And when they catch a glimpse of it, they are propelled forward. I was never like that. I never had a master plan. Never had any clear objectives, really.' He pauses as if he's weighing the ramifications of what he's just said.

He started performing on the sidewalks when he was 12, gaining instant popularity with people of all ages. When he was 15, a talent scout from New York spotted him and suggested to his grandmother (his mother had died the year before) that he start performing in the big city. 'That kid had magic coming out of his eyes,' noted Samuel Hunt, former program director at Radio City. 'He would stand in front of you and do one of his tricks, never taking his eyes off of you. When he was done, you'd feel as if it wasn't a human performing the trick. He was that good. But then he would show you how he did the trick, and would then do it again, and you still wouldn't have a clue how he'd done it. That's when you knew you were in the presence of greatness. Or the devil.'

His stage career was a short-lived one, however, ending after only two shows. Something about his magnetism, his electrifying presence, didn't quite transpire on stage. The crowd felt it, the promoters felt it, but most of all, he felt it. He took a year off magic, refusing all requests to return to his street performances. 'He would sit in his room all day and do nothing,' his grandmother said once in an interview. 'I would go up to him and say - kid, you've got a special talent, and if God gave you this gift, you need to use it. But I was better off talking to the walls. Nothing would change his mind. Nothing, of course, but that little girl.'

On December 14, 1992, Stacy Connolly was waiting for

her mother to pick her up from school. When 30 minutes had passed and the mother hadn't arrived yet, Stacy decided to make the three mile walk back home on foot. It was a cold winter day and heavy snow had fallen the night before. In one of those freak accidents life deals us sometimes, a speeding pickup truck failed to stop at a stop sign. To avoid colliding with a passing car, the driver swerved violently to the right, leaped onto the sidewalk and ran over Stacy. The driver was none other than Megan Connolly, Stacy's mother, who was rushing to pick up her daughter from school. Stacy lay in a coma for the better part of that winter. The Connolly's tried everything, from experimental medical treatments through blessings from various religious figures, but Stacy would not wake. Behind closed doors, the doctors began talking about pulling the plug. On a bright morning in April, Stacy's mother made a trip three blocks down from their house. It would be her third visit to a young man whom Stacy had spoken highly of. A year earlier she had seen him perform some magic tricks and could not stop raving for days. Megan Connolly had no idea whether magic could help her daughter, but when your child is lying in a coma, you don't rule out anything.

All this happened such a long time ago, that hearing him recount this story, this miracle of how a young girl woke up from a coma after receiving a visit from a young man who simply lay his hand on her forehead, could lead you to underestimate the importance of this event in his life. But after the Connolly incident, he returned to the world of magic and never looked back.

And now he's been locked in a Perspex cube for 30 days. Without food, without human interaction, without radio or television.

Most people, when asked for their opinion about his stunts, tend to fall into two camps. Those who think he's insane and those who think he's crazy. After all, why lock yourself in a cube for 44 days when modern life is as lonely and alienated as it is? But there is a third camp. A group of people who, like him, are not driven by some guiding light, some set of lofty goals, but something else altogether. You can spot those people amongst the crowd. They look at his box and wait to catch his eyes. When they do, they don't wave or shout anything, but simply nod.

In the last interview he granted me before leaving for his self-induced exile, the one where I asked him about what drives him, he said something I hadn't quite understood at the time, but now suddenly makes so much sense. 'Sometimes it's not about where you want to go and what you want to achieve. Sometimes it's about where you're coming from and how fast you need to run away from it.'

#51

'Come here for a second, baby. I want to tell you something.

'You know how on our first night together we played this game that you invented? You know, the Truth Game, where you can ask whichever question you want to ask and the other person has to answer? Do you remember which question you asked me, the single one I told you I could never answer?

'Well, I think I'm ready to tell you the answer now.'

The phone rings and it's my Mom on the line. I could have thought of a hundred times where a ring from her could have really gotten me out of a sticky situation. But now, just when I'm ready to pull my heart out and lay it on the table, she calls.

'Yes Mom, of course I'm coming. I told you so. No, I don't think it's rude not to call Aunt Bella when I visit. Mom, I haven't seen her since I was five. Yes, I know she loves me more than the others. No Mom, I'll never forget to visit you when I visit. Mom! Stop it! Enough with the guilt trip. I love you and I'll see you next week, OK? OK, send my love to Peggy. Bye. Love you too, Mom. Bye. Mom, I'm hanging up now. Mom!

'Nineteen years ago I went to summer camp in the Rocky Mountains. It was one of those adventure camps that my parents thought would help develop my masculinity. Those were the 80s and I guess parents worried about that kind of stuff back then.

'For some reason my parents were frantic that I'd get lost somewhere between Seattle and Denver airports. My Mom was convinced that I had to wear clothes that stand out, so she had me wear a pair of red corduroys and a neon orange sweater. How they let me on the airplane in that outfit is something I'd never understand. To humiliate me even further, I had to wear a 9x12 sign on my chest:

HELLO!

MY NAME IS

MICHAEL KRAZTMAN

IF YOU FIND ME

PLEASE DIAL 206-323-4353

'Needless to say I couldn't have bid my parents farewell fast enough. I threw the sign into the nearest garbage can I could find. The first thing I did on the plane was take off my sweater and hide it under my chair. The pants, unfortunately had to stay on.'

'I was picked up together with four other kids in Denver. Not a word was spoken for the next two hours, as we made our way towards Camp Skokomish. I was convinced it had something to do with my red pants, but it probably had more to do with the simple fact that we were all barely teenagers.

'Camp was great. By the end of the first week we had all the friendships and rivalries to last us a lifetime. They say that once you pass a certain age, say 20, you don't really make friends any more, only acquaintances. I had made good friends at Skokomish. That's where Tom Reynolds and I met. You remember - he was the guy who called us the night before our wedding to apologize he couldn't make it.

'There were lots of activities at Skokomish. Most of them had to do with river life. We learned how to camouflage ourselves, how to fish and how to paddle. At night, we would all get around the campfire and listen to Indian tales about Buffalos and evil spirits.

'On the seventh day of camp we woke up to what looked like another regular day of fun and activities. We were going to spend the afternoon white water rafting, and the camp instructors were tense, checking again and again to make sure we had our life jackets on. I was on a raft with five other kids: Jordy Hubbard, Alice Kelly, Mark Blanchard, Tom Reynolds and July Maynard. There were five rafts in the water and ours went before last. It was only later that I'd learn that this was because our rafting instructor hadn't guided a group before.

'At first the water was calm, and I remember Tom Reynolds complaining to the instructor that this ride was for girls. Five minutes later, Alice and July began screaming. Five minutes later, we were in grade four rapids, and Tom looked like he was about to scream. There didn't seem to be much sense in trying to use our paddles in those waters. The river was taking us for a ride and any attempt we would have made to alter course seemed like a bad joke.

'I was sitting behind Jordy Hubbard, so I'm not really sure how we got so close to the raft in front of us, but suddenly I was in the water. It felt like some big hand had plucked me out of the boat and thrown me into the river. Swimming wasn't an option here, only a reflex-driven effort to keep my head above the water. I drifted for a bit, spotting someone next to me here or one of the rafts there. But overall, there wasn't much I could see. The sound of roaring water around me was deafening, and for the first time in my life I thought about my own mortality.

'Suddenly, I felt something dragging me under the water. I tried to shake it off, but it didn't let go, as if I picked up some weight along the way. A minute later I realized I had. Mark Blanchard was holding onto the back of my lifejacket. Somewhere along the way he had lost his and managed to latch on to mine. I began swallowing more and more water and all my attempts to stay more above water than underneath it were failing.

'I yelled at Mark to let go but he didn't. He just hung on to me, not even trying to swim or anything like that. I tried to release his grip from my lifejacket. I knew that he would get us both killed if he didn't let go. But he didn't. So I elbowed him. I elbowed him so hard you could hear something break, amidst the roaring water and all.

'Two hours later, they found Alice Kelly's body. Just before dusk they found Mark's.

'You see, baby, sometimes life twists your arm into doing things you'd never dream of doing. And then you spend the rest of your life running away.'

#52

'Blow it up!'

'What, the whole thing?'

'Yeah! Blow it up!'

He looked at her face. 'God, she's beautiful,' he thought to himself, as he crouched above the control box.

She was wearing a blue sweatshirt with the words 'Duke University' on the front. It was a fairly new sweatshirt and it was at least two or three sizes too big for her. 'Surely it's from an old boyfriend or lover. Or some guy she just slept with,' he thought to himself.

'What would it take to get her to wear my sweatshirt?' he wondered, looking at his faded Old Navy one.

They were sitting in a small, damp room, the kind maintenance men kept their supplies in. On the floor was a control box of some sort, not unlike the kind kids use to fly a remote-controlled plane. From the box, a multi-coloured cable made its way to the wall, where a small hole had been drilled the night before. From there, the cable made its way through the thick grass that separated the Georgetown Geriatric Research Unit from the Clarence Archer Biology Building. When the cable reached the wall of the Biology Building it stopped. There, it was met by 50kg of explosives. Enough to cause an irreversible amount of damage to something, or someone.

'What are you looking at me like that for?' she asked him.

'Like what?' he answered, though he knew exactly what she meant.

'Like I'm some kind of animal. Like I'm some kind of rare species. Something to be studied and explored.'

'I don't know what you're talking about,' he said.

'You men are all alike. You talk and talk and talk, but when it's time to do something about it, you don't have the balls.'

'But this was my idea in the first place!' he answered back.

'Oh, listen to you... "It was my idea in the first place..." Then push the button. Come on, push it.'

At first he'd thought that something had gone wrong with the wiring. He'd pushed the button, and the red light indicator did go on. But that was it. He pushed the button again. There was a loud explosion and the room shook. Then there was quiet.

She looked at him in disbelief. Her face was pale. He looked at his hands. They were trembling.

'You... you... you pushed the button...' she said.

'I can't believe you pushed the button. You just pushed the fucking button... fuck!'

He got up and felt his head spin a bit, though not in a bad way. Outside there was a commotion. They could hear people running out of the labs and meeting rooms into the corridor. He looked at her. She was still leaning next to the control box.

'Come on, let's get out of here,' he said, offering her his hand. She didn't move.

'Anna, let's go.'

She slouched back and leaned on the wall next to a stack of paint containers.

'We can't stay here. Sooner or later they'll come looking for us.'

'You pushed the button...' she repeated in disbelief. 'You fucking pushed the button...'

'Anna, what's wrong with you? Get up... let's get out of here.'

'I... I can't believe you did it...' she said, holding her head in her hands.

'What?' he shot back. 'You just told me to push the button about 10 times. What did you expect me to do?!'

'I don't know...' she answered softly. 'Nothing, maybe.'

'Well, it's a bit too late for nothing. So get up from the floor and let's get a move on it.'

He bent his knees and tried to take her by the arm. She didn't move.

'Anna, you're not helping me very much. If we don't leave right now we'll be in big big trouble.'

'I didn't know...' she said.

'Of course you did!' he said, raising his voice. 'You helped me lay the cable through the grass. You helped me put the explosives in the bag. You even got us the detonator. What do you mean you had no idea?!'

'I had no idea...' she said, her eyes moist with tears.

'Anna, what on earth are you talking about?'

'I had no idea you cared that much...'

#53

'Nothing you're going to do can change this, you know.'

'I know. I'm ready'

'OK. Let's go.'

I slam the door and put my seatbelt on. John is driving

and I'm sitting shotgun. As my belt clicks in place he looks at me with that look of his that makes me feel like I've done something really childish. Normally, I would have looked back, confused, and would ask, 'what?' Now I simply don't care.

We're driving down route 125 from Middlebury to Green Mountain National Forest. It's a short ride, only 15 minutes or so but the views never cease to amaze me. Though I've been living in this part of Vermont for over 10 years, something about the mountains here gives me a rush time and time again.

John accelerates the car, knowing I'll ask him to slow down. I look at him and before I get a chance to open my mouth he takes his foot off the gas pedal and smiles.

I've never seen so many people on this road. Hundreds, thousands of people maybe. When did they all come here? Why did they all come here?

We're only doing 50mph, but the banners and the signs are all a blur to me. I can see my name on them, but still can't fathom that all these people would come here just for me.

I open the window and let the cool wind blow through my hair. John looks at me and shakes his head. I lean my arm on the door and feel that part of the window that didn't slide all the way down. I rest my chin on my arm and look straight ahead. It's impossible to focus on anything this way. All you see is a frame - a girl on her daddy's head waving, two older folks shouting something. The face of a young woman.

'Stop the car!'

'What?'

'Stop the car, John!'

'Steve, we're not there yet.'

'I know we're not there yet, John. Stop the car.'

The car comes to a standstill and is immediately surrounded by people. John reaches out and grabs me by the arm.

'Steve, if you leave now, you won't be able to come back. You know.'

'I know.' I look back at him and want to say goodbye. Something in my throat blocks any attempt to speak. I open the car door and step outside for the last time.

I killed a girl on the road a few months ago. Nothing I can do to change that now. It was late at night and I finished my shift at the mill. I had a couple of beers with the boys and headed back home. I was drunk. I offered her a lift and for some reason she accepted. The rest you probably know.

John offered to drive me in to the ranger's station. That was my only condition. Didn't want no police car to pick me up. Didn't want to go to the police station in town. I would give myself up only to the forest ranger, and only if John would drive me there. The chief of police said yes and someone leaked the whole plan to the press. And now there are 500 people here, calling my name, screaming revenge.

I didn't expect to see her, though. Didn't even call to say goodbye. She loved me, that much I knew, and after I'd done what I'd done, her life would be hell. So what would I have said on the phone?

But now she's here, amongst the crowd. And I need to see her. Need to tell her something before I go. And it's weird that my brain is still processing, with all the kicking and punching that's going on. They'll kill me these people. These people I was once a part of. People don't take murder of a young woman too easily here.

I look up from the ground. I can't hear anymore and my eyes have already started swelling up. But I swear to God that I can see her. I open my mouth to say something and nothing comes out. Nothing.

#54

'Tell me a story, Daddy.'

'OK. Would you like to hear about the little prince?'

'No.'

'Would you like to hear about the gold-hearted flower?'

'No.'

'Would you like to hear about the scary dragon?'

'No. I want to hear about the friendly dragon.'

'The friendly dragon? Honey, I don't know any friendly dragons. Aren't all of them big and scary?'

'Not this one.'

'And does this friendly dragon have a name?'

'Sheldon.'

'Sheldon? That's a pretty peculiar name for a dragon.'

'Yes. It's cuz he's a pecoo-lee-ar dragon.'

'OK. Sheldon it is. And why is Sheldon so friendly when all the other dragons are so scary?'

'Because he's not afraid.'

'Afraid? What isn't he afraid of, pumpkin?'

'Of people, daddy. Sheldon wasn't afraid of people.'

'Ahhhh, I get it. OK. Here goes...

'Once upon a time, in a far away land, lived a dragon named Sheldon. Sheldon had two dragon parents - Mr and Mrs Droog, and two older dragon brothers, Bouk and Mouk.'

'No, daddy. Bouk and Mouk aren't good names. You have to give them really scary names.'

'Hey, who's telling the story here, you or me? OK, OK, I was just joking. So Sheldon lived with his parents and two older brothers Bootroos and Mootroos. Bootroos and Mootroos were the scariest dragons in the whole world, and Sheldon's parents were very proud of them. They were so scary that even Sheldon's parents didn't dare tell them to clean up their rooms or do their homework. At school, none of the other kids would even look into the eyes of Bootroos and Mootroos.'

'What did their eyes look like, Daddy?'

'Oh, their eyes are too scary to describe, honey.'

'No, no, I want to know. Tell me what their eyes looked like.'

'Their eyes were green. Dark green. And in the middle of each eye, was a black slit. And when they would get angry, that black slit would get bigger and bigger and bigger, until their whole eye was black.'

'What were Sheldon's eyes like, Daddy?'

'Oh, Sheldon? He had kind eyes. They were blue like the colour of the sky. And they always smiled.'

'His eyes smiled?'

'Yes, pumpkin. Sheldon was such a friendly dragon, that even his eyes smiled. But Sheldon would often get into trouble. The other kids didn't like him and they often played nasty tricks on him.'

'Why didn't they like him, Daddy?'

'Maybe it was because of his scary brothers, or maybe they felt that he was not scary enough like all the other dragons.'

'What kind of tricks would they play on him?'

'Oh, they would blow fire up his backside, and make fun of his droopy ears and the way he flew.'

'Sheldon couldn't fly well?'

'No. He had a lazy wing, and when he tried to fly, he always ended up flying in circles.'

'Daddy?'

'Yes, darling?'

'I'm getting tired. Could you tell me how come Sheldon wasn't a scary dragon like his brothers?'

'Of course, sweetheart. It all happened when Sheldon was a little boy. One day he and his two brothers went playing in the woods and got lost. It was the first time they had ever gotten lost and Sheldon was very scared. As night fell, Sheldon and his brothers breathed flames out of their noses to see their way and to warm themselves up. After walking for hours and hours, the three decided to go to sleep under a big tree. Hours passed by and suddenly the sounds of galloping horses woke them up. They found themselves surrounded by 20 riders, all dressed in black. The riders were on a mission from the Evil Queen to go hunting for dragons. The three brothers tried to blow fire out of their noses, but they had used their noses so much earlier that nothing but snot came out.'

'YUCK!'

'The leader of the riders was a tall and handsome knight. He got off his horse to get a better view of his successful catch. It wasn't every day that he and his men caught a dragon, let alone three. Bootroos and Mootroos were shaking with fear as the knight drew closer. But Sheldon, who had never seen a human being before and was happy that someone found them, just smiled. Surprised, the knight said: "And what might be the name of this little dragon who smiles?"'

'Sheldon! Sheldon! His name is Sheldon!'

'That's right, darling, that's exactly what he said to the knight. "Sheldon?" asked the knight. "My name is also Sheldon!". "Well," said Sheldon the dragon, "maybe we can be friends then!?" Bootroos and Mootroos almost fainted. Not only were they surrounded by a group of riders sent to hunt them down by the Evil Queen, but their little brother dared talking to a human being.'

'Daddy, Daddy, did the two Sheldons become friends?'

'The knight was so impressed with Sheldon's friendliness that he decided then and there to become his friend. In the morning, the riders brought Sheldon and his two brothers back home to their worried parents. Bootroos and Mootroos told everyone that they had scared the riders into bringing them back home. They told everyone how the knight was so scared that Bootroos and Mootroos would kill him, that he agreed to show them the way out of the forest. But with all their storytelling, the two brothers knew the truth. They knew that the only reason they returned home safe and sound was because of their little brother, Sheldon. Sheldon who couldn't breathe fire out of his nose properly, had droopy ears and couldn't fly straight. Sheldon, the friendly dragon.'

Bang! Bang! Bang!

What on earth! Who's this pounding on my door?

Bang! Bang! Bang! Bang!

This time the pounding is even louder.

Oh Lord, what should I do? Who knows what kind of crazy person could be on the other side? Maybe if I don't do anything they'll just go away? But what if they just want to make sure that there's no one home so that they can break in? On the other hand, what kind of burglar raises such a racket before they break in? Maybe it's a new technique they're using? Maybe it's psychological warfare

Bang! Bang! Bang!

Oh dear. This doesn't sound good. Sounds like they're strong as well. Strong enough to break this door down if they wanted to. I told Jimmy to put in a stronger door. 'Jimmy,' I said, 'I don't feel safe with this door. It's made of wood. Wooden doors aren't strong.' But did he listen? No. Got me one of those fake-oak doors installed. I told him, 'Jimmy, your mother is an old lady. Now is not the time to be cheap on her. I need a solid steel door.' But Jimmy wouldn't listen. He tried to convince me that the wooden door was more expensive than the steel one. As if. All I can tell you is that in my days we had a lot more respect for the elderly. A lot more respect.

This would never happen if Jacek was still alive. He'd install an electric fence around the house if I asked for it. But now? Now all I got is this plywood door between me and the world.

Maybe they got scared and ran away. Or maybe they're just waiting for reinforcement to arrive? How am I supposed to go back to sleep now? As if it's not enough that I have trouble sleeping. As if the new butcher working at Schlemer's isn't giving me the evil eye? As if I didn't have enough to worry about.

And now my bed is cold again. Oh, for crying out loud! Don't these people have any respect for the people who built this country? Didn't their parents teach them any manners, waking me up from my nap!

Bang!

Dear Lord, this is the end of me. I knew this would happen. I knew this is how I would go. Killers, killers are breaking into my home and there's no one here to help me. Oh, I wanted to install that panic button a long time ago. Only God knows how many times I asked Jimmy to install it. What does he do? Offers to bring in a live-in helper. Did I ask him for a live-in helper? No! Did I ask for someone to live in my house, snooping around in my bedroom? Looking through my clothes? No! So I said to him, I said to him, 'Jimmy, if you want to kill your mother, just be a man about it and shoot me. Shoot me! Just don't get someone else to do the job for you.' So he never installed the panic button. Never got me a helper either.

Bang! Bang! Bang!

All right! All right! I'm coming. I don't care if it's Jack the Ripper on the other end of the door. I'll show him what I'm made of. The special frying pan in the kitchen! The big one I put aside for emergencies. Now, where is it? Ha! That'll teach them a lesson, messing around with old ladies.

Bang! Bang!

Just a second! Can't you see I'm in the kitchen! Well... the nerve some people have! What am I, an athlete or something? I can't fly, you know. You've waited so long to bang on this door you can wait another minute. Jacek would have never let something like this happen. Those scumbags would have been running home to their mommies by now. Always a strong person he was, my Jacek. Had a weak heart though. Got him early.

Now to open this contraption. For goodness sake, you have to be a university professor to open this door. I told my Jimmy, 'Jimmy, all I want is for you to put in a steel door with four locks. A steel door with four locks - that's all I'm asking for. Put in the steel door and you can leave me to die peacefully.' So what does he do? He puts in a wooden door with a computerized lock. Computerized lock! Who ever heard of such a crazy thing? Now when I want to leave the house I have to punch in a number! I swear on my mother's grave, it's just another way to keep me locked up here at home.

Oh! Jimmy! You scared the hell out of me! What are you doing here?

#56

'So you want to know how it all started? Hmmmm. Let's see. It must have been 1946. Jack and I had just gotten married a year earlier and were expecting little Ruthie.'

As she says this she leans back in the lilac-coloured sofa, as if reclining will help her memory back-track through all those years. I can't help but notice how incredibly beautiful she is. At 82 she exudes more vitality than most people in my class. Her eyes are hazel-brown, her hair is almond-coloured with streaks of grey. Her skin is dark olive, the only reminder that she hails from the old country. That, of course, and her sense of style, which makes me, draped in sweatpants and an oversized Gap sweatshirt, look like some kind of soccer Mom. She looks at me with a combination of confidence and curiosity and continues to tell me her story.

'All those young men coming back from the front, looking for work. It wasn't easy. Plus, we had little Ruthie on the way. So Jack joined General Electric as a salesmen. He was good, my Jack. "Jack could sell ice to the Eskimos", is what they used to say about him. But all that travelling meant that I was spending more and more time on my own.'

'Were you angry at him for leaving you alone so often?'

'Angry,' she chuckles and slaps her hands on her knees. 'I could never get angry with my Jack.'

She pauses as if scanning selected scenes from her life, the corners of her mouth change shape slightly, becoming somewhat tighter.

'But I must admit that at times I was a bit jealous.'

'Jealous?'

'Yes. You see dear, back then women didn't get to do much but stay at home and take care of the children. Jack would come back from all these exotic places; New York, San Francisco, Atlanta, and there I was, 26 years old, had never seen a skyscraper, had never been on a plane, had never even seen one up close.'

'So you started making stories up?'

'Yes. Well, at first I didn't think of them as stories, not the kind you'd read in a book or anything like that. There were stories I used to tell Ruthie and then Adam and then Michael. They were my first audience, I guess,' she says and chuckles again in that beautiful laughter of hers. She is so elegant that I feel acutely aware of all the elegance that I've never possessed. I may have travelled to Paris and Rome, but this woman who has never left her town, had never left her home, in fact, for over 50 years, is better-travelled in ways I will never be.

'I can't remember who it was, but one of my girlfriends convinced me to start writing my stories. I sent a few of them to the local newspaper. The editor personally came to visit me one day. Couldn't believe that a woman could write such adventures.' She gives me a knowing look, the kind that only women can share. 'Needless to say he became a believer after that.' We both burst into laughter and she pours me some tea from a pot it's been simmering in for the past few minutes. It's an exquisite little artefact, this tea pot. No doubt sent to her by one of her admirers around the world. With 42 books in as many languages, she's one of the most popular writers alive and her sitting room is a living testament to all her fans.

'So when did you... em,' I begin asking uneasily.

'When did I stop leaving the house? It's OK for you to ask. That's what everyone wants to know. People are funny like that, they're always afraid of asking the most obvious questions. As if I'm not aware of the fact that I'm a strange ol' lady,' she says to me and smiles in the most disarming way.

'I think it was when Michael was four. By then I had three books published and an advance for another. Then one day it all stopped. I would sit down in front of my typewriter and nothing would come out. This went on for a few weeks until Jack took me aside. Jack always knew when something was not right with me. "Emily," he said, "whatever it is you're worried about, you have to let it go." He was right of course, but there was nothing I could do. I felt that if I would leave the house and go outside I might find out that things are not what they seem. That what I write about, all these exotic places and mysterious people, don't really exist. I was scared, I guess. Still am a bit now. Scared that all those things I imagined don't really exist.'

#57

You are so predictable. You, who could argue with me for hours about how unequal society is, yet stare at me in disbelief for giving a homeless person a five pound note. You, who preach for love and harmony, yet never called up your Dad and said, 'I love you'. You, who thinks voting is a duty, yet cannot tell me the difference between right and left. This story is for you.

Ten years ago, give or take a few months, I was travelling in India. The visit was unexpected. I was on my way to China to meet with some government officials on the construction of a big science park when my plane had to make an emergency landing in Bombay. We flew too close to a cumulonimbus - a massive cloud structure that normally houses a thunder storm or two. The electrical storm we ended up passing through did not seem that dramatic from my window, but apparently it put some of our navigation systems out of synch and the pilot decided not to take any chances.

There were no direct flights from Bombay to Shanghai and my options were either to spend the next 24 hours taking a combination of five connecting flights, or to take the train to Varanasi, and fly out directly from there. It was Thursday evening, and my meeting with the Chinese wasn't until Monday. I decided to take the train.

Bombay's Victoria Terminus is a massive complex. It is so big that it has its own weather system. Except that the weather in Victoria is a choking combination of soot and exhaust fumes. It's a place you do not want to spend more time in than absolutely necessary. In my case that would be 43 minutes. 43 minutes that would change my life.

I had heard many stories about the petty thieves in Asia. How someone would come up to you, dressed in a suit, speaking impeccable English, only to swindle you ten minutes later through some scheme or another. And so when a silver-haired man dressed in a tailored suit approached me, I was mentally prepared.

'Good evening, Sir.'

'Ehhh, no thank you.'

'No thank you, Sir? Why, I only wished to bid you a good

evening.'

'I... I'm sorry, good evening to you too,' I muttered, suddenly feeling self-conscious of how suspicious I'd become in the course of the three hours since I got off the plane.

'Thank you. Though I can imagine better places to spend a fine evening,' he answered.

'Yes, yes, so can I,' I answered back, still resisting the urge to engage in conversation.

'Where would that be?' he asked.

'Where would what be?' I replied.

'That better place. Where would you rather be right now?'

I was caught off guard. Part of me wanted to stay out of this conversation, to be left alone. But it was too late for that now, and I figured that I wasn't going to let anything happen anyway. I glided my hand over my breast pocket, making sure my wallet was still there.

'I'm not really sure,' I said. 'There are so many places I can think of, I wouldn't know where to start.'

'To be frank, Sir, nor would I.' There was a brief silence before he continued. 'But where would you end?'

'Excuse me?' I answered, not really in the mood for any philosophical discussion.

'If your life was to end today, say, in seven minutes, where would you rather be?'

I felt uncomfortable. Hypothetical situations are part of my daily life. When you're designing massively complex building sites, 'what if?' becomes an habitual question. But I had never thought about my own mortality in that way. And so I allowed myself to be drawn into the conversation.

'That's an interesting question,' I answered, surveying the man again. He was well-dressed by any standards, let alone in comparison to most of the people in the station, who wore nothing much more than a piece of cloth around their waists. His fingernails had been manicured recently and he wore cufflinks. His tie was black, and his shoes were made of fine leather. The man knew how to make an appearance.

'I guess that if I had seven minutes, there wouldn't be much time for fancy meals, or even seeing too many people. I'd want to see my wife, and my little girl and tell them that I love them.'

'And if you had two minutes left? If you learned now that in two minutes you'd be gone, what would you do?'

I began feeling uneasy. His line of questioning seemed to lead nowhere.

'I don't know,' I answered, deciding that it was best to try to end this game as soon as possible. 'I would probably try and speak to someone, you know, anyone, so that if I wasn't with my loved ones I could at least pass on some kind of message to them.'

My train was approaching the platform rapidly, and a mass of people began running towards it. I was pushed and shoved with the strength only a collective mob could muster. I lost my balance and only thanks to the sheer density of the crowd, did not fall down. Instead, it was if someone was pushing me closer and closer to the tracks. The train was almost at the station, yet it didn't look like it was slowing down at all. Too close to the tracks now, I have absolutely no power to stay on the platform. In front of me, one or two people spill over the platform and fall onto the tracks. The train is closer, only 30 feet away. I feel nauseous and my throat is dry. And as I look away from the tracks, refusing to believe that this is happening, I see the old man. And in a quiet, calm voice that I can hear clearly amidst all the shouting, he says: 'What is the message?'

#58

'I was never close to my parents. My father hated me and I

don't think my mother had what you Americans call a "maternal instinct".'

We are sitting in the First Class Lounge at JFK. It's a plush little space that looks more like a Philippe Starck hotel room than an airport lounge. The room is sparse. A big sofa shaped like a pair of big, red juicy lips. A rectangular glass table with seashells underneath it. A huge vase with green bamboo sticks surrounding one very tall orchid. Two chaises longues draped in velvet. Whoever designed the space had a lot of artistic freedom.

And artistic freedom is what we were meant to discuss here today. I've been trying to get an interview with her for eight months. Must have spoken to her agent in Paris a dozen times. I have tried to track her down at a fashion show in Madrid, during a book reading (her fifth) in Tokyo and in a nightclub in Moscow. So naturally, my first question today is what made her change her mind about giving me an interview.

'I'm not,' was all she answered. And so the rules of the game had been laid out. She would talk, I would listen.

'I wrote my first play when I was 14. It was a parody on the French elite. It was set in, how do you call it, a kindergarten?' I nod and take a sip from my coffee. 'Half way through the year, when all the questions of hierarchy have long been settled by the children, a new girl joins the class. She is smart, remarkably pretty and very sharp.

Unfortunately she is also black.'

'Unfortunately?' I ask. 'For who?'

'For the other girls of course. Making fun at someone's colour, when you know they are brighter and more beautiful than you is the easiest thing to do. But even children know that in mocking someone else, you only mock yourself. And so by pushing her away from them, the other girls ended up pushing themselves from who they thought they were. It all ends up quite badly.'

I am not sure I understood the play, nor its conclusion, but that is the norm with her work. You don't really understand it. Yet something about it captivates you, draws you closer, brings you back for more.

'That play was a turning point for me. I realized that what went on in my mind could have an impact on other people.'

'How did your parents react when they read your play?'

'Oh, they didn't read it. My parents couldn't care less about what I wrote. They heard about the play from my schoolmaster. Apparently it was provocative enough to feature in the weekly staff meeting. My teacher decided that I stole the play from some unknown French play writer and I was ordered to write a 10,000 word essay on plagiarism.'

'That's crazy,' I said. 'What does a 14-year-old girl know about plagiarism?'

She smiles mockingly. 'Apparently, you do not know many 14-year-old French girls.'

I decide to remain silent for a while. There was no use trying to appear smarter than I was. We had never met before, but already she had managed to make me feel as though she knew me inside-out.

'I wrote the first draft of "The Lie" in a fortnight. It was an analysis of ten great works in art, history and science. From Beethoven's Fifth to Max Plank's theory on electromagnetism. It showed how each and every one of these discoveries had, in fact, been made before. How none of the people we admire for being responsible for these "creations" were really the ones to make them. They were simply very talented liars.'

She tips her cigarette holder into my half-empty coffee cup, crosses her legs seductively and looks into my eyes. 'Coffee is bad for you, you know.'

She looks into my eyes. If she is blinking, she is doing so way too fast for me to notice. Everything about her has to do with being present. Her intensity scares me, but like a deer caught in the headlights, I cannot look away. She takes a long puff from her cigarette and blows it out in perfect rings of smoke, all without taking her eyes off me. I stare, mesmerized, like a teenager who notices his next door neighbour taking off her bra.

'So, Mr. Sullivan. My plane leaves in 45 minutes. What would you like to do until then?'

#59

You could see the terror in their eyes for miles. The mosque, which used to be the largest, and certainly the most visible in Baghdad, was reduced to a pile of stones. The stones, oddly enough, were all the same size, not larger than a man's palm. Funny-looking stones, Marcy thought to herself, oblivious to the fact that so many people around her were screaming, running around with their hands on their head, their clothes bloody with the remains of 87 people who found their death here only 15 minutes ago. These stones, she said to herself, look like they're made from mud. No wonder the whole mosque fell to the ground like a stack of cards. But the stones were also very beautiful, for on one side, each stone was covered with turquoise lacquer. The kind you'd find on a Bulgari egg, or on the ceiling of the Sistine chapel. Marcy could only guess that these stones were all part of the roof, and that they all formed some sort of picture. But a picture of what? Unlike the ceilings of

Christian places of worship, Muslims, much like Jews, did not have pictures of their sacred deities. But if you're not allowed to paint the ceiling with holy images, what do you paint it with?

Before she could think of an answer, she found herself on the ground - slammed into it by a group of people going nowhere in particular, but going there very quickly. And that's when she started hearing the voices around her. Most of them were screams - there were still over 200 people who were lucky enough to be alive (though some of these were clearly better off dead, with their missing limbs, eyes, faces). Some were just yelling at the sky - as if the bomb which reduced the mosque to rubble came from above (it didn't - it was carried by a large milk truck). Others just kneeled on the floor, head in hands, and cried like little children. Only here there were no mothers to console them - only fathers, brothers, uncles. Men. It was almost as if the carnage had given everyone the right to behave like children again, to expose their weakness, to shed their everyday covers of manliness and confidence and to do what most of them hadn't done since they were five. Here, they could cry.

She had already taken five rolls of film before she was pushed to the ground. No one really noticed her. She might have been the only woman in the area, but covered from head to toe in her black 'chador' she was almost invisible. And so she lay there on the ground for a bit longer than she normally would have. Listening. Listening to the screams, the cries, the sorrow. Listening to her heart beat steadily, a constant reminder that, against all odds, she is alive. She can see. She can record all this so that everyone reading the next issue of Time Magazine will see what happened here today and... and what?

She got up on her feet and began taking pictures again. She might be 25, but she's seen her share of bodies in the past three years. First there were the bombings in Pakistan, then the war in Afghanistan, now the war (and its far more deadly aftermath) in Iraq. So many bodies. So little time. Her mind starts drifting away. The men are looking at her in fear, though this is not because of her sex, but because of her demeanour. Confident, tall (taller than most men in the middle east), she moves with ease from one place to the other, almost oblivious (at least to the common observer) of the horror around her.

But more than anything, what captures the attention of the men who are looking at her is the fact that she is covered with blood. Red over black always makes the best impact when you go out, her friend Sarah said to her once. 'Dressed to Kill' she called that look. Sarah had a name for every outfit. 'Roll over and die', 'Drop-dead gorgeous', 'Femme Fatale'. It's only now that Marcy realizes that all these outfits are somehow linked to killing, or death, and she wonders how that factoid had escaped her for so many years, especially considering the fact that she was the one who found Sarah in her dorm bathroom, wrists slit and all.

And now she was walking on what used to be the biggest

mosque in Baghdad, covered in the blood of 87 martyrs, recording the scene of the crime for millions of people to stare at (for about 3.4 seconds – at least according to Time Magazine Photo Editor's Field Manual). Walking as though she is the devil's personal photographer – taking stock of his work in this godforsaken city, bringing back the pictures to show him how good was the day's catch (and where he needs to improve for future incidents). And it was only after three more rolls that she noticed that all those men who were looking at the sky, or holding their heads with their hands, or supporting one another, all those men were kneeling on the ground, facing her, bowing to the devil's photographer.

#60

///START SOUNDTRACK///

///ZOOM IN ON DEAN///

'I got a song in my head, though I just got out of bed. I got a song and I'm feeling strong!'

///FADE SOUNDTRACK///

'Millions of Americans are waking up with a song this morning, just like they have been in the past three weeks. Welcome to Sing-Sing, the greatest craze to spread across the continental US since Pet Rocks and Hoola Hoops. It starts something like this: one day you receive a letter in the mail. The letter usually comes from someone you know - a friend, a colleague or perhaps a family member. It comes in an orange envelope with a large Smiley etched on the back. Unsuspecting, you open the envelope and start reading:

///CLOSE-UP ON DEAN HOLDING A LETTER. WE CAN JUST ABOUT SEE THE WORDS///

'Dear Marcus, I know it's been a while since I wrote you, but I wanted you to help me with something. No, I don't need any money, and no, you don't need to come and visit me. All you have to do is to write a short song, right now. Tomorrow morning, I want you to call seven people and sing them the song you wrote. It could be a friend, a colleague or perhaps a family member. Do this for seven days and you will feel the difference.'

///CUT TO A HUGE BUILDING. THE CAMERA SCANS THE ENTRANCE SIGN WHICH READS 'US POST OFFICE DISTRIBUTION CENTER - URBANA ILLINOIS'. THE PARKING LOT IS JAM-PACKED./// ///CUT TO DEAN, MEDIUM SHOT///

'I'm here at the US Post Office Distribution Center in

Urbana, Illinois. As you can see, there's a lot of post running through this sorting center, the biggest in the US.'

///CUT TO THE SORTING MACHINES, ENVELOPES ARE BLAZING THROUGH THEM ON A SERIES OF CONVEYOR BELTS. EVERY NOW AND THEN WE CAN SEE AN ORANGE ENVELOPE PASS BY///

'...But ever since September, the amount of letters being processed here has doubled'.

///CUT TO HARRY STANTON, REGIONAL OPERATIONS MANAGER///

'We never used to have a full parking lot. I mean, sure, I'd have to walk a few minutes each morning, because by the time I get here all the good spaces up close to the entrance are taken, but the parking lot was never full. Now it's crazy - ever since that little girl made that phone call to her grandmother... now we have to bring in part-time workers to help us with the load.'

///CUT TO A WELL-KEPT SUBURBAN STREET. ALL OF THE HOUSES LOOK THE SAME EXCEPT FOR ONE. WHEN THE CAMERA GETS CLOSER WE SEE THAT IT'S COLOURED ORANGE. BUT THAT'S NOT THE ONLY THING THAT CATCHES OUR ATTENTION. IN FRONT OF THE HOUSE, AND ALL THE WAY DOWN THE STREET FOR AS FAR AS THE EYE CAN SEE, ARE PEOPLE STANDING IN LINE, ALL MUMBLING SOMETHING TO THEMSELVES.///

///MEDIUM SHOT - DEAN APPROACHES ONE OF THE PEOPLE IN THE LINE, A MIDDLE-AGED WOMAN WITH STRAIGHT BLACK HAIR AND A SMILEY PIN ON HER LAPEL.///

'Hello Ma'am, could I ask you, how long have you been waiting here?'

'Well, I came here first thing in the morning, so it must be, what, seven hours now.'

'And why come all this way to stand in line?'

'Why, of course, to sing to Heather!' And as the camera zooms in on the woman's face she begins to sing: 'All the trouble I have seen, all the places I have been, mean nothing to me, mean nothing to me. All the sorrows I will sow, all the places I will go, mean nothing to me, mean nothing to me. 'Cause I've got God, I've got God on my side. Yeah I've got God and there's nothing to hide.'

///DEAN TURNS TO ANOTHER PERSON STANDING IN LINE. THIS TIME IT'S AN OVERWEIGHT MAN WEARING A FADED IOWA UNIVERSITY T-SHIRT AND A TRUCKER HAT. THE MOMENT THE CAMERA ZOOMS IN ON HIM HE STARTS SINGING:///

'Been on the road for so many years. Driving at night through a river of tears. Home is where I park my 18-wheeler. One day she'll be back, I can almost feel 'er.'

'Yes folks, there's no mistaking here. This is a national phenomenon. It all started when a little girl called Heather Malone called her grandmother one morning and sang her a song. She did so for the next seven days, calling her each morning with the same song. Her grandmother, Harriet Mills, was so moved, that she in turn wrote a song and called her sister, Connie, for seven days in a row. Connie was so overwhelmed that she too wrote a song. But unlike Heather and Harriet, Connie decided to call seven people every day. And that was how Sing-Sing was created.'

///THE CAMERA IS NOW FOLLOWING DEAN INTO THE HOUSE. WE ENTER THE LIVING ROOM WHERE WE SEE A TRAY OF MILK AND COOKIES ON THE COFFEE TABLE. ON THE SOFA, LYING IN WHAT SEEMS LIKE A MAKESHIFT BED IS HEATHER MALONE. BESIDE HER IS HER MOTHER, AND STANDING IN FRONT OF THEM IS A WOMAN IN A BLACK LEATHER OUTFIT. UNSURE WHETHER SHE SHOULD START SINGING OR NOT SHE LOOKS AT HEATHER'S MOTHER. HER MOTHER NODS BACK WITH A FAINT, WEARY SMILE, AND THE WOMAN STARTS SINGING:///

'Baby it hurts too much, the cut's so deep. I can see you now, only in my sleep.'

///ZOOM IN ON THE WOMAN IN THE LEATHER OUTFIT. SHE IS UNCERTAIN WHETHER TO KEEP ON SINGING. THE CAMERA SHIFTS FROM HER MUMBLING THE REST OF THE SONG TO THE SOFA, WHERE WE CAN SEE, NOW

THAT WE ARE CLOSER TO HEATHER, THAT SHE IS FAST
ASLEEP.///

'Why do you always do this to me? Why do you always make
me feel so...so... Fuck! I hate you!'

The door slams before I even get a chance to get off the
bed. She just went down on me and mid-way I asked her if
she felt like watching the game. It wasn't that she wasn't
doing it right or anything. It's just that I completely forgot
about tonight's game. It's the end of the season. This game's
important.

Needless to say she didn't want to see the game. Didn't
even want to finish what she started after I tried to convince
her that, really, I was only joking.

At first she just looked up at me from down there. I get
turned on when she looks at me while she's doing it. But
this look, this look was more spite than sultry. More pain
than passion.

She was silent for the first few seconds. Still holding me

in her hand. Then letting me drop like some tree that's just been chopped down.

She pulled on her shirt, sat on the edge of the bed and zipped her boots. Then I saw the first of many tears rolling down her face. She was too hurt to even wipe them off.

I looked at the bedside table. Sun Tzu's 'Art of War' had been there for the past six weeks and all my attempts to get past the first ten pages had failed. The clock read five minutes to kickoff. Fuck! Why couldn't I wait another five minutes. She'd be done and we could watch the game together.

I get off the bed and put my shorts on. Calvin Klein had an ad in the 90s with Marky Mark wearing a pair of shorts just like the ones I have on right now. Around him circled a slim model. No words, no music. I bought my first pair of CK's after watching that ad.

I walk to the living room and turn on the TV, killing the sound. I'm watching the pre-game preparations. Watching, but not watching. Another game, another season, another girl.

The referee flips a coin and my team loses. The other team gets to choose which direction they play first. In the top right-hand corner of the screen an hourglass appears, seconds trickling down next to it. The game has just begun and already I want it to be over. Don't care who wins. Don't care who gets injured, don't care who makes it to the nationals this year. I just want it all to be over.

There's a knock on the door. She's back. Earlier than I expected. Part of me is angry at her. Angry that she won't let me slide, let me fill with self-hatred. I get up slowly and stand near the door. I want to hear her breath on the other side. I want her to knock again before I open. She knocks again and I open the door, not knowing what will happen once it's open.

It's Mrs Schwartz from upstairs. She is dressed elegantly, as always. She is saying something to me, something that has a sense of urgency to it. I can see little beads of sweat forming on her brows. Something is wrong. I can't hear a word she says, but something is wrong. I tell her to wait. Tell her that I'm just going to put some pants on. She asks me to hurry and I don't. I'm back at the door and she's not there. I go upstairs and walk through her open door. Inside I hear her sobbing softly. I call her name out but there is no answer.

'Yurek! Yurek! Please, please don't do this to me!'

I walk towards her voice and enter her bedroom. She is sitting on the bed, and as I enter she turns her head and looks at me with a look that is a combination of fear and despair. On the bed, Yurek Klein, her husband of 45 years is lying motionless. His eyes are open, staring at some random point in the ceiling. The room smells of sweat and urine. I walk towards her and say the first thing I can think of: 'Is he OK?'

Yurek Schwartz is not OK.

I walk away from the bedroom and find their kitchen. We've been neighbours for three years, yet I've never been to their house. Why is that?

I find a glass, delicate and far too small for my own taste. I know it's not from here. I know they've had this glass for many years. Brought it over from the old country. The old country. There's a water filter standing near the sink, but I fill the glass with tap water instead. I head back to the bedroom when a set of photographs hanging on the wall captures my eyes. A young couple, dressed in their finest clothes, is sitting close to each other. Their expression is hard to read until I see that they are holding hands. Another photograph shows the same couple looking into each others' eyes, smiling.

The sobbing turns into crying and I suddenly remember where I am. I walk back to the bedroom and look at Mrs Schwartz, her head lying on her dead husband's chest. His eyes are still open, as if waiting to hear her report back whether his heart is still beating.

I take a few steps forward, not knowing what to do. I should call an ambulance, but for some reason I don't. If she asks me to, I will. But she doesn't.

The delicate glass is still in my hand. I raise it so that it's between me and the bed. I look through the water and see a warped image of Mr and Mrs Schwartz. I draw the glass closer and sip the water. For some reason I let out a long 'ahhhh', as if I were walking in the desert for the past three days and just had my first drink. Mrs Schwartz looks at me befuddled. I am not sure what to do, so I finish the water.

Mrs Schwartz raises her head from her husband's chest and with her hand adjusts a silver strand of his hair. I turn and leave the room. I head to the door, passing the photographs without looking at them again. I notice the glass in my hand and change direction to the kitchen. There, I put the glass on a small Formica table and pull out one of the two wooden chairs. I lean my forehead on one of my hands, using my elbow to support it. I look at the glass from above. There's a little water left, a little reminder that until not long ago this glass was full. I stare into the glass and see a tiny ripple suddenly moving. Then another one. And another. And another.

'What are you, stupid?! Give me that!'

'What? Who's ever gonna look in my pockets?'

'Are you an idiot or are you trying to get both of us arrested?!'

'Dude, calm down. You're not gonna get arrested.'

'You bet your ass I'm not.'

And then he shoved the small bag down his shorts.

Benny was always like that. Always knew how to get into clubs without waiting in line, how to take in ecstasy pills without being caught, how to end up in the toilet stalls with some Russian chick giving him a blowjob. Yeah, Benny always knew.

'Eli! Eli! Where the fuck you at, man?!'

Benny was giving me his death stare. He had somehow negotiated with the bouncers to let us in, without realising that I had gone to get some smokes. When I came back he was ready to strangle me. 'G, what's wrong with you? Why you want me to look like a dick in front of these guys?!'

But Benny didn't wait for an answer. In seconds he was downstairs and I followed like a soldier, taking one look at the never-ending line behind me. We were in, as always. We were lit, as always.

Even before I opened the basement doors it was clear that tonight was drum & base. I could feel every bone in my body reverberate as the deep beats attacked every solid object on the dance floor. It was like being in Africa or something - everyone getting ready for some tribal dance, everyone putting their masks on. I'm telling you, it was...

'OK Shakespeare, I think we get the picture. Just tell us what happened next.'

Like I said, Benny disappeared pretty much from the start. I walked around for a few minutes and when I couldn't find him at the bar I went to look for him in the toilets - first the men's, then the women's. I thought, you know, maybe he got lucky early on or something. But he wasn't there.

'But in your statement you said that you saw him one more time before the end of the evening.'

Yeah, well, I kinda did and I kinda didn't.

'Listen, you little fart, you're in such deep shit, you're gonna need an oxygen mask to keep breathing. If you want your momma to recognise her little boy's face, you better stop fuckin' with us!'

I'm not fuckin' with you, man. About an hour after we came to the club I was dancing like crazy. I was so loaded I completely forgot about Benny. I was dancing with this cool chick. Man, could she move. We started kissing. We were all sweaty and stuff and she started licking the sweat off my neck. So at first, I didn't really notice the tapping on my shoulder. But then someone punched me in the back and I turned around, not really pissed off, just kind of surprised. I turned around and saw Benny standing behind me.

'Did you notice anything peculiar about him?'

Yeah, that's what I'm trying to tell you. It was Benny's face, but his body was like half his usual size. Benny's a big guy, you know, but this person standing in front of me was like, tiny. He was also wearing different clothes. Benny came into the club with an Atari t-shirt. This guy was wearing a black t-shirt with nothing on it.

'Did he say anything to you?'

If he did I wouldn't have heard anything man, that place was louder than an airplane's engine.

'So then what happened?'

Then the girl I was with stretches her arm out and grabs my head, turns it back towards hers and starts kissing me again. I turn my head back to look at Benny, but he's gone.

'So what did you do?'

I freaked out man. What would you do?

'So why didn't you call the police, or security?'

Are you out of your mind? I'm in a club, I've just taken my second ecstasy pill, and you expect me to call the police telling them I just saw my best friend, except he was wearing someone else's body? I might have been tripping man, but I wasn't stupid.

'Eli! Eli! Man, what's wrong with you? You want me to look like a dick in front of these guys?! Come on, they're letting us in.'

I'm following Benny past the bouncers. I look behind me and almost stumble. Didn't I pass the same line, the same bouncers only a couple of hours ago? And where are the police detectives that were questioning me?

Benny is already at the bottom of the stairs, opening the club doors, spilling out the deep base beats. I follow him, calling his name, asking him to wait for me, shouting that I don't want to get arrested. He waits until I reach the bottom of the stairs and holds the door open for me. He grins and wraps his arm around my shoulder, squeezing hard.

'Dude, calm down. You're not gonna get arrested.'

#63

'Frank Sinatra?! The singer?!'

'No, honey, the cab driver.'

'Come on, you're joking! There's no way you met Frank Sinatra!'

'I sure did.'

'Then how come this is the first time you're telling me about it?'

'Dunno. You never asked.'

'Never asked?! Never asked?! You know how much I love his music... My God, I can't believe this. Look, look at my arm, I've got goosebumps all over!'

'Look, it's not like we were close friends or anything. It was just a business partnership.'

'A business partnership?! My husband and Frank Sinatra were business partners?! Richard?!'

'Martha?'

'Look at me for a second. Are you kidding me? Are you pulling my leg? Because if you are, I'm never going to speak with you again.'

'I ain't kiddin'.'

'What... what kind of business were you in with Frank Sinatra?'

'Music.'

'OK. Ahhhh, can you be a bit more specific?'

'Song writing.'

'Richard Drake. If you think I find this game amusing, then I've got news for you. I happen to appreciate Frank Sinatra a great deal and I don't appreciate you making fun of him, nor me, for that matter.'

'I thought I was done playing this game
Playing this game of love
But every time she whispers my name
The sun just shines from above.'

'OH MY GOD! You... you did not. No... that's not possible!'

'I thought I had set down the rule
Never to give away my heart

But just as I try to play it cool
I'm still a fool, fool for your love.'

'Honey? Honey, don't cry. I didn't know this was so important to you.'

'You... how could you not know? I have all his records. All of his books. For crying out loud, Richard, I even have Frank Sinatra slippers. What other clue were you looking for?'

'I'm sorry. I just never thought this would be such a big deal. I only wrote a few of his songs.'

'A few?! You mean you wrote more than one?'

'Emmmm, yeah.'

'How... how many songs did you write?'

'473.'

'What?'

'473. I wrote 473 songs.'

'I think I'm going to faint. I can't believe this is happening. Richard, you're an accountant for crying out loud. Since when did you become a songwriter? And for Frank Sinatra of all people... I... I'm not sure what to do about this right now...'

'Well, considering the fact that they've already been written, I'm not really sure there's much you can do.'

'That's not what's bothering me.'

'It's not?'

'No, Richard. What's really bothering me is that your wife of 42 years apparently doesn't know the man she's living with.'

'It's still me, Martha. What difference does it make if I wrote a few songs?'

'A few songs?! A few songs?! You write 500 songs, you write songs for Frank Sinatra, you write "Castle Rock" and you ask what difference it makes?'

'Don't forget "Quando Quando Quando".'

'What?!'

'"Quando Quando Quando"'

'You did not!'

'I did.'

'You did not write "Quando Quando Quando"!'

'There's a moon over Rome,
 Twice as big as back home.
 Is the reason for this
 Your intoxicating kiss?'

'Richard, when were you in Rome?'

'1960.'

'1960? That's the year we met. You never told me anything about Rome.'

'I thought it was better that way.'

'Who is she?'

'Who?'

'Richard, stop playing dumb. Who's the girl from the song?'

'No one.'

'Richard Drake. If you don't start telling me the truth, I swear to God I am packing my things and moving to my sister's.'

'Martha, I don't think it's healthy to dwell in the past.

Why can't you let bygones be bygones?'

'I can't let "bygones be bygones" Richard, because I'm starting to feel as if I've been living in a lie for all these years. First you tell me that you and Frank Sinatra were business partners, then you tell me you wrote hundreds of songs, including "Quando Quando Quando". What's next Richard? Are you going to tell me that you and Sinatra had an affair?'

'Richard?'

'Richard?!'

'By the time you read this, I will be on my way back to Nigeria where I will be executed. My flight leaves in a few minutes. If you are reading this message, maybe you can still save my life.'

'Andrew! You there?!'

'Yeah... I'm, I'm here. Just a minute, Mom.'

'There are two secret service agents waiting for me outside the toilets. They are taking me back to Nigeria, where I am a high-powered official. I came to this country to seek asylum, but the Nigerian government knows I know too many secrets. Now they've found me and want to take me back.'

'Andrew, hurry up in there. Your father is waiting for us at the gate.'

'OK Mom, I'm coming.'

'My friend, if you are the kind of person I think you are, all I ask is that you call this number below and ask to speak to Minnie. Minnie is my wife. Please tell her that you have a message from Lawrence. Tell her that Lawrence says that he loves her more than the moon loves the earth. Tell her that Lawrence always did what he thought was right for his country. Tell her Lawrence will meet her over the mountains. Thank you my kind friend. Yours, Lawrence B. Madalu.'

'Andrew - don't you know we've got a plane to catch? What's wrong, honey? Are you feeling OK?'

'No, Mom, I'm... I'm OK.'

'Andrew smells like pooh! Andrew smells like pooh! Andrew smells like pooh, yeah, you know who!'

'Katherine! Stop making fun of your brother. Andrew,

take your backpack and let's go. Daddy's probably worried by now.'

'Dad?'

'Yes, son?'

'What's Nigeria?'

'It's a country in Africa. Why?'

'Dad?'

'Yes, Andrew.'

'Can I make a phone call?'

'A phone call? We're boarding the plane in five minutes.'

'Ummmm, I know, I just want to call aunt Betsy and say goodbye.'

'Aunt Betsy? But you said goodbye to her last night, don't you remember?'

'Emmm, yeah, but I forgot to tell her some stuff. Can I call her, Dad? Please?'

'Well, ahh, sure son. Here's some change. There's a phone booth just over there. Just be quick.'

'Seven, One, Eight, Three, Three, Six, Seven, Eight, One, One.'

'Hallo? Hallo? Who's that?'

'Andrew.'

'Andrew? Andrew who?'

'Andrew Brody.'

'What you want, Andrew Brody?'

'Can I speak to Minnie?'

'You speaking to her. Now be on your way, boy. What business you want with me?'

'I have a message from Lawrence. He says he'll meet you over the mountains.'

'Who is this?! Is this some joke you pulling on me?!'

'No, ma'am. Lawrence wanted to tell you he loves you more than the moon.'

'Boy, if you playing tricks on me I be spanking the living daylight out of you! How you know me husband's name?!'

'From the airport. I saw it in the bathroom. He said he

always did what was right for the country.'

There's a long silence on the other end of the line. Then sobbing. From the corner of his eye, he can see his father signalling him to put down the phone. When he doesn't, his father gets up and starts making his way towards him.

'I... I have to go now, Mrs. Minnie. He loves you very much.'

I've been teaching this class on existential philosophy for eight years now and some things never change. Somewhere after the second or third lesson, one of the students, usually a woman, would ask me how Sartre could have had so many abusive affairs with women (and men), yet at the same time carry the motto 'hell is *other* people'. It's a good question, and one that deserves to be answered. The only problem, the only thing that causes me to cringe time after time after time when someone asks me this, is that I am the worst person to answer it.

'He wasn't physical at first. Let me rephrase that. Ed always had physical presence. He's a strong man, well-built, you've seen him. He carries himself like a God. When he enters the room, one thing is clear - Ed McGovern has arrived. More than anything else, this presence, this vitality, was what made me fall in love with him in the first place.

'"Fall in love." It's funny how often we forget what our most common phrases actually mean. No one wants to fall. Falling hurts. Yet we do it again and again, craving, in fact, for it to happen.

'Ed was the chair of the engineering department at the time and I was a young philosophy professor. There were several cases of sexual assault on campus that year and the press were having a field day. The university President set up a student-teacher committee to find ways to "eradicate the problem". I was cynical about his real intentions and felt he cared more about managing the media than protecting the women in his university. But when you're on track to become a tenured professor, the last thing you want to do is cause trouble. So I joined the committee.

'Five minutes into our first meeting I knew that Ed would be my husband. It's hard to explain the appeal behind a charismatic person. There is something threatening about the confidence and certainty they have about themselves, and Ed had more than his share of these. The meeting was over in less than 20 minutes, and when we adjourned, Ed got up from his chair and said to everyone: "Folks, we made great progress here today. I knew you wouldn't let me down."

The funny thing was that no one had said a single word throughout the meeting. The eight of us just sat there, eating out of his hand, hanging on to every word he said. And to make matters worse, when he was done, we actually felt proud of ourselves. Actually felt that we did the right thing.

'So, nine months later I did the "right thing" and got married to Ed. The first few months were heaven. I started teaching a new course and Ed had his hands full with his department. Then one night I came back late - some students had invited me for coffee and Kafka - and Ed was sitting in the kitchen, fuming.

'I knew something was wrong from the minute I stepped in. Even before I saw him I could sense the tension in the air. I think I said this before, but there's something about his presence that just fills up the entire house. I walked in, gave him a kiss on his head and went to the fridge to start preparing dinner. I must have rambled on for a few minutes before I noticed he wasn't really paying attention to what I was saying. I took one look at him and my blood froze. There was something so intense about his face that I thought I was going to die right there on the spot. Immediately I knew I had done something wrong. But what?'

'"Ed? Honey? Are you OK?" I asked him, edging closer to him, kneeling next to him and putting my hand on his leg. I don't really remember what happened next. The paramedics said I had a minor concussion. I'm sure it seemed serious, otherwise Ed himself wouldn't have called them in the first place. I don't know why I didn't call the police or something like that. I think the fact that he called an ambulance, even though it was him that hit me, made me feel like he cared.

'Things got gradually worse after that. He broke my jaw twice, and I can't remember the amount of times I landed in the emergency room with a fractured wrist or ankle. His assaults were always very brief, very to the point.

'I came to know when to expect his "sessions" and simply lost myself in thought when they happened. I thought about Jean Paul Sartre, the French philosopher, who talked about how we needed others to mirror ourselves. How we needed other people to justify our own existence. You see, when Ed hit me, more than anything else in the world, I felt alive.'

She's looking around the room now. Twelve students are staring at her, some in awe, some in disgust, some in pure shock. 'Does anyone have any other questions?'

'It's not for us to decide. You're the princess and I'm the prince, and I'm coming to save you from the evil witch. So you have to lie down and play dead and I have to come and kiss you.'

'Yeah, but how come you always get to play the prince and I have to be the princess? It's not fair!'

'It IS fair. You're playing the girl and I'm playing the boy. The rules say that the evil witch always casts her spell on the girl, so you have to be the one sleeping and I have to be the one saving you from her. That's how everyone plays the game. We can't change the rules, it's not for us to decide.'

'OK. But I want to have a talking part as well, I want to say something after you save me.'

'OK. You can say, "Oh, prince charming. You are my hero, you saved my life! I will love you forever."'

Alex wasn't happy, that much I remember. But I would always have it my way, would always get to play the prince, fight the evil witch, save the princess. Our games turned into daily routines: come back from school, fight the witch, save the princess, go home. Some games I could never get tired of.

One day after school I came to Alex's house and it was clear that something was wrong. The front door was unlocked so I let myself in. There was broken furniture all over the place and lots of screaming. Part of me was scared but the other part of me was so used to playing the prince that it was easy to make believe it was all a game. I found Alex shaking, hiding under the kitchen table. So we hid there, waiting quietly. I asked Alex what had happened, but the only response I could get was more and more tears. Quiet tears, the kind you cry when you know that crying out loud could put you in harm's way. So we did the only thing a six-year-old can do when his life is thrown up in the air like a deck of cards. We played our game.

Except this time I couldn't run upstairs as though I'm climbing the tower. Somebody was up there and as evil as I imagined the witch to be, whoever was up there seemed more evil. I really wanted to fight this evil witch, but it seemed like a bad idea. To start off with, there were two people fighting upstairs, and the state they were in, it didn't sound like Alex's parents would appreciate my chivalry. All this seemed to be fine with Alex who was lying on the floor beside me, eyes shut, and with a face so beautiful I just knew I would never meet anyone with a face like that.

And I was right. Two weeks later Alex's parents finally decided to pack their bags and head in different directions. Alex's Dad went back to San Francisco, and Alex's Mom decided that it was best for both of them if they moved back to Canada. Alex and I wrote to each other every day. Sometimes we would ask our parents to help us with difficult words, but mostly we just drew pictures - I'd draw a prince, Alex would draw a princess and we would send our drawings back and forth, each time one of us completing what the other had begun. Then school began and the daily letter-writing slowed. First to weekly, then to monthly, then to none at all.

That was twenty years ago.

I ended up going to school in upstate New York and then won a scholarship to go to Columbia University. I had no idea where Alex was, though someone said something about a Toronto ballet company.

It was the last day before summer break and the campus in Columbia was buzzing. I had just finished making plans with friends to go out to the Hamptons for the weekend when I heard someone calling my name. It was Ned. Ned and I weren't close friends in high school, but both of us were happy to discover that the other made it into Columbia.

Ned looked pale. 'What's up, G?!' I asked him.

'Yeah, ahhh, have you heard about Alex?'

'Alex? What about Alex?'

'He's dead man. He died this weekend.'

Dead.

My princess was dead.

'They say it's AIDS but I don't know, man.'

'Some things are not for us to decide.'

'What's that, man?' Ned asked. But I just closed my eyes and blew one, long, final kiss.

'So tell me when you're gonna let me in!'

'NO!'

'Whaddya mean "No"?! Tatiana, you can't stay in the bathroom forever...'

'YES I CAN!'

For reasons that are beyond me, she has no Russian accent whatsoever when she shouts.

'Tatiana, what do I have to do to make you come out?'

'NOTHING!'

She's been in the bathroom for over an hour now. Under normal circumstances I would let this storm ride and wait for her to come out. But I really need to go to the bathroom, though if she finds out, she's bound to stay even longer.

'Tatiana, is this about last night?'

She doesn't answer, but I can hear her sniffing from behind the door. Last night we went out for dinner at this new fusion place. We were at the dessert stage when an obnoxious bunch of investment bankers landed next to our table. There must have been six of them, most in their early thirties.

'Bring us a case of your finest Champagne!' one of the bankers yelled towards the waitress.

'And don't forget to get undressed on the way back!' said another, causing all his friends to burst into laughter.

Tatiana and I returned to our dessert when one of the bankers, an Abercrombie & Fitch mutant who's name could only be Chad, leans towards me and says: 'Pardon me for being so brash, but do you realize that your girlfriend is the most beautiful woman in the world?'

'Thanks,' I answered and turned back to my ginger tiramisu.

'Thanks? I don't recall giving YOU the compliment! I

gave it to her,' he says, brushing his hand on Tatiana's bare shoulder.

Tatiana turns her head, somewhat annoyed.

'Great. Both of us are really happy,' I say, making a slight move towards his hand, which is enough to make him draw it back quickly.

The waitress, still dressed, brings the bankers their Champagne. Corks pop, glasses clink and bad jokes are told. Tatiana and I drink our espressos, eat our fused desserts and get up to leave. As Tatiana stands up, the bankers next to us become silent.

Now, I must admit: Tatiana IS a very beautiful woman. But I never understood how any man could gawk at a woman and expect to get her... attention?

'How do you do it, man?' the Chad-unit asks out loud.

'Very easily...' I answer, put Tatiana's coat around her silky shoulders, and leave the restaurant.

And now I'm dying to go to the bathroom, only I can't because Tatiana has been holed in there for over an hour. As I consider using the sink, I hear Tatiana snivelling louder than needed.

'Baby, listen, if it's about last night, then whatever it is,

I'm sorry. I didn't mean it. But you should really come out now...'

'NO!'

'But, baby, I said I'm sorry...'

'YOU'RE NOT SORRY!' she answers.

This is the tricky part. On the one hand, if I argue that I am indeed sorry, she'll ask me to explain in detail what I'm apologizing for. But since I don't actually know, doing so could actually get me into more trouble. On the other hand, if I don't insist that I'm sorry, she'll stay in the bathroom till my bladder bursts.

'Baby? Tatiana?'

'What?'

'I love you...'

She doesn't answer. That is a good sign.

'Baby, come out. I need to tell you something really important.'

'What is it?' she asks softly.

'I need to see your eyes to tell you this,' I say. My legs are crisscrossed now. One wrong move and things could get messy.

I hear her walking towards the door.

'Do you really love me?' she asks from the other side.

'Baby - open the door and I'll show you just how much I love you.'

She opens the door. I've been dreaming about this moment for over an hour.

I push the door and her to the side. Now, inside the bathroom, I dash towards to the toilet, pull my pants down and relieve myself.

Tatiana is contemplating what to do, clearly in a state of shock.

I look at her, trying not to lose grip of the matters that are at hand. She looks back, then looks in the mirror. She opens the cabinet drawer, takes out a little brown bag and starts putting some lipstick on.

#68

At this height breathing becomes more and more difficult. The normal senses of weight, distance and time get bent. What seemed like an hour, took only a few minutes. What seemed like the weight of an elephant, was simply your normal backpack. What looked like a ten mile hike was actually a short walk.

I am not sure why people come here. Depending on how you look at it, it's either the end of the world, or its beginning. I assume some of them lost something along the way and thought they'd find it here. Others must have come here for the opposite reason - seeking to shed some old skin and return to wherever they came from reborn.

I came here for her, I admit. There was no question of not joining her. Yes, on the face of it, the idea did sound crazy: three weeks in the South Pole, tracking the last leg of Robert Scott's fatal journey from 1912.

I have no idea where she got this sense of adventure from. Her mother's idea of an adventure is going to a new spa. As for me, I can't even say I like adventures. Never had much yearning for the unexpected. Life deals us surprising cards without our intervention, so why shuffle the deck?

But I could never say no to Jeanie. When she wanted to buy a motorcycle at age 17, I put my foot down and said 'no'. Two weeks later I was at the Yamaha dealership buying her an XS 400. Somehow she convinced me that a big bike will make other drivers notice her better. That's for sure. Then there was the question of hiking to the Everest Base Camp. Why, I asked her, after learning a bit about the immense physical requirements needed to ascend the 'mother of all mountains', could she not simply fly there? She responded with a look that needed no elaboration and left me with a strong feeling of old age and irrelevance.

But now I'm here. This is our second week, and I must admit that until three days ago it was the most difficult, scary, beautiful and magnificent thing I had ever done. Being here with my daughter only made the experience all that more emotional. I love her very much. I think back at all the challenges I had when I was younger. God, life seems so complex before you have children. But when Jeanie came to the world, everything became clear. I wasn't Norman Foster. I was Jeanie's Dad.

And now Jeanie's Dad is dying. I'm not sure which came first, the frost bite or the altitude sickness. The doctor, before he froze to death two nights ago, confided in me that any of the two could kill me if the evacuation team doesn't arrive within 24 hours. They haven't, and I have mixed feelings about being given this extension to my life.

I buried Jeanie three days ago. She was the first one I

found, covered in three feet of snow. The wind was so strong, that when I woke up everything was white. There were no tents to be found, no backpacks. No dogs. Nothing. By sheer chance, the tarp that covered my tent remained intact, creating a kind of an air mattress between the tent and the elements. I remember opening the tent's zipper, only to find a wall of dense snow in front of me. If you told me it could snow that much during such a short period, I would call you a lunatic. Now it is me who is losing his mind.

The doctor helped me bury Jeanie and Thomas, our guide. It took us close to an hour to find them in the first place, then another five to carve out a pair of shallow graves. The doctor had signalled our HQ to rescue us, but judging from the condition of the radio, we were fooling ourselves to think anyone would have gotten our signal. If not for Emma back home, I'm not sure I would have wanted to return. How could I? What would I tell her? That I couldn't protect our little baby? That I managed to do it for 22 years, but have now failed?

But now that burden has been taken off of my shoulders too. I will die here, most likely before the night falls. I look back at my handwriting and see it fading steadily. In my brain, air bubbles are starting to aggregate. Soon, I will drown in my own fluid. Unless I freeze before that.

I ate one of the dogs today. I had already given up on life, but, in a cynical triumph of body over mind, my own hunger mechanism forced me to seek food. Since all the packaged goods we had were buried under six feet of snow, all I could find was one of the dogs, who somehow managed to be only partially covered with snow. It tasted like frozen chicken.

If you read these lines, you've probably found our camp, or what's left of it. Do not feel bad about not arriving here earlier. There was not much you could have done, save for bringing back home a broken man with advanced gangrene in his two legs. Do not feel bad that you didn't make sure we had prepared better for this expedition. Thomas was the best guide in the world. But when God intervenes, even angels have to stand aside.

I spent the better part of the last 48 hours trying to understand, to comprehend, what had happened. I couldn't. There is simply no way to make sense out of such a horrific experience. My conclusion was that it did not happen for a reason. What reason could justify losing your daughter?

But I do know this. I do know that what you do now counts. Not the big things, like which job you take, where you live, or even who you marry. What counts are the little things. That person on the street you wanted to stop by and talk to. That girl in the shop you wanted to ask out for a coffee. That friend you've grown distant from yet did not dare phoning her to find out why. Those are the things that matter most. Those are the things you should pay attention to.

#69

'You wanna know how I feel, motherfucker? You really wanna know how I feel?! How the fuck do you think I feel?! No, wait a second, YOU tell me how I feel. Look at me and tell me how I feel?!'

'Ummmm, angry?'

'Damn right I'm angry! What else?! Look closer, what else am I feeling?!'

'Emmmm, depressed?'

'Depressed?! Depressed?! Why, you little asshole! Depressed?! I'm not feeling... Well, of course I'm depressed! How would you feel if someone took all your money and ran away?!'

'Well,' says Malcolm, 'technically he didn't run away with the money.'

'Oh? Well, technically I'm not going to kill you right now! Technically, I didn't lose my life savings on that stupid idea of yours! Technically we're still going to Las Vegas! Sure, Malcolm, technically, it's all hunky dory.'

So here I was, wearing my Elvis outfit, in a cheap motel room in Nevada. The furniture here is sparse. A twin bed. A chair, a round wooden table with a green ashtray that will never clean again. The carpet is the colour of vomit, which seems to fit the numerous unidentified stains scattered across it. The bed is made, though the cigarette burns on the cover give you the impression that this room was built for drama, not sleeping.

And drama we had this morning. See, Malcolm and I are partners. We're, what you call, in the entertainment business. I'm the best Elvis impersonator this side of the Mississippi, and Malcolm, well, Malcolm is my agent. This morning Malcolm made a phone call in which he learned that the booking agent he used to book me a show at the Grand Palace in Las Vegas is gone. With him were $15,000. My $15,000.

'Look, I think we should just get in the car and drive to the Palace, speak to one of the bosses and...'

'...and become the laughing stock of Las Vegas?! No thank you!'

I step into the bathroom to wash my face. The basin must have been white when it was manufactured, though you wouldn't guess by looking at it. I let the cold water run for a bit and splash it on my face. Drying it with a ragged towel. I look in the mirror, only to find that one of my sideburns has come off, making me look like Elvis after a head-on collision. I can feel the familiar burn creeping up from my stomach to my throat. I take two pills and realize that all this time Malcolm has been talking to me through the door.

'...and eventually you'll thank me.'

'Right now the only person who should be thanking anyone is you, Malcolm,' I say, barging back into the room. 'I trusted you, man, and now I'm fucked. That gig was supposed to change everything. That gig was supposed to make me a star. "A star of the stage", you said so yourself.'

I slouch in the small wooden chair. I'm not a big person, but this chair might as well have been swiped from some kindergarten.

'So what are we gonna do, Malcolm?'

Malcolm is on the phone, calling up the Grand Palace. He is standing next to me, talking into the receiver, but I hardly hear a word. I'm tired and sad. So many months, so many rehearsals. So many renditions of Heartbreak Hotel. And all for nothing.

'Great! So we'll see you tonight! Mr Cohen, thank you so much for this opportunity. You won't regret it!'

Malcolm put the receiver down and looked at me as if I'm supposed to share his glee. 'See! I told you I'll take care of things. You, my friend, will be on stage tonight! Grand Palace - here we come!'

'You're kidding me, right? I'm going on stage tonight? What happened? Did they find the agent?'

'Don't worry about the agent. We're all good!'

'Whadya mean, don't worry about the agent? You said they were never gonna let me on stage as Elvis unless we book it through an agent.'

Malcolm isn't responding, which isn't a good sign.

'Malcolm? Malcolm, look at me. I'm not going on stage as Elvis, am I?!' He nodded and looked away from me.

'OK, then what am I going up on stage as?!'

'Well, ehhh, do you know Peter Pan?'

'Malcolm - I ain't going up as Peter Pan! I ain't dressing up in green tights and wearing a funny hat!'

'No, no, they don't want you as Peter Pan.'

'Oh, well, that's good. I guess I could be a pretty good Sheriff.'

I get up and look at myself in the mirror. I definitely

have that certain tough look.

'Tinker Bell.'

'What did you say?

'Tinker Bell. They want you to play Tinker Bell'.

'But it's a collage, Daddy! It's a collage.'

It doesn't look like a collage any more. The garage door is open, and Mike Korma is standing outside, peering in, hands on waist. Inside, just as it has been for the past six months, is his prize, his treasure, his new Hummer H2. The H2 doesn't look new anymore, now that it's covered in blood and gunk and unidentified animal parts. No, it doesn't look new at all. Mike Korma isn't sure what it does look like. He's still in a state of shock.

Six months ago he made the 200 mile trip to Rick Johnson's up in Wakipa Bay. Johnson's isn't the only dealer stocking this new breed of Hummers. Dick Nelson from Sugar City is a lot closer than Johnson's, but Mike went to high school with Rick Johnson, and more than a favour to an old high-school chum, he knew that Rick would pass the word that Mike Korma has arrived. Mike Korma has made the grade. Mike Korma has an H2.

Or had an H2.

Mike wasn't really sure this was his truck anymore (General Motors, who made the H2s, would never dream of calling them 'trucks', but that was Mike's way of convincing his wife that he actually needed an H2, and in ways she never understood, used it to justify the $50,000 bank loan they took out to buy the beast).

'Daddy,' she said in a soft voice, 'you're not aaangry with mmmme, arrrrre you?'

Angry? No, angry was not the word Mike Korma was looking for to express an emotion so raw, he wasn't sure a definition of it existed in the dictionary. And so instead of trying to answer his six-year-old daughter, he just kept on looking at the truck from a distance, frozen in disbelief, knowing that if he entered the garage his nightmare may well come true.

'Ahhh... honey, could you tell me what happened here?' he asked his daughter. She was standing next to the humongous yellow truck, with something small and furry in her hand. It was only now, now that he had taken two more steps closer to the garage that he could see the fans.

He had two of those installed when he bought the H2. GM recommended storing the truck in a 'cool, well-ventilated space', and resisting his temptation to install an air-conditioner for the garage (and saving himself from an imminent divorce had he done so), Mark Korma decided to install two very large, high-powered, ceiling-attached fans. Except now they didn't look much like fans, but more like some bloody art installation. From each one of the fan wings, hung by a string of some sort, dangled an animal, or what was left of it. On the left fan it was easy to identify Rufus, their miniature poodle, his afro mane somewhat collapsed and drenched in blood. On the other fan he could just about make out their cat, Tabby, or at least Tabby's head. The rest of her was missing. All that was left on the other four fan wings were limbs, dangling in mid air.

'Molly? Wha... what on earth did you do here?'

'I just wanted the animals to have some fun, Daddy, you know, like in the amusement park. So I built them a merry-go-round.'

'You... Built... Them... A.... Merry... Go... Round. OK. And why all the blood, Molly, why all the blood?'

'Well, Rufus told me that he was really hot and suggested that if I turn on the fans all the animals would be a lot happier.' Molly stepped closer to her father, causing him to take one step back.

Rufus didn't look very happy right now, especially given the fact that his head and body had been detached for quite some time.

'But, Molly... They're all dead. All the animals, they're dead. And my truck. My truck is...' And with this she ran and jumped into his arms. Paternal instincts ruled that he had to catch her, though what Mike Korma really wanted to do was run away. Molly wrapped her arms around his neck tightly and whispered in his ear. 'Daddy, I'm a very lucky girl, you know?' Mike Korma couldn't quite register that last statement. Somehow the word 'lucky' didn't quite fit with the scene in front of his eyes. 'Why are you a very lucky girl, Molly?' he asked, with the first signs of exhaustion showing in his voice. 'Because Chester left me a good luck charm!' Chester, one of the two family rabbits, was nowhere to be seen, as was the case with Casey, his better half. 'Here - you can have it!' And with this she took one of her arms off Mike Korma's neck and held, very close to his face, the mangled foot of what used to be a very white rabbit.

I close my eyes and let my head drop. I'm somewhere between really tired and really drunk. Or maybe I'm just cold. I can feel his hand through my jeans stroking my knee. I'm not really sure where this is leading to, but it feels good.

I open my eyes and raise my gaze not to meet his but to meet hers. That blond girl who's been staring at us since we came in. We're not a couple or anything, at least not yet. It's our first date and I'm not really sure where this will lead to. But like I said, I'm tired, and drunk enough not to be too uptight about it. What will be, will be.

But she's looking at us, no doubt about that. I wonder if her boyfriend notices. Surely not. Men can have a woman on the verge of nervous breakdown in front of them and know nothing about it. But her female friend doesn't seem to pick up on the glances she's throwing at us either. But there's no hiding, every now and then she's checking him, or me, or us, out.

And that feels kinda good.

'Let's go,' he says, caressing my hand. I came here in my car, which was simply a testament to how many bad dates I've had recently, and how low my expectations for this night were.

'I think you should drive,' I tell him, handing him the keys. 'I think Miles should drive,' he answers and hands them back to me. I smile, and only then realize that I have no clue what he's talking about. We step outside to the cold night. It's been snowing all night and central a location as we're in, outside there's nothing but silence.

Nothing quite like the sound of a city on hold.

I know this sound. This sound of nothing and everything at the same time. I was seventeen, visiting Paris for the first time. At 10pm my parents were already fast asleep. I was not. I had my own room, 300 Francs and 12 hours before I had to report for breakfast. I got dressed in an outfit I picked up near Les Halles earlier that day. I didn't show it to my mother, and that was a good idea. Fat chance she would have paid for it if she saw it before I handed it over to the cashier. I take the elevator down to the lobby, looking at myself in the mirror. Or is it really me I'm looking at? God, please don't let this elevator get stuck on the way. Please don't make it stop. Not now.

Down at the lobby I approach the concierge and ask for a cab. 'Where to, mademoiselle?' he asks. I realize for the first time that I haven't got the faintest clue where I'm heading, and blurt out the name of the only club I've ever heard of in Paris. 'Le Bain Douche, s'il vous plaît.'

As my cab approaches the club I already know this was a bad idea. It's Friday night and outside there must be at least 100 people standing in line. It's December, it's freezing and I'm wearing the shortest black little number known to man. Or girl. 'Should I wait for you?' my driver asks. Me? Wait for me? I'm thinking in my head. I answer no.

Something inside of me is charged. I'm not sure what, but it doesn't quite fit with the word 'teenager' any more.

I remember seeing a documentary by Desmond Morris once. It was all about body language and the little, almost imperceptible cues we send each other. I remember how little details about how you looked at someone, what poise you held, the stillness of your gaze, had an amazing impact on other people.

I slam the door behind me and walk straight towards the doors. I'm not looking at anyone. Not at the people standing in the VIP line, not a the selector, not at the bouncers. I'm walking in.

I am here, I have arrived.

Inside, still shaken from the fact that I managed to make my way in without being stopped, I take off my jacket and hand it to the girl at the counter. I make a u-turn and head towards the bass beat. I'm not sure why I'm here, nor what I'm to do now that I am, but the deep sounds hit me in the stomach and I am drawn to them like moths to a flame.

Someone taps on my shoulder. I turn around and it's the coat-check girl. I look at her, confused. She holds out a ticket. Yes, of course, I forgot the ticket. I apologise profusely in the little French I know. She smiles and gives me a little kiss. On the lips.

I turn back towards the dance floor, feeling as though I could be wearing nothing and still feel like a million dollars. So this is what it means to feel alive...

I was a shy teenager. Didn't really have a reason to be, but when you grow up in a town that has the population the size of a busy street in New York, you don't get to practice your social skills that much. I order a drink from the bar and find a wall to lean against. I look.

I like to look. People are fascinating animals. Especially women. I like men, always did, but I find them predictable. Once you figure them out, which I did when I was 16, there's not much more you need to know to get them to do what you want them to do. Women, however, are a different story. Women change. Constantly.

There're these two girls on the dance floor. A tall skinny woman with short black hair and almost no breasts. No bra as well. She's dancing with a little blond bomb, short, curvaceous, sexy. Very sexy. It's obvious they like dancing. And each other. Very much. A few minutes of self-criticism pass before I finally realize that the blond is looking at me. Almost looking through me.

I like that.

I'm not sure who's responsible for it, it certainly isn't me, but the next thing I know, I find myself dancing behind the blond girl. Her back is exposed and I can see the thin film of sweat covering it. I want to do something about it, but I'm scared. I look at the tall black-haired woman. I'm not sure she likes the idea that I've joined their duet. Sweet and considerate as I am, right now I don't give a fuck. What I do give a fuck about is the blond girl who's leaning back closer and closer to me. Our eyes never meet but I know that she knows that I want her. And that scares me. And I like it.

Four hours later I leave the club, or at least my body does. A part of me, an old part of me, is left behind. I step outside to the most amazing scene I have ever seen. It's white and cold and silent. The only sound you can hear is the snow falling. I never knew snow could make a sound until that night.

I start walking, oblivious to the fact that it's 4am and I'm walking alone on the streets of Paris. I walk for half an hour before my feet start to hurt way more than I can bear. I signal a cab and go back to the hotel.

'So, where will it be tonight, Sir?' his driver, who I presume is Miles, asks.

He looks at me in a look that hovers between utter calm and complete arrogance. 'China White, Miles. Tonight we're going to China White.'

His hand is resting on my knee. I lean back into the leather seat, and close my eyes.

#72

'It's all about experience. Everything in this life is about experience. You can't just jump out of a plane and be an astronaut. You can't just get on a ship and be a captain. You can't just hold on to a hockey stick and be a hockey player.'

'A space ship.'

'What?'

'A space ship.'

'What about a space ship?'

'You said, "you can't just jump out of a plane and be an astronaut". Astronauts don't jump out of planes. They jump out of spaceships.'

'Yeah, OK, whatever. But do you understand what I'm telling you?'

How could I not understand, or at least appear to be understanding. Here I was, 17 years old, getting lectured by my Dad, the dean of the history department. Professor Alex Thompson. God, that sounded so official. When you grow up in a small town like I did, you use whatever card life deals you. And being able to say that my Dad was a professor was a pretty high card, until now. See, when you're nine or ten, it's really important that your Dad is smart. Because even if you're not so good at sports, or you don't look very cool and you can't do the moonwalk like Michael Jackson does, there's still hope. There's still hope that at least one of your parents is smart, or good at sports, or looks cool (though God help you if they can do the moonwalk). But at 17 it's all about you. And today it was all about me. I'm in bed and there's no way I'm going to school today. It's almost the end of the year. I've sat down long and hard on my does-my-ass-look-too-big-in-these-jeans and did all my tests. Unlike last year, I failed none of them. But tonight we have the school play and there is no way on earth I am getting on stage in that dorky outfit.

OK, let me back-track for a second. I forgot we're not best friends yet and that some of this may be confusing to you. That's a good thing, since maybe that'll make you feel a bit like I do. Confused. Stuff has been happening for the last couple of years that is freakin' me out. I'm not even talking about the usual stuff that girls go through when they're growing up. That was years ago and I'm kind of used to the fact that every once in a while my body acts as if it has a mind of its own (and I act as if I have none). What freaks me out most is my Dad. Since we're on a first name basis here, allow me to be blunt: my Dad is a dork. If you want to know where my looks come from - look at my Dad and put on a pair of tits. OK, take off a few years, but you get the picture, and it ain't pretty. Many Dads are dorks, and in that my Dad would be no different than many others. But about 3 years ago, my Dad had what my Mom calls a 'mid-life crisis'. For the first year, Dad would constantly fight with Mom, with the final scene being something like this: Mom: 'Melvin, what the hell is it exactly that you want?' Dad: 'What I want?! What I want?! What I want is to be alive?!' And with that he would slam the door and go sit in his car for an hour, before crawling back inside. If that wasn't weird enough, the year after my Dad sold his car and bought a Harley. My Mom freaked out. Before this, my Dad didn't even ride a bicycle. I mean, it was Mom who taught me how to ride a bike. But one morning while we were having breakfast without speaking to each other (which was common in the Thompson residence), Dad spurts out something like, 'Life is too short', as if he read it off the back of a cereal box. That evening he showed up in leather pants and a leather jacket which had 'Hell's Angels' written on the back. Needless to say, that Mom and I had a seizure on the spot, but the only thing we manage to convince Dad is to get a regular Harley Davidson jacket. There's one thing worse in life than being a Hell's Angel – pretending to be one.

But wait, it gets worse. You know, looking back, what was then a really bad phase, wasn't that bad after all. Mom and Dad still loved each other, and they sure loved me. So what if Dad installed a basketball hoop on the garage door and started lifting weights? At least he was Dad. But then he had to stick his thing into that bitch, Melanie, who's just five years older than I am. God, how gross can you be? Sleeping around with someone who's almost triple your age? Anyway, I don't blame that bitch Melanie. It's my Dad's fault and Mom and I are making sure he pays for it.

Which is why I have no plans getting out of bed.

'Dad, there is no way I am going to school today and there is no way I am going to be on stage tonight.'

'But honey, if you don't show up, how will they put on the play?'

'I don't care about that stupid play. I mean, who watches Star Trek anymore? Who wants to watch Star Trek on a school play? How stupid can you get?!'

'Listen, honey, that's what I'm saying. It doesn't matter what the play is about. It doesn't matter which character you're playing. The only thing that matters is that it's an experience. The more experiences you have, the better your life will be.'

I looked at his face in disbelief. Could he be any more out of touch with this world?

But something about his determination made me get out of bed. I got up, dressed up, put my Star Trek uniform in my bag, and went downstairs. Today, for the first time in my life, I'm going to be in space.

#73

Some people think I'm stupid. Momma says not to pay attention to what other people say. Sometimes I pay attention. Like the other day, I was walking down our street to visit my Nana and some kids called me a retard.

Every day at five I go to Nana's and watch Speed Racer on TV. Nana doesn't like me watching Speed Racer. She says it promotes recklessness. I'm not sure what recklessness is, but I think it means a bad person.

I asked Momma if I'm a bad person. She said that I don't have an ounce of badness in me. Sometimes at school I want to be bad. I'm in a special class for special people. I like my teacher. Her name is Miss Collins. It's spelled with two Ls. Miss Collins always speaks very slowly when she's talking to us.

One day my friend Danny asked Miss Collins if she was stupid. Miss Collins sent Danny to see the principal. Danny started crying. He didn't mean to hurt Miss Collins. He just wanted to know if she talks real slow because she's special, like us.

I live on Canoe Road. I don't know what a Canoe is, but Momma said it's like a small boat. I think it's a silly name for a street. Or a road.

67 Canoe Road. The Millers. That's us. Gladys and Stevie Miller. That's Momma and me. Momma said I had a Dad once, but he had to go on a special mission to Africa and won't ever come back. My Dad is a famous hunter. He hunts Cheetahs and Tigers and Elephants. My Dad is very brave. Momma doesn't talk much about Dad. One time she said that I've got my Daddy's good looks. I think that means that I can see really well.

I have x-ray vision. I can see things that other people can't. Except I stopped telling people that I have x-ray vision. One time this kid on our block, Bobby Higgins, was making fun of me. So I told him that he had cancer. He said that I was bullshitting. I told him that I had x-ray vision and that I could see his brain. Bobby didn't believe me, but asked me what I saw in his brain anyhow. I told him that he had cancer all over and that he was going to die very soon. Maybe even later today. Bobby started crying and ran home to his Momma. When I came back home Momma told me that I have to stop making things up. She told me that I have to stop scaring kids and telling them they are going to die. I don't know how Momma knew what I told Bobby Higgins. Maybe she has telescopic hearing.

On the first day of school Miss Collins told the class that something tragic happened. I didn't know what that word meant, but Miss Collins had tears in her eyes so I figured it was a bad word. Miss Collins told the class that Bobby

Higgins was dead. A boat hit him on the last day of summer camp. I raised my hand and asked Miss Collins if Bobby was hit by a Canoe. Miss Collins said that what I said was not funny.

Tomorrow Momma and Nana are taking me to Sizzlers. Sizzlers is my most favorite restaurant in the world. The steaks there are the biggest in the world and the French fries are real big, not like the ones in McDonalds. Even Nana likes Sizzlers. Nana is really old and skinny like a scarecrow. I don't think Nana eats anymore. Except when we go to Sizzlers. Nana really likes the barbecue wings. She says they are to die for. One time after she said that I started crying. I didn't want Nana to eat any more barbecue wings, because I thought she was going to die. Nana said it was just an expression. I don't know what an expression is.

The real reason I like going to Sizzlers is secret. It's a secret reason, so you have to promise me that you won't tell. Promise?

I have a special friend in Sizzlers. Her name is Marsha and she's a grownup. Marsha is a very nice woman. She is a very important person. She has four Sizzlers stars on her shirt and a nametag that says, 'Hi, My Name is Marsha!' on it. That's how I know her name. Marsha is very nice to me. Every time we come to Sizzlers she has a different present to give me. One time I got an airplane. Marsha said it was a replica of the Concorde. I don't know what the word replica means, but I think it's a good word. Another time Marsha gave me a little backgammon board. Momma and I used to play backgammon a lot until we lost one of the dice. I think Momma hid it because she was tired of losing all the time.

Some people think I'm stupid, but maybe it's them that's stupid. People wouldn't call me stupid if they knew that I am an official MVC. That stands for Most Valuable Customer and it's the highest rank you can get at Sizzlers. Marsha said I am the only MVC in town. Maybe next time I'll see Marsha I'll tell her about my x-ray vision.

#74

I knew it was bad the moment I woke up. My eyes opened, then instinctively shut as the shower of broken glass flew in my face.

We spun for three, maybe four times, then came to a standstill. I looked over to Marty, who seemed more in shock than physically hurt. I knew he fell asleep at the wheel. Don't ask me how. I just knew.

Both of us looked at the back seat. Harris was lying on the floor with his hands over his head, like people do when they fear a bomb is about to drop.

I asked Marty what had happened, but he couldn't explain, could hardly talk, really. His gaze was fixed at some distant point in the horizon. Slowly, he raised his arm in the air and pointed. I looked out of his window and could see smoke rising from the field. Marty and I looked at each other. Terror spread on his face.

'My Dad's gonna kill me when he hears about this,' Marty said.

'Your dad may be the least of our worries Marty,' I answered and opened the door to go check the car we had hit.

'No,' said Marty, grabbing my shoulder. 'Don't.'

'But Marty, we hit another car. Someone there might be hurt. We've got to go and see what happened.'

'Don't. Please. Let's... Let's just move on,' he said as he turned the ignition key. The car wouldn't start.

Harris lifted himself up from the floor and pushed his head between Marty and I. He had a cut on his forehead that bled a bit, but otherwise seemed fine.

'Marty's right. We should drive on. There's nothing we can do.'

'Wha... what?! "Drive on?!" We just hit someone! It's clear

that someone has been hurt. How can we just drive on?!'

'If we stay here any longer the police will arrive. When they do, they will take us to the station. When they do, my parents will be notified. When they are, my Dad will throw a fit. And when that happens,' he said, poking a finger at my chest, 'Marty boy will be in deep trouble.'

'Seems to me as if Marty boy is already in deep trouble,' I fired impatiently and opened the door. 'I'm going out there.'

Marty grabbed my arm again but this time I was determined to leave. Outside, the air was cool and quiet. Aside from the hiss of our own car, nothing else could be heard. I began walking quickly towards the smoke, then started running. What was I doing? I don't know any first aid. Why didn't I send Marty and Harris to go get some help?

By the time I was done asking myself all these questions, I had made it into the field. A silver convertible was lying on its back, smoke coming out from underneath. If anyone was in the car when it overturned they didn't stand a chance.

It's surprisingly quiet. Shock does that to you. It shuts off non-critical inputs, enabling you to focus on the task at hand. Which in my case was... what?

Marty must have hit the ignition again because now I

could hear our car running. Surely they wouldn't leave me here?

'Hello?! Hello?!' I call out in the general direction of the wreck. No answer. I look under the car, preparing myself for the most gruesome scene. No one there.

I realize that what must have happened was that the driver and whoever else was with him were thrown out of the car. I begin circling around, hoping I find someone, while at the same time hoping I don't.

I make two or three circles and see nothing. Then, just as I'm about to go back to our car to join Marty and Harris, I hear a faint sigh. I walk towards the sound and find two men lying fairly close to each other, both with their heads facing down to the ground. Something strikes me terribly odd about the whole situation, but I'm not sure what.

Though there's not much blood anywhere, the shape in which the two bodies are lying leads me to believe that neither will leave this place alive. I move closer to them and then understand what bothered me earlier. The two men are dressed in exactly the same clothes I saw Marty and Harris wearing only minutes ago.

There's another sigh, and I move closer to the man dressed in Marty's clothes.

'Are you OK?' I ask, though it's clear he isn't. And as I'm

standing there, looking at the two men in front of me, I notice a third body lying nearby. This one wearing the same clothes as I am.

#75

'Are you trying to approach them as the Press, or should I bring you in from another side?'

I've worked with Marcus for more than three years now, and he never ceases to surprise me. It's as if by the time I pick up the phone and give him his orders, he's got it planned, multiple scenarios and all.

'No, not Press this time. I did that with Sanyo and the Foreign Minister swore that my foot will never step on Japanese soil again.'

'OK, then we'll have to go in with Vladek,' Marcus said, with clear signs of discontent. And after a short pause, we both said the same sentence, 'You know how much I hate working with Vladek,' and burst into laughter. 'Yeah, I know buddy, but this time I don't really have a choice. The European Commission is voting on this next week and my client... Well, you know how it is.' 'Ya, I know,' answered

Marcus, his 'Ya' sounding very German. 'OK boss, I'll talk to you on the 15th. In the mean time, do everything I wouldn't. Sayonara.'

And that was it.

It's always strange leaving a city you got to know and love. This time it was Stockholm. Two years in Stockholm. Man, time definitely passes faster the older you get. I can still remember my first week here, walking down Kungsträdgården to watch all the local beauties, taking a boat to Lake Mälaren. I used to think that if I didn't attach myself to places, didn't meet people or see the sights, it would be easier to leave when I had to. But as you grow older you realize that life is not a rehearsal. It's the real thing. And if you try too hard to get things right, you'll wake up one morning with a user's guide to a life you've never lived.

Now I had to focus. For the past 18 months I've been working for a client, let's call him 'Mr F'. Mr F. has special needs. One of them is isotopes. Isotopes, for those of you who slept during chemistry class, are atoms that have the same atomic number but different mass numbers. You don't really need to know more than that. In fact, it's better you don't. All you need to know is that Mr F. needs to change the course of a certain decision about to be taken in a certain committee in the European Commission. The head of that committee is Olaf Laarsen. Laarsen's wife and kids live in Stockholm. You with me, right?

18 months ago I befriended Laarsen's wife. When in doubt, I always go for the wife. They never suspect anything and they're always dying for a meaningful relationship. And so for the past 18 months I got to know Uta Laarsen well. Very well. Some people in my profession would argue too well. But as I said, when you're driving at full speed, you don't have time to look at the scenery. If you do, you're dead. And though I've never slept with Uta Laarsen (that would be foolish and unprofessional), I did get to know her daily habits extremely well. Our morning coffees became one of them. I knew a lot about her, and everything about her husband. She knew nothing about me, and everything.

And now it's 9:27. In three minutes, we'll be meeting downstairs at Mocha, our favorite café. In three minutes she will give me a peck on both cheeks, tell me I look wonderful and ask me when I bought the black turtleneck sweater that I've been wearing for most of our morning encounters. It's 9:28. In two minutes, I will sit down at my favorite table, a copy of the local paper in hand. I don't speak, and certainly cannot read Swedish, but took a vow not to let that stop me from scanning the headlines each morning. Like I said, life is not a rehearsal. It's 9:29. I stand up from the single wooden chair left in my apartment. There's nothing here but this chair. The movers were here yesterday and for some odd reason, as if they knew I'd need it this morning, forgot one wooden chair. I fold the chair, lean it against the wall near the door and step outside. I walk the two floors downstairs, gliding my hand on the cold railing. I can feel every bump on the metal, every imperfection of its black coat of colour. It's 9:30. I open the main door. The wind is cold and refreshing. The sun is out. Uta is already sitting at our table. She doesn't see me yet. I walk up to her, stand behind her, admiring her auburn hair. This woman has the most beautiful hair I've even seen.

#76

'Enjoy Cock!'

That's what her t-shirt said.

'Hi,' he said, 'my name is Raj.' 'Hi Raj, my name is Sandra.' Sandra, he thought to himself. Slutty Sandra. He kept on saying those two words over and over in his head until he heard a question coming out of his mouth:

'So, do you?' he asked, looking at her breasts, feeling strange that he was both horrified he asked her the question and charged from how powerful he felt being that forthcoming.

'Sure,' she said. 'Doesn't everyone?' And with that she gave him a wink. Confident as he was feeling at the time, there was no way he could have taken that wink to mean anything but despise.

'Never go out with a Punjabi girl.' That's what his mother used to tell him and his brothers. 'They're cheap, they're trashy, they have no respect for their mothers.'

And now he was facing one. It was pretty clear that Sandra didn't have respect for anyone, Raj included, but he wasn't sure about the cheap and trashy part. She WAS wearing that racy t-shirt, which, this much he was sure of, had no bra beneath it. And those fishnet stockings ended only a bit higher than her miniskirt. And those high heel shoes, and the fact that... damn, that skirt is short. Yet short as it was, she was quite capable of ensuring that neither Raj, nor the other people in the break room, would have a clue as to whether or not she was wearing any underwear. Her legs, which were kept at quite a distance from each other when she was standing, had super-glue qualities when she sat. It was as if they were connected to each other not just at the base, but also throughout their length, so that when she was sitting, even the most minute movement of one leg would immediately shape the movement of the other, so that the only gap between them started no higher than the ankles.

He wasn't paying any attention and he knew it. Someone was talking to him and a group of others who were sprawled on the sofa. The speaker was trying to make eye contact with all of them, and Raj was giving her a hard time. Or was it Sandra giving Raj the hard time.

Not really sure what to do now, just knowing that sitting and staring at her fixing a sandwich at the kitchen counter was not enough. The shoot would start soon and he'd have to take his position in the control room. She would have to take her position on the set, where the question of whether or not she was wearing any underwear would become irrelevant.

Chaala! Chaala! Let's go, people, we've got a movie to shoot!

And before he knew it, it was only him and her in the kitchen.

A can of coke was on the counter. He wasn't thirsty, but neither could he think of any other excuse to approach her. He tried getting up from the sofa in one quick move, but failed, and he almost fell back into his seat, if not for the armrest he balanced himself on. Her back was facing him, but he still felt stupid for making that little fumble. He walked towards the coke can, but found himself standing directly behind her. Realizing that, if anything, she could hear his breath. She held out her long arm and picked up the coke can, turning her hand, robot-like, 45 degrees to the left, serving him the can without actually turning her body.

'Look,' he asked, as he took the beverage in his hand. 'Can I ask you a question?' 'Let me guess,' she said, still with her back to him. 'You want to know if I really like fucking men I've never met before in front of the camera?' He was speechless. That this is what she was about to do in less than five minutes was not news to him. But hearing her say that burnt his skin.

He was closer to her now, almost breathing down her neck. He could see that her hands where laid flat on the white counter, fingers spread wide, as if they were about to support her whole body. She didn't move. Didn't even breathe, as far as he could tell. So this is how it felt, he said to himself. This is how it felt before you take something you want without asking for permission. This is what it felt to be a predator.

'I can't hear a thing! Juni - I can't hear a thing! Wait, let me walk out of the studio. Stupid cell phone - never works when you need it!' The set designer marched out of the studio, oblivious to the two of them. 'Look, all I can say is that the fucking scaffolding has been here for 48 hours, and if you don't get the contractor to stop the work, then we can't shoot the bar gang-bang scene. Unless you want to hear jackhammers in the soundtrack.'

The set designer was out of the building now. Raj noticed he had a can of coke in his hand. He looked at it, looked at Sandra's exposed neck, then looked back at the can. He turned away from her body and flipped the can lid, so as not to spray her with the foam. She ran her hands through her hair and walked into the studio. He took a swig from the can, liquid dribbling down his chin.

#77

'Quantum Mechanics? Nigger, what the fuck do you know about Quantum Mechanics?'

'I don't. That's why I signed up for the seminar.'

'Fuck that shit. You're not fooling me with that story. What's the real reason you signed up for this seminar?'

'I want to learn about Quantum Mechanics.'

'Bitch, you don't even know what Mechanics is, let alone Quantum Mechanics!'

'So?'

'So? SO?! So who you foolin' with signing up to that seminar?'

'I'm sorry, Alvin. I don't understand what you mean.'

'Don't "I'm sorry Alvin" me, nigger. I want you to tell me what's the real reason you signed up for this seminar when we had already agreed that you're taking a seminar with ME on Malcolm X.'

'What, like I can't change my mind?'

'"What, like I can't change my mind?" Dude, you sound like a little girl. What's wrong with you?!'

'Nothing's wrong, Alvin.'

'Bitch, you keep calling me Alvin and I swear I will kick your ass so hard you'll be prayin' for your mamma to come and take you home.'

'What?'

'What?!'

'Why are you looking at me like that?'

'Why?! Why?! I'll tell you why. I am looking at you like that because my eyes do not believe what they are seeing. And my eyes do not believe what they are seeing because a minute ago they thought they were looking at my man, Tyron. The same Tyron, who was going to take the seminar on Malcolm X with his homeboy. The same Tyron who has just informed his homeboy that he's declined to learn about his past AND HIS FUTURE, and signed up for some white boy course on some theoretical, infinitesimal, sub-atomical particles.'

'Can't we take the Malcolm X seminar next semester?'

'Next semester?! NEXT SEMESTER?! Bitch, are you out of your mind?! Do you know what's gonna happen by next semester?!'

'No.'

'No?! NO?! Well, let me tell you what's going to happen. By next semester, you're gonna find yourself sitting in the back of the bus. By next semester, you're gonna have to sit on a special park bench. By next semester, homeboys won't be the only ones calling you "nigger". That's what's gonna happen by next semester.'

'What are you talking about?'

'What am I talking about?! What am I talking about?! I'm talking about your people, that's what I'm talking about. I'm talking about your pride. Your heritage. I'm talking about standing up for your rights and doing the right thing!'

'And taking a seminar on Quantum Mechanics isn't the right thing?'

'OF COURSE IT ISN'T THE RIGHT THING!!!'

'What's the right thing, then?'

'Nigger, please tell me that I'm tripping. Or that you're tripping. Or that we're in some kind of parallel universe.

'Cuz I don't think I can take this shit much longer.'

'Tyron, look at me.'

'I AM looking at you.'

'No, you're looking in my direction. I want you to look AT me.'

'OK.'

'Now, tell me what do you see?'

'I see a tall black man with an afro that needs restyling.'

'Man, I don't know why I'm even talking to you. This "black man with an afro" shit ain't what you're looking at, fool. You're looking at a disenfranchised, underprivileged Nubian. You're looking at a man who is taking his life in his hands and is shouting, "No longer will I be raped by The Man".'

'Who's the Man?'

'That's it! I'm going. You take your Quantum Mechanics seminar and shove it where the sun don't shine. But don't you come crawling to me and my brothers when the university doesn't let you graduate, or when you find there's no work for you when you graduate, or when some white guy at the golf course asks you to carry his bags, thinking you're the caddy. Don't come crawling to me, 'cuz I won't care.'

'Alvin?'

'WHAT?!'

'What's a Nubian?'

#78

'Each day I wake up with the realization that I am responsible. I am responsible for the deaths of all these people. People I've never met. People I knew nothing about. All gone... Mothers, fathers, sisters, brothers, husbands and wives and children and grandparents and uncles and...'

And here he pauses for a second. With his eyes tear-filled and shiny, he looks at me to see whether there's even a hint of comprehension in me. To see whether I can really understand where he's coming from - not just on the rationale level - but on the emotional level, too. To know whether I feel in my stomach what he feels every waking hour.

The first thing you learn when you become a therapist, is that you and the patient are not the same. That may seem obvious, even simplistic, to most people, but to be a good therapist you have to be able to put yourself in your patient's place. Sometimes, and I'll be the first to admit, we get carried away. Sometimes we sleep poorly, or don't sleep at all. Sometimes we go home and take our patients on our backs. Sometimes we just break down and cry, for some burdens are too heavy to carry, even if they're not your own.

Talal was one of those patients. In a former life he was a train driver. He'd been with the rail company for 12 years and had a spotless track record. Then, one day, he lost his concentration. He failed to see a car that had got stuck on the rail crossing. When he did see the car, it was too late. Though he pulled the brakes a good 50 meters before reaching the crossing, his train still hit the car at a speed of over 120km/h. Under normal circumstances, such a collision would make little, if any difference to the 20 ton locomotive. But in Talal's case, things were different. The train he was piloting that day carried a heavy load of nitro-glycerine. Through a combination of bad judgement on behalf of the train dispatcher and poor maintenance of the train's load-balancing mechanism, the impact with the little Peugeot car set a chain reaction which caused the nitro-glycerine to ignite and explode.

The fact that the train was making its way through one of Europe's most populated cities turned the accident into a tragedy. At the end of the day, the body count was 134. The number of injuries came in at ten times that number. Talal came out of the whole ordeal without a scar. At least none that the eye could see.

Though the railway company recognised that Talal was not directly responsible for the accident, it was forced to suspend him from his job until the investigation was over. After spending three months at home, so traumatized that he could not get himself out of bed, Talal finally called me. Actually, it was his wife who called me and brought Talal to my clinic. The railway company keeps a list of specialists it uses in case of emergencies, and I was one of them. I did not expect to hear from Talal earlier. Trauma patients take their time in approaching professional help. Some never do.

'I think about that question every day, you know...' he starts again after wiping his tears. 'And the truth is, I don't know if it would have made any difference. I don't know what would have happened if I had seen that car 50 meters earlier. The investigators said that most likely the result would have been the same. But that doesn't matter, you see. I was there, I was in charge of that train. I was responsible. And now all these people... so many people...'

He goes silent again, his gaze fixed on my eyes. I know it's not me he's looking at, but some random point between us. Some point he can hang on to long enough to suspend the realization that he's still alive. That he's not dreaming. That these feelings and thoughts he has will be an integral part of his life till the day he dies.

'My youngest one, Khalid, he comes back from school one day. Doesn't want to talk to me, doesn't want even to come to my bed and give me a kiss. His mother forces him. So finally he comes to my room, but does not come close. His mother is pushing him from behind to come closer to his father, but he refuses. She yells at him: "Show some respect to your father, Khalid! Can't you see he's not feeling well?!" And do you know what he answered her? Do you know what this seven-year-old boy said to his mother? He said, "This is not my father. My father was not a killer"...'

Sometimes I ask myself whether I'm really helping Talal. Whether there's anything left to help with. It was quite clear the man would never work again. The simple fact that he made his way out of bed and to my clinic was quite miraculous. But I had doubts whether he would ever be able to break away from obsessing about what had happened on those tracks.

Not all cases are like that.

A few years ago I had a young man come in to the clinic. He crossed a red light, driving at 90 km/h and killed a mother and her baby. He showed up in my clinic because the court sent him there. We spent 45 minutes together before I sent him back home. For someone who had taken the lives of two people, and destroyed the lives of at least five or ten family members, he seemed incredibly at peace with what had happened. At times during our session, I felt more sadness about the whole event than he had.

'Tell me, Talal, what would these people, these people who died in the accident, what do you think they would tell you if they met you, say, in the afterlife?'

Talal raises his head and looks at me, his face turning sideways like that of a dog expressing confusion upon hearing a strange voice.

'But they're dead, you see. All those people... dead.'

#79

'I don't know why I'm doing this. I guess you could describe it as a calling. If making movies can be considered a calling.'

I must have seen this interview, his last interview, a dozen times. He died three days after they taped it, which only adds to its already haunting qualities.

Though some would consider him a good cinematographer, or a good director, not many would feature Eugan Kurovski on their top ten list of best directors.

I do.

I think what this man did in his movies was so profound, so unique, yet so poorly understood, that he stands shoulder to shoulder with the likes of Akira Kurosawa and Alfred Hitchcock. He may, in my opinion, be standing even a bit higher than them.

You see, until 'Barefoot', his first movie, the world was split into two camps: the realists and the romanticists. The realists wanted to create movies that mirrored life, with all its pleasures and pains, its ups and its downs. The romanticists argued that if you want to see a movie about real life you could go out to the local pub on any given night. For the romanticists, movies were simply another form of storytelling. A vehicle to take us as far as possible from our miserable day-to-day existence. In 'Barefoot,' Kurovski created a dreamscape that puts Alice in Wonderland to shame. In that, he was talented, but not more talented than most other directors of his generation. Kurovski's real talent was to create this dreamscape in the mind of a twelve-year-old-boy. Atilla, the hero of the story, suffers from obsessive compulsive disorder, a rare abnormality that causes its victims to engage in obsessive thoughts and compulsive acts. Someone who suffers from OCD could walk around all day convinced that he left the gas burning on his stove, or be compelled to perform an activity, say, washing his hands, over and over and over, often resulting in physical injuries.

'Barefoot' begins with the camera following Attila as he walks down a street with a little knapsack on his back. It is early in the morning, and the streets are almost empty. Atilla is skipping from one leg to another. The scene is a fairly long one, taking a good 15 minutes. At first, we are led to believe that Atilla is simply a playful little boy who left his home early for a walk. But as the scene progresses, we notice a number of peculiarities.

First, for someone who is engaged in a playful activity, Atilla does not seem to be enjoying himself at all. His face shows strong discomfort. Then, there is the issue of skipping. As we become familiarized with his motions, we realize that he is hardly moving forward. There is something methodological, painfully methodological even, about his skipping. We notice that more than the act of skipping there is an act of repetition. An act that Atilla is compelled to carry over and over. Third, we notice that there are setbacks to his routine. Every now and then he stops skipping, turns around and walks back ten or twenty steps, only to begin skipping again, as if something with the way he covered that last stretch of gravel was imperfect.

Kurovski belongs to that elite group of film directors who can make the banal seem exciting. Directors who can take an everyday event and turn it into a Greek tragedy. Who can take a little boy's walk and turn it into a heart-wrenching struggle for dignity. And we instantly know this film is about dignity; losing dignity and the battle for regaining it. For as the camera follows young Atilla, it becomes clear to the viewer that what should have been a fairly short stroll is taking, in fact, ten times longer. For if Atilla leaves his home early, by the time he reaches his destination, two hours have passed by.

There are no clocks in the opening scene. Kurovski would never have mocked the audience's intelligence in such a way. But there is not a single person in the audience that fails to notice that the scenery around Atilla changes. Bit by bit we can see more people on the street. A few horses drawing carriages. A slight change in the shadow caused by the moving sun. Little things which carry great weight.

And just as the viewer is held in the spell of this young boy who seems physically capable of walking his route, we are thrown another morsel of information: the boy is walking to school. And then it dawns upon us. Every day, this boy of twelve leaves his home two hours earlier than the rest of his friends, so that he can wrestle with his predicament and still make it on time for school.

In the same interview mentioned earlier, the interviewer asks Kurovksi where he draws his ideas from. 'Was there really a little boy named Atilla? Was there really a headmaster who learned his life's lesson from talking to one of his students?' Kurovski looks at the interviewer and answers, almost without thinking: 'I do not know what really exist. I do not know if there is an "Atilla" or a "Headmaster". I do not know even if there is a "Kurovski". All I know is that humans suffer. And in our suffering, there is great dignity. And that is the only real thing in life.'

The speedometer reads 55 miles per hour. Today I have no problem staying within the speed limit. I've got the roof down and we're heading West, me and my honey. I look at her and she looks back, eyes covered with a pair of chic sunglasses I picked up for her in Paris. She takes her left hand and lowers the glasses a bit, enough to reveal her big, beautiful, brown eyes. She bats her eyelashes and we both start laughing. And then it all slows down, almost to a halt. Everything seems to move in slow motion. My eyes focus on the corner of her mouth, where her seductive smile announces its appearance long before the rest of her face catches up. And then I'm thrown back to that night. That damned night.

It was a simple plan - surprise Cath on our first year anniversary and escape with her to Paris. We'd spend a week in the city, then another travelling through the French countryside. Cath always wanted to visit Paris. She'd never been to Europe, never even travelled outside the US (unless you count Tijuana). On her bedside table she kept a picture of her Mom, taken somewhere in the 60s. In the picture she is sporting a short, almost boyish haircut, with a scarf tied around her head. She looks intently into the camera, the Eiffel tower behind her. It was only after we got married that Cath told me that the person who took that picture was not her Dad but a lover her mother picked up while she and Cath's Dad were on sabbatical in Paris. Eventually he found out and returned to the US, alone. Cath was born nine months later.

The flight to Paris was half-empty. It was February and all the Christmas travellers had long since returned to their offices. When the stewardess asked us whether we'd be having any wine with our meal, we both answered yes. When she asked us whether we would like red or white wine, we both answered, 'Champagne.' Such was the nature of our relationship - completing each other in almost every possible way. Cath never did handle her alcohol and shortly after the Champagne arrived she became very tipsy. She began kissing my face, my neck, my earlobes, all while her hand made its way towards my lap. I felt a bit uneasy. Public display of affection was something I never saw at home. Even kissing in public made me self-conscious to the point of discomfort. Cath, on the other hand...

'I want to do it,' she whispered in my ear, in-between flicks of her tongue.

I chuckled and said nothing.

'I want to do it. Here.'

'Are you serious?' I asked her. She was.

'You've been reading too many magazines,' I answered, managing to kill her enthusiasm immediately. I do this sometimes. I don't mean to, but when she surprises me, I simply don't know what to say. So I say the first thing that comes to mind, which is usually such a fumble, I wonder why I don't simply keep my mouth shut.

Cath falls asleep ten minutes later and so do I. When I wake up, her head is leaning on my shoulder. God, I love this woman.

In Paris we take a cab to our hotel. Cath is glued to the window like a little kid. She points out all the major attractions we pass. Here's the Place de la Concorde and the Arc de Triomphe. There's the Notre-Dame Cathedral and Les Invalides. And there's the Eiffel Tower. Cath looks at me, then back at the tower. She puts her hand on my leg, searching for my hand. When she finds it, she squeezes it hard and says, still looking at the window: 'I love you.'

Three hours later, the jet lag catches up with us and we crash in our hotel room. It's only 8pm but despite our airborne nap we both drop like flies. Around midnight I wake up to the noise of running water. Cath is taking a shower. When she steps out, I gasp. She's wearing a sexy black combo - black bra and black underwear with black stockings and a suspender belt. 'How we doing, lover boy?' she says in a mock-French accent. I signal her to come back to bed. 'Later, Cherie. First, we go out and play.'

I get dressed and we leave the hotel. While I sort out opera tickets with the reception desk, Cath is talking to the concierge. He's good looking and not that much older than we are. They both laugh a few times. Cath always had a way with people, especially men.

'Where we goin', angel?'

'On a little adventure,' she says, smiling at me. 'Hold on tight.'

It was weird seeing Cath like this. In all our time together. she's never been afraid to express herself (or her sexuality, for that matter), but there was something intense about her that night, like she was determined to take the lead, without really worrying (or caring?) whether I followed or not.

We stepped outside the hotel, hand in hand. It was freezing, and I kissed Cath on her head. She smelled great. Our concierge signalled a cab, and when it stopped near the entrance he stuck his head through the passenger window and had a word with the driver. I give him a tip and we climbed in. Inside I noticed the driver studying us through the mirror. I wondered what we looked like to him. A young couple on their honeymoon? Two lovers stealing a night away from their partners?

Ten minutes later, we were making our way through narrower and narrower streets. Finally the cab stopped. 'C'est ici,' the driver said in a not too friendly tone, as if a couple with more finesse would have chosen a different destination. I remember Cath complained once that the French are the only people in the world who feel it is their responsibility to judge you about EVERYTHING. I didn't understand how someone who'd never been out of the US could utter such a generic statement, but now I was thinking she might have been on to something.

Outside the club with no name stood two massive bouncers, both with dog collars around their necks. Cath took me by the hand, and guided me through the doors.

At first I couldn't see a thing. We went through a series of curtains that cut off all visible light. Finally, we entered the club. I gasped. I've been to clubs before, but this, this was nothing like I'd ever seen before. To start off with, everyone was dressed in black. Then there was the fact that not everyone was, actually, dressed at all. Some people were wearing masks, some were in leather. Some wore outfits I didn't even know existed.

I was hesitant, and Cath felt it.

'We don't have to stay,' she said.

'No... no, it's ok,' I answered defiantly, though I didn't feel like it.

'Let's get drunk,' she said, giving me a wink.

'What would you like?' I asked her, trying to gain my composure.

'An orgasm,' she said, grinning.

I smiled back at her and tried kissing her on the mouth.

'Not yet,' she said. 'In a bit.'

I was getting annoyed. But this trip was my gift to her, and I wasn't going to spoil it. I ordered us both Champagne, and leaned on the bar, waiting. It was like being on the set of a movie, only this time you're one of the actors. I looked at Cath. She was glowing, and I wasn't the only one who picked up on that tonight. Cath was exchanging looks with a tall, incredibly pale and incredibly beautiful woman. She was not wearing a top, and both Cath and I had a hard time not staring. Cath stepped back until the small of her back touched my front. She turned her head and said, 'I think she likes us.'

'I think she likes you,' I answered, not without a touch of jealousy.

Someone tapped my shoulder and I turned around. Our Champagne was ready and I spent a few seconds trying to fish out the right amount of change. Apparently I overshot quite widely as the barman smiled wildly when I told him he could keep the change, which is probably the reason he took my hand and gave it a long, warm kiss.

When I turned back to Cath I found the tall blond woman whispering something in her ear. I saw Cath's eyes widen and that smile of hers starting to build. I hugged her from behind and kissed her neck, trying my best to blend into the atmosphere.

'She likes you,' she said.

'Who does?' I asked, trying my best to hide the fact that I knew exactly who she was talking about.

We stayed like this for a while, scanning the room, sipping Champagne, kissing and holding each other as if we'd fall off of the edge of the world if we didn't.

'Have you ever thought about other women since we met?' she whispered in my ear.

'Baby, you know I'd never cheat on you,' I answered.

'That's not what I asked. I asked if you'd ever thought about other women?'

I didn't answer. Instead I turned and ordered us another drink. This must have been our third or fourth glass, because even I started to feel my head spinning.

'Because tonight I'm letting you play around a bit...' Cath whispered again in my ear, only to break into a long giggle.

The blond woman reappeared and approached us. She held her hand up and I went to kiss it. But before I could rest my lips on it, she turned around and guided me away from the bar. I took Cath by my other hand and we made our way through the crowd. When we reached the end of the room, our new friend opened a door and took us through to another chamber, this one even darker, partially covered in smoke. Cath let go of my hand and disappeared. The blond took me forward a few steps and turned to face me.

'Your wife is a very lucky woman,' she said in a heavy French accent, holding her mouth very close to my ear. 'Very lucky,' she said, this time flicking her tongue in my ear. I pulled back, only to feel Cath holding me from behind.

'I want you to kiss her,' she whispered in my ear.

'Cath, that's... that's crazy...'

Suddenly I felt her hand in my pocket, making its way to my member. 'Just do it,' she whispered.

So I did. I hadn't kissed another woman in more than two years, and doing so made me feel ashamed and excited at the same time. Cath kept holding me from behind and fondling me from the front.

'Do you want her to go down on you?' Cath asked me. I didn't answer. I just closed my eyes and kept on kissing the blond woman. This went on for a while, and when I tried to grasp hold of Cath's hand I discovered that she was gone, and in her place was now only the blond woman, who by now had opened my zipper and made her way into my pants. Where the hell was Cath?

I couldn't think straight anymore, and I couldn't see anything around me. The room was spinning and the blond woman was looking into my eyes as her hand kept on massaging me. I thought I noticed a movement to my right, but before I could figure out whether there was something there or not, I felt something wet and warm closing over my member. I looked down, horrified. There was the blond, on her knees. This had gotten out of control. I pushed her back, but she held her ground. I ran my hand through her hair and she gasped loudly. Cath is going to kill me.

Once again there was a motion to my right, and this time I could see the silhouette of another couple next to us. The man was holding the woman's head in his two hands. She too was on her knees. I was getting more and more excited, especially given the fact that now the woman to my right and the blond woman were holding hands.

I returned my attention to the blond. Someone had turned the lights up a bit and I could see her face clearly now. Beautiful, chiseled, focused.

The man next to me was breathing heavily. I felt charged and disgusted at the same time. And then I looked again, and saw her.

Cath. It was Cath kneeling next to the blond, in front of that guy.

Something broke inside me that second. It's as if someone took a samurai sword, cut me open, and held the sword steady above my heart. Any little movement on my behalf would spell instant death.

We were supposed to stay two weeks in France, but we left the day after. No words were spoken after the club, and none during the flight. Numerous times after that, Cath tried to explain, but I was having none of it.

This was three years ago.

It took me a year to get over my anger, and another year to understand what made me angry in the first place. I can't say that my scars are unnoticeable. They still hurt from time to time. But somewhere along the way I had to make a decision. Either I accept what happened that night as a given fact, or I stay locked in that club for the rest of my life, never leaving, never seeing Cath again.

And so I made the only choice I could - I chose Cath. In the end, I found that as hard as you look, sometimes you don't find any answers. Sometimes there are only questions.

But I also found that some questions are more important than others. Like the question of whether what happened was important enough to leave the woman I loved. And when I looked at it that way, suddenly there was no question left.

#81

'Are we out of time?'

'Three more minutes, Jack, and remember to ask her about her affair with Tom Cruise.'

'We're back and with me is Tara Thompson, who stars in "Giving Birth", which opens this weekend in cinemas across the US. Miss Thompson, I know you don't like to talk about your personal life, but we've all seen the pictures of you and Tom Cruise in the papers. Does Penelope Cruz have anything to worry about?'

'Don't answer, honey. You don't have to answer him. Just say "no comment".'

'Edith, for crying out loud, she's not the Chief of Staff, you know. I told you before, if your daughter wants to be a

Hollywood star she'll have to get used to the fact that her life doesn't belong to her anymore.'

'Sssshhh. I want to hear what she says!'

I don't know what to say. I've waited all my life for this break. I worked hard. Damn hard. I've mopped floors and waited tables and played the roles of every fruit known to man in more TV commercials than I care to remember. All for this. For a chance to get on the big screen. And now I don't know what to say. I mean, I knew this question was going to come up, and Tom and I agreed about what would be said and what wouldn't. But now, faced with the question, on TV, in front of the nation, I'm not really sure what to say.

'Why isn't she answering?! Oh my God! Phil! Phil! You get on the phone right now and tell Marcus that if this little bitch makes anything out of her little friendship with Tom we'll be over her with a steamroller.'

'Marcus, whatthefuckisgoingon?! Whad'ya mean you don't know! She's your client, you're her agent, what's not to know?!'

'Ssshh! I think she's going to say something'.

'Jack, I'm really happy you asked me this question. It seems that everyone wants to know whether I slept with Tom Cruise or not.'

'Oh, my God. Edith! Edith?! My little baby had sex with Tom Cruise?!'

'Oh, shut up, Howard and let me watch. For God's sake!'

'Phil. Tell me I'm dreaming, Phil. Tell me this is a nightmare. Tell me this isn't happening.'

Good. The look on his face is priceless. If this movie bombs, at least I'll go down in the pages of history as the only actress who's ever managed to surprise Jack Cogan, the king of night-time TV.

'Yes, eh... well, there has been some speculation about what exactly went on between you and Tom.'

'Jack, we've got 60 seconds left. Get her to spill the beans. Now!'

'Yes, I know. Sometimes it feels like the nation doesn't have any other worries. In a way, I guess it's flattering. And in a way it's kind of sad. But I understand it. People are curious, and people love controversy. And it is true that Tom and I are close friends.'

'Close friends, my ass. Phil, get on the phone to Marcus and tell him that if the twat says even one more thing about Tom, we'll sue her! And him! Tell Marcus we'll sue him and everyone he knows!'

'Jack, twenty seconds. Let's get a move on it!'

'Yes, well time is running out, and I'm sure our viewers at home are dying to find out just how close your relationship with Mr Cruise is.'

'Yes, it's a close relationship, Jack. Tom is a wonderful person, far more intelligent than most people are aware of. Most people don't know, for example, that he has a Masters degree in literature. Did you know that, Jack?'

'Marcus! I'm warning you. Tell your client to keep her mouth shut!'

'Jack, we're gonna lose this one. Five, four, three, two, one and cut to titles!'

'Ladies and gentlemen, I'm afraid that's all we have time for tonight. Please join me tomorrow when I'll be hosting PJ Harvey. Until then, good night from us all in the studio.'

'So, did she?'

#82

it's late and the last of the guests has just left. good turnout tonight. people had a good time.

but now that they've all gone home it's just her and me left. the silence that fills the space left behind by the dj is painful. more than an absence of sound it's the presence of a very distinct, heavy noise. it's the sound of us, together, but not.

never stop living. never stop lying.

jake took me aside at a certain point and told me that i look like shit. he said that i'm fucking up my life and her life at the same time. said that he's tired of seeing me run after the white rabbit. jake was off his head with coke when he said that. he was also right. jake's always right.

it didn't used to be like this. not at the beginning. at the beginning it was great. or was it just great sex? now, now it's just... it just is. the unbearable lightness of being. it takes no effort, but kills you in the process.

in a minute she will look at me with a sad smile and tell me she's going to bed, asking me if i'm going to stay up for long. i'll tell her no, when in fact she knows the opposite.

i'm a deep sleeper, but for the life of me cannot fall asleep after a good night out. or a good night in. or just a night in.

why is this so hard?

just don't go back to her, my mom said. mom was right. mothers always are. except, of course, when it comes to choosing their own partners. god, i could write an anthology about her partners. weirdos of the world unite.

'in a minute babe.' in an hour.

i look at the evidence left behind. a dozen bottles of red wine lying in various directions, as if we had just completed a multi-team version of truth or dare. spin the bottle, then dare to move to the next group, who doesn't know you, and doesn't care, and will make you suffer.

beer cans, glasses, some full, some empty, some broken. just like people, i guess.

someone wrote something on our wall. now i remember she said to me something about that earlier, but i paid no attention, just like i always do. i guess i just have slow ignition. you know, it takes time between someone telling me something and me comprehending it. i'm not stupid or anything, it's just that I've heard so much bull in my life, that i don't take anything at face value anymore. if it's important, it'll sink in.

who the fuck writes on a wall in somebody's home?

i don't trust people. i used to, but i don't anymore. i know myself too good by now, and i know i can't be trusted, though, fuck if i'd ever admit it in her face. trust is like virginity. once you lose it, you ain't got it anymore. and i don't care how many plastic surgeries you take your trust through, the people who need to know, will know.

the dj was excellent tonight. for a while, i thought it was me spinning the records, not him. i came up to him and told him he's the best dj in the world. told him his choice in music is unsurpassed. he said thanks, but that really has nothing to do with him. i asked him what he meant as he brought the crowd to a craze. i'm not playing the music, he said. the music is playing me. i nodded as if i understood and went away.

but the truth is, i didn't. i've never done anything naturally, never just stood there and let it flow. and so no music has ever played me, no book has ever read me, no woman has ever felt me. i'm never here.

until now.

now i feel cold, and scared and miserable. and what i thought would comfort me - the thought that i can't go on like this - only frightens me more. for if i leave all this behind, where does that lead me?

i sit on the sofa and put my feet up on the bizarre metallic coffee table she picked up in some flee market. i always hated that coffee table.

i stare directly ahead - trying to focus on the writing on the wall. i squint my eyes real hard, as if that would make a difference. as if i hadn't gone through ten lines of coke and that many tequila shots.

i cry, wiping the tears off as fast as they flow. my knuckles are painted black from the mascara. the tears are gushing now and my white shirt is getting an addition of wet polka dots. dot dot dot.

i get up from the sofa and blow my nose with a Kleenex. i step closer to the white wall and stand in front of it. someone took great care to use the best handwriting they could to write three words.

open your eyes

There's something about growing older that nothing prepares you for. It's that feeling you get every once in a while, sometimes on a Sunday morning, sometimes on a Monday night. At first you assign the feeling to the changing patterns of the weather, or to your partner's altering mood, or simply convince yourself that you're feeling the blues. And that works for a while. But then another week, another month, another year passes by and you have this growing realization in your head that this isn't just a phase - it's your life. Something isn't turning out as planned. Something is missing. You. You are missing from your life.

And so, three years into our marriage it came that we were getting divorced. Being the rationalists that we were, Couples Therapy was out of the question. If we couldn't sort out our own relationship, what good would it do to bring in an outsider? And so it happened that on the exact evening we were planning to sit down for The Talk; that first talk in which we cease to be husband and wife and begin the painful process of being something else; the first talk in which we would discuss our divorce; it happened that the power generator on Canal Street blew up in flames.

She lights up some candles and plugs her iPod into the portable speakers. Minimal Pain is on, playing 'Devotion'.

/The look in your eyes tells me all I need to know
Sometimes it's what you don't say
If you don't believe that this love can grow
Just tell me so and I'll be on my way

But baby, don't lie to your heart/

We both listen to the song, glass of red wine in our hands. That song always meant the world for us. More than any paper documents or legal agreements. We used to listen to this song so many times and just look at each other, look into each other, and know.

The first to speak tonight could be accused of breaking up our marriage. So no one says a word. The song draws to an end, then starts again. I don't mind and neither does she.

Where do we go from here? How do you get used to being one again, when you've multiplied already? How do you move from being 'we' to being 'me'? Which parts do you cut, which do you leave?

The wooden floor is cool and dry. I move my fingers over the grooves that years of walking have carved. I stick my fingernails and pull back. Can I stand the pain? Will I let go before they come off?

'Do you love me?'

/Before you came there was only me
Now us is the only thing that I can see/

'Don't. Don't answer,' she says. 'I know it's not fair of me to ask.'

There was a time when she didn't have to ask. A time when she knew the answer to that question, and others. A time when I did as well. But that time has gone and now we are walking on a tightrope. Walking on a tightrope in the dark.

I take her hand and bring it towards my face. It is heavy, as if it's playing neutral, waiting to see where all this will lead to. I glide the back of her palm over my cheek. She feels the wetness of my tears and pushes her hand deeper into my face, as if to assure herself that I am really crying. I take her hand in mine and kiss it, tasting my own salty tears. She stops breathing and I begin licking her hand, like some little boy licking the chocolate coating off a candy bar. Her palm stretches, flexes out, as if it was laying in a really awkward position for a really long time. My tongue darts out and moves over her fingers, taking short stops at the webs between them.

/I'll stop the ticking of the clock
Stop the world from turning round
But I can't stop you if you choose to walk
I can only put my arms around you
And tell you how I feel/

I put my arms around her and want to whisper something in her ear. Something true. Something real. Instead I just hold her.

I take the iPod in one hand and click the forward button.

The same song starts again. 'Don't bother,' she says. 'It's the only one I've got.'

Acknowledgments

Writing might be a solitary activity, but it takes a village to get a book out.

The book would have never been written if not for my muse, Tami Zori. She was my first audience and kept her word to give me feedback on every story I wrote, every day. Her word made it easier for me to keep my word to my growing list of readers, which included Alexis, Amanda, Amit, Amparo, Arian, Bruce, Bryce, Chris, Daniel, Gerard, Gulzat, Ike, Isabel, Jason G, Jason M, Jess, Jessia, Joanna, Klaudia, Marielle, Maya, Melissa, Michal, Miles, Naomi, Nargiz, Nerolie, Nick, Ray, Sandra, Seth, Shai, Shuki, Sian, Simon, Yarah and Zack. I thank you all from the bottom of my heart for reading what I wrote, even when you didn't like it (and weren't afraid to say so).

Writing a book is one thing. Getting it published is another. This book would have never been published without Uri Fruchtmann. It was during lunch at The Electric that Uri asked me whether I would send him any of my stories. After I did, he suggested I meet Franc Roddam, the famous film director and now, the equally famous publisher. The rest, as they say, is history.

I wish everyone to have a publisher like Franc. Writing and publishing a book has a lot of ups and downs. The ups you can usually deal with on your own, but with the downs, I was lucky enough to have Franc to show me the way up.

Samantha Hill at Ziji provided us with invaluable help –
just when we needed it most, while Jim Garden braved
dozens of revisions to bring the book to its current design
format.

If you've heard about this book somewhere, it's because
the folks at Colman Getty PR did an amazing job. Without
Dotti Irving's leadership, the ingenuity of Ruth Cairns and
the of commitment of Jane Opoku, this book would have
been unheard of.